THE PRINCESS
OF NOWHERE

THE PRINCESS
OF NOWHERE

PRINCE LORENZO BORGHESE

AVON

An Imprint of HarperCollins *Publishers*

HarperCollins books may be purchased for educational, business, or sales promotional use. For information please write: Special Markets Department, HarperCollins Publishers, 10 East 53rd Street, New York, NY 10022.

FIRST EDITION

Designed by Diahann Sturge

Library of Congress Cataloging-in-Publication Data is available upon request.

ISBN 978-0-06-172161-8

10 11 12 13 14   OV/RRD   10 9 8 7 6 5 4 3 2 1

This book is dedicated to my mother and father,
who have been married for more than forty years.
They have taught me that communication
is the secret to a successful marriage.
Without it, love cannot grow, nor can it be complete.

ACKNOWLEDGMENTS

So many people were a major part of the process of putting this book together, from early on in life in the form of inspiration right up to now—too many to thank but a few I have to.

To my brother and sister, grandmother, aunts and uncles, and the rest of my family, I'm so proud to have you all in my life! And, of course, to my parents for leading by example. My editors, Lucia Macro and Esi Sogah, are amazing, and I could not have shaped this book without their guidance. My agent, Ian Kleinert, thank you for getting the ball rolling. I would also like to thank a friend who is a professor for advice and assistance with the process of researching and writing this book, whose help was enormous. And lastly, I would like to thank all the people who have been a part of my life and have made my journey thus far so very special. You know who you are. Please know I will never forget you or the wonderful moments we have spent together.

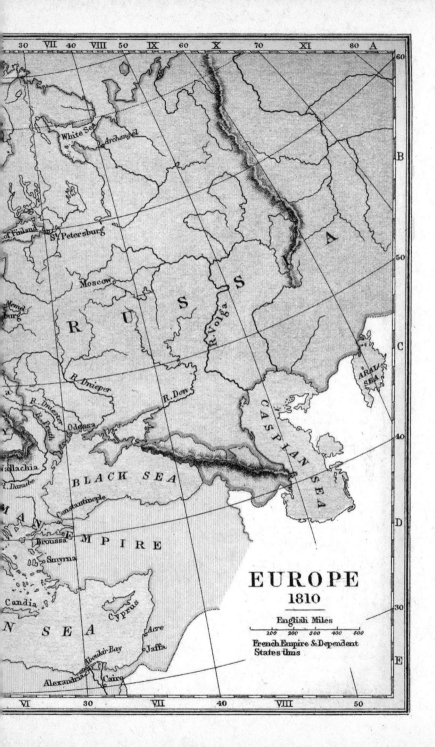

EUROPE
1810

English Miles

100   200   300   400   500

French Empire & Dependent
States thus

Pauline's Family

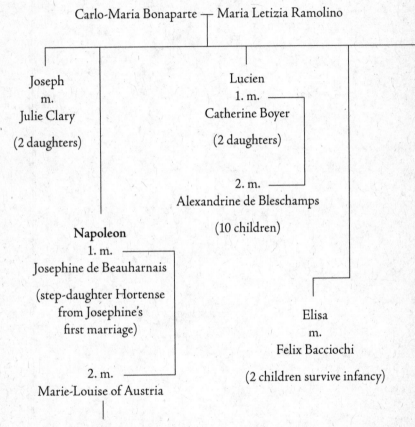

Carlo-Maria Bonaparte — Maria Letizia Ramolino

Joseph
m.
Julie Clary

(2 daughters)

Lucien
1. m.
Catherine Boyer

(2 daughters)

2. m.
Alexandrine de Bleschamps

(10 children)

Napoleon
1. m.
Josephine de Beauharnais

(step-daughter Hortense
from Josephine's
first marriage)

2. m.
Marie-Louise of Austria

Napoleon II

Elisa
m.
Felix Bacciochi

(2 children survive infancy)

Louis
m.
Hortense de Beauharnais

(daughter of Josephine)

(3 sons)

Caroline
m.
Joachim Murat

(4 children)

Jerome
1. m.
Elizabeth Patterson

(1 son)

Pauline
1. m.
Victor Emmanuel Leclerc

Dermide Leclerc

2. m.
Catherine of Württemberg

(3 children)

2. m.
Camillo, Prince Borghese

Camillo's Family

Marcantonio, Prince Borghese — Anna Maria Salviati

Camillo, Prince Borghese
m.
Pauline Bonaparte Leclerc

Francesco
m.
Adele de la Rochefoucauld

Maria

Marcantonio,
Prince Borghese
1. m.
Lady Gwendoline Talbot

Agnese

2. m.
Therese de la Rochefoucauld

(10 children)*

Camillo

Scipione

* Agnese's younger half-brother Francesco
is the author's great-great-grandfather.

CHARACTER LIST

> † deceased before story begins
> [not mentioned]
> *fictional*

BONAPARTE FAMILY

Mother: Letizia (Madame Mère)
Uncle: Cardinal Fesch, Letizia's stepbrother
Brothers and sisters:
Joseph (wife Julie)
Napoleon (wife Josephine; second wife Marie-Louise of Austria)
Lucien (second wife Alexandrine)
Elisa (husband Felix Bacciochi)
Louis (wife Hortense, daughter of Josephine)
Pauline (also Paolina, Paoletta)
Caroline (husband Joachim Murat)
Jerome (second wife Catherine of Württemberg)

LECLERC FAMILY

Victor Emmanuel Leclerc†, Pauline's first husband
Dermide Leclerc, Pauline's son
Adolphe Leclerc, Victor's uncle and Sophie's grandfather
Sophie Leclerc, Victor's cousin (once removed);
    ward of Napoleon
Charles Speare, British officer on Elba, Sophie's husband

BORGHESE FAMILY

Camillo Filippo Ludovico, Prince Borghese
Anna Maria, Dowager Princess Borghese,
 Camillo's mother, widow of Prince Marcantonio
Francesco Borghese, Camillo's younger brother,
 later Prince Borghese
[Marcantonio Borghese, Francesco's son,
 Prince Borghese, named for his grandfather]
Lady Gwendolyn Talbot, wife of Marcantonio
Agnese Borghese, daughter of Gwendolyn and Marcantonio

PAULINE'S HOUSEHOLD
(FIGURES SERVE AT VARIOUS TIMES)

Madame Ducluzel, housekeeper
Doctor Peyre
Carlotta, nursemaid
Nunzia, Sophie's maid
Auguste de Forbin, count, Pauline's chamberlain
Felix Blangini, music master

CAMILLO'S HOUSEHOLD

Maxime de Villemarest, secretary
Matteo, manservant
Bettina, family attendant, sister of Matteo
Doctor Vastapani, court doctor at Turin

OTHER IMPORTANT CHARACTERS

Luigi Angiolini di Serraverra, Italian diplomat
Gian Andrea Visconti, young Milanese aristocrat
Chevalier de St.-Luc, royalist French agent in Rome
Prince Georg, heir to Grand Duchy of Mecklenberg-Strelitz
Antonio Canova, sculptor
Duchess Lante della Rovere, Camillo's mistress (and cousin)

THE PRINCESS
OF NOWHERE

PRELUDE

His Excellency Prince Camillo Borghese and Her
Excellency Princess Pauline Bonaparte Borghese
invite you to celebrate the last evening of Carnival
at their Villa on the fourteenth day of February
in this year of Our Lord Eighteen Hundred Four.

Everything glittered.

In its verdant setting just beyond the old city walls
of Rome, the marble facade of the miniature palace
reflected light from hundreds of lanterns—some hanging
from the upper stories, others on dragon-headed poles fixed
in the ground at intervals around the building. Carriages lined
the drive, lamps gleaming. Fountains splashed in the moonlight. Servants in gold-trimmed livery and powdered wigs
carried trays of glasses filled with champagne. In the supper
room, glazed fruits in marzipan were stacked on gilt dishes.

The guests, in fantastic costumes and even more fantastic masks, were a kaleidoscope of silk and jewels and feathers. Their eyes burned with a gay, fierce intensity; their gestures seemed to leave trails of sparks in the air. They darted from one activity to the next, drinking, eating, laughing, dancing, flirting. Tomorrow was Lent. Tomorrow would bring ashes and penance and gravity. But tonight was still *Carnevale,* and once again the Borghese family had opened their villa for the traditional masked ball marking the final hours of the eight-day celebration.

The February night was mild, and many couples were taking a turn in the small formal gardens encircling the building. Their walls and geometrically patterned hedges offered a few dark corners, but between the extra lighting and the hovering servants, no one interested in a serious indiscretion would find them adequate. The wilder (and unlit) groves beyond the neat walls offered better opportunities. That is why the hostess of the ball was now several hundred yards away from the nearest lantern, running down a tree-lined path with a masked cavalier in pursuit.

Pauline was not running very fast. After all, she was planning to be caught. Her pursuer, however, had been injured recently, and Pauline considerately paused on the far side of a fountain to let him rest. He did not seem to understand the rules of the game. Instead of pausing in his turn, he strode around the fountain and fell dramatically to his battered knees, with only a small gasp of pain.

"Angel! Goddess!" he said, stretching out his arms. "I beg you, flee no further! I mean you no harm!"

Pauline found this declaration extremely disappointing.

Her suitor evidently failed to see her scowl in the dim light, because he continued in the same melodramatic tone, "I shudder when I think that in the darkness you might fall or tear your lovely skin on a bramble! Slow your flight, my queen, and I will slow mine!"

Flowery declarations were commonplace in Pauline's life, and this one sounded depressingly familiar. It was repeated almost word for word from the libretto of a popular operetta about a coy nymph. Why did men believe women wanted lovers to fall on their knees and declaim bad verse?

She had thought St.-Luc more promising than most of the young men she had met since arriving in Rome. He had followed her through the crowds at a masked revel on the third night of Carnival and, after a series of ever more suggestive remarks, had finally seized her and tried to kiss her. She should have let him have that kiss, Pauline thought. But some imp had prompted her instead to display her power. She had twisted away, smiling. "My kisses must be earned, sir, not stolen!" she had scolded.

"How may I earn them, then?" His black eyes had challenged her.

She thought for a moment. "In exchange for one of the Barbary horses. One horse, one kiss."

The riderless horses were sent racing down the Corso just before sunset every evening during Carnival, and by the time they reached the end of the street, at the Piazza Venezia, they were very dangerous to approach. Prudent Romans watched the finish from balconies in the *palazzi* surrounding the square and placed bets on the aftermath of the race as well as on the contest itself. As the horses spilled into the plaza, daring young gentlemen would prove their courage by attempting to grab and subdue a slippery, furious animal who outweighed the would-be handler by upward of a thousand pounds. Even trained grooms were often injured in the process, and the ever-present possibility that the horses would maim or kill someone ensured a large and enthusiastic crowd each night.

"And if I capture two?"

"Two kisses—and a lock of my hair."

"What if I am even more ambitious?" he asked softly.

"For three horses, you may name your own reward," she said equally softly, very pleased with the turn the conversation was taking.

He bowed. "In that case, I shall take three."

The Chevalier de St.-Luc had been as good as his word: he had caught three horses, one on each of the fourth, fifth, and sixth nights. He had also acquired two broken ribs and a badly bruised knee. That had not prevented him from limping across the piazza to the Palazzo San Marco after each triumph and saluting Pauline, like a gladiator saluting an empress. It was a dramatic sight: below, the bloodied cavalier, the sweating, trembling horse; above, in the midst of the wealthy spectators on their hired balconies, the exquisite young woman, her dark curls framing her mask. By the third performance, the revelers were more focused on this romantic display than on the winning horse.

Pauline was never averse to being singled out for public admiration by conquering heroes. She had rewarded St.-Luc in full view of the crowd. After the first victory, she nodded and smiled. After the second, she blew a kiss. After the third, she tossed down her glove, with a note inside: "Find me at midnight Tuesday at the ball given by the Prince and Princess Borghese and you may claim your true prize." It was signed not with her name but with the device on her carnival mask: a swan.

This was the great fiction of Carnival. For eight days, Roman society wore strips of gilded pasteboard on their faces and pretended not to recognize each other. The fiction made many things possible. Pauline Bonaparte Borghese, the new bride of a papal prince, could not openly encourage an exiled enemy of her brother Napoleon to seduce her. But a masked beauty could smile on a masked admirer. Everyone might be well aware that the lady behind the swan feathers was the Princess Borghese, and that the gallant with Harlequin silks across his face was the royalist envoy seeking papal support for the restoration of the Bourbons to the throne of France. But who would violate the unwritten laws of Carnival by saying so out loud?

Unfortunately, St.-Luc's public wooing was not adapting well to more private circumstances. Chivalric adoration was all very well in a large piazza, but now, in the deserted clearing by the fountain, Pauline was hoping for something less bookish.

She looked down in exasperation at her kneeling worshipper. Over the gentle splash of the fountain she could still hear, faintly, the music and laughter of the ball. Had she left all that gaiety for badly delivered lines from an operetta? "Get up," she said suddenly. "Take off your mask."

He climbed slowly to his feet. "But we must remain masked until dawn. That has always been the rule."

"Take it off!" She tore off her own, a shimmering concoction of gold and swan feathers, and tossed it aside. It landed in the fountain and floated, rocking gently in the moonlight beside a marble seahorse.

St.-Luc swallowed, then untied his own mask and let it fall. He was not as handsome as her husband, Pauline thought resignedly. His features were a bit irregular, and his dark hair was coarse and straight. But he had tried to steal a kiss, and he had wrestled with rearing, sweating horses in front of half of Rome for her sake. Above all, he was French. Pauline was desperately homesick.

"Do you know who I am?" she said.

He nodded.

"You have known from the first." It was a statement, not a question.

"Yes." It was little more than a whisper.

"If you dare, then, monsieur, meet me in two minutes at the Temple of Diana." She pointed down the path, where white columns shone faintly at the end of the alley of trees. Then she walked away without looking back.

After ten paces, she flung off her domino.

After twenty paces, she stopped and untied her jeweled sandals.

As she vanished, barefoot, behind a marble pillar, she was slipping her gown off her left shoulder.

Camillo Borghese was looking for his wife. He had not been looking very hard, at least not at first. The satisfaction of escorting Rome's greatest sculptor through rooms full of masterpieces collected by his ancestors was something to be savored. It was impossible, in any case, to move very quickly in the crowd. As host, he had forgone a mask; for his part, Canova disdained them. They were therefore a striking and recognizable pair— the tall young prince, with his open, wide-browed face and soft brown hair; the aging sculptor, with his intense stare and slightly stooped posture. Every few feet, another guest came up offering greetings and compliments to both men.

A servant hurried by just as one group of guests had turned

away, and Camillo beckoned him over. "Have you seen the princess?" he asked in a low voice.

"No, Excellency."

"Would you find her, tell her there is a special guest I wish her to meet?"

"Certainly, at once." The servant bowed and retreated.

This was the third servant he had waylaid. He looked around the room distractedly, hoping to spot Pauline.

"Diana," the sculptor was saying. He spoke loudly, so as to be heard over the music and conversation. "I shall represent the princess as Diana. With a bow, and a stag by her side." He paused, frowning. "No, not a stag. The stag has been done; it is trite. Perhaps a dog. A *lévrier*. What do you think of that notion, Your Excellency?"

"A goddess? A pagan goddess?" Camillo stopped scanning the room and turned back to Canova. "Are they not usually represented nude?" He was slightly shocked at the thought of a naked statue of Pauline but tried to conceal his reaction. Canova still had the power to make him feel very unsure of himself.

Camillo was no longer the gangly schoolboy who had fled in embarrassment a dozen years earlier, when he had come upon the artist sketching in one of the villa's galleries. In total silence, Canova had studied the sixteen-year-old with the same dispassionate thoroughness that he had given to the Roman mosaic he was copying. Then, without saying a word, he had turned back to his sketchbook. Camillo had avoided meeting the artist for years afterward.

Now, however, Camillo Borghese was a grown man. A prince. A prince who was offering Canova a spectacular commission. He had invited the sculptor to the ball to make the final arrangements for the new piece. And Canova, who had no love for the Bonapartes, had nevertheless consented eagerly. What sculptor would not want a chance to create a life-size portrait of Pauline Borghese? At twenty-three, she was universally acknowledged as the most beautiful woman in Europe, Venus to her brother's Mars. Camillo had conducted all the preliminary negotiations in confidence; he had thought it would be a splendid surprise for Pauline to bring Canova to the ball and announce the portrait as part of the festivities.

"Diana wears a tunic," the artist said. "In any case, the princess would only model for the head." He looked around impatiently. "Did you not say you would present me to her? Or has she already retired?"

Where was she? He had sent servants out into the walled garden twice; he himself had been searching the rooms (admittedly with many interruptions) for nearly half an hour. His eye fell on the youngest of Pauline's attendants, and with a hurried excuse to Canova, he pushed his way through a knot of drunken young men to the corner where she was standing.

"Sophie, do you know where Pauline is?" he said.

She flushed. "I am sorry, Your Excellency," she said, not meeting his eyes. "I saw her earlier when you were both receiving guests, but now it is so crowded. She—she was complaining that her mask was uncomfortable, so that she might have changed it for another, and perhaps, if she went outside, she took a domino as well."

He saw Sophie's hands clenching her skirt, but he did not need that telltale sign to know that the girl was lying. Sophie idolized Pauline and shadowed her everywhere on public occasions. What is more, even if Pauline had changed masks and thrown a domino over her costume, the hooded cloak could not fully conceal Pauline's distinctive costume of gold tissue or the even more distinctive sandals, decorated with intertwining jeweled straps. Each strap had cost more than Camillo's entire outfit.

"Is she on the terrace?"

"Yes, I think so. Yes, I saw her there a few moments ago." Then, as he glanced toward the doors that led out to the terrace, she added hastily: "Or perhaps—perhaps she has gone back to the supper room."

Lying. Lying, lying, lying.

A familiar, bitter taste filled the back of his mouth. But he concealed his anger from Sophie and managed a crooked smile. "I will look for her there, then," he said.

He would not find her. She would not be in the supper room, or on the terrace, or in the formal garden. The grounds of the villa covered acres and acres of land. She could be anywhere—by the lake, in one of the grottoes, in the ruins. He certainly could not send servants after her. Nor could he leave his own ball to search for her, especially with Canova frowning at him and looking more and more suspicious. Camillo was trapped at his own ball with an offended genius and five hundred guests, and Pauline was off under a tree in the dark with someone's tongue down her throat.

PROLOGUE

Rome, 1845

Sophie had arrived a little early, and now, just outside the doors into the salon, it suddenly occurred to her that there might still be people—most likely male—admiring Pauline.

"Wait here, Agnese," she said, looking down at her companion. "I don't think your father would want you to go in if there are strange gentlemen visiting. Give me a moment to make sure that Matteo is alone."

Agnese hoisted herself obediently onto a marble bench. Her feet dangled high above the floor; she was very small for a nine-year-old. "Bettina says that the men who come to see Aunt Paolina are wicked," she observed, looking sideways at Sophie. "Bettina says that if I go to see her, she will have to pray for me."

"Bettina prays for you every night in any case," Sophie pointed out. The old nurse was probably praying right now, while she waited in the carriage. Praying was one of her favorite activities, especially when it involved Agnese. Bettina—and most of the population of Rome—had idolized Agnese's mother, a beautiful Englishwoman who had died while tending the poor during an epidemic. The entire city had mobbed the streets for Princess Gwendolyn's funeral, and there were reports of miracles at her tomb. Agnese, in Bettina's eyes, was the only surviving child of a saint.

Unfortunately, another one of Bettina's favorite activities was comparing Agnese's mother to her predecessor as Princess Borghese, Pauline Bonaparte. Bettina called them the angel princess and the devil princess. Sophie was fairly sure that Bettina had told her nursling all the lurid tales about Pauline by now. Still, Sophie did not want Agnese to overhear the sort of comments that gentlemen frequently made during their visits to this particular part of the villa. It was one thing to hear your old nurse talk about Jezebel, and another thing to hear a stranger snigger and make lewd remarks.

She hurried across the corridor and went through the double doors. No one was there except Bettina's brother Matteo, another ancient Borghese family retainer. He was trimming the wicks on the candles, glancing possessively every so often at the young woman in the center of the room. She was always shown by candlelight to important visitors, and apparently Matteo had decided that the daughter of one princess deserved proper ceremony when visiting another.

The woman was reclining on a massive, funereal daybed, one arm propped on the cushions and the other resting gently on her thigh. Her garment had slipped down to her hips, where it lay in a suspiciously appropriate V-shaped fold just below her navel. Above that fold the bare skin stretched up smoothly: first the soft abdomen, then the ribs gently curving out to support her small breasts, then shoulders, neck, and the proud little chin. A mocking half-smile on her face suggested that she was well aware of the effect her appearance created.

No matter how many times Sophie walked into this room, the effect was always the same. No one—*no one*—could be that beautiful. But Pauline was.

There was a faint sound from the corridor, and Agnese peered around the edge of the doorframe.

"May I come in now?" She did not wait for an answer but skipped over to stand by Sophie. "Oh!" she said. And then, after a long pause, more softly, "Is that Aunt Paolina?"

"Yes."

"I didn't think she would look like that." Agnese was staring, rapt. She gave a tiny sigh that told Sophie Pauline now had another worshipper at her altar.

"Would you like to see something very special about her?" Sophie looked meaningfully at Matteo.

He frowned. "Today?" He glanced significantly at the black rosette pinned to Sophie's bodice.

"*She* always loved it," Sophie reminded him.

Matteo bowed slightly and moved around behind the daybed.

"What is the special thing? Is it that fruit?" Agnese peered doubtfully at the apple in Pauline's hand.

"No, not the fruit. Stand here." Sophie took her little cousin's shoulder and pulled her back a few feet. "Now watch." She nodded to Matteo, who pressed a lever with his foot.

The bed began to move.

First it shuddered, and Pauline's arm, perched on the backrest, shuddered with it. Then she and the mattress and the coverlet and cushions and ornamental base all swung sideways. The entire ensemble was rotating slowly, circling in the candlelight. A low hum beneath the floor was the only sound in the room. Agnese was delighted; she clasped Sophie's hand and squeezed it in her excitement.

Pleased with the effect of her surprise, Sophie waited until the piece had completed three full circuits and then nodded once again. The servant stooped; the daybed grumbled and jerked and finally came to rest in precisely the position it had occupied at first. On her marble pillows, in her marble draperies, Canova's statue of Pauline Borghese smiled her marble smile and settled back into immobility.

Agnese's awed silence lasted only a few seconds after the piece stopped moving. Then the questions poured out. Where was the motor? How did Matteo make it start and stop? Did any of the other statues in the collection move like this one?

Matteo showed her the concealed lever, which Agnese insisted on trying out for herself. Her little foot could not shift the mechanism, however, and Sophie had to help her. After two more tries, she finally stamped hard enough to set the motor in gear without help. Sophie had to drag her away, reminding her that the carriage was waiting to take them to the church.

"Bettina!" Agnese shouted as soon as the carriage door opened. "I made the statue turn! Without Sophie's help!"

Matteo's sister muttered something about works of the devil and crossed herself. She had never seen the statue. Before it had even been completed, she had announced that she would not cross the threshold of any room that housed it, and she had advised her brother to resign his position at the villa when it was brought back to Rome. When Matteo climbed in, she moved as far away from him as possible and gave him a pointed glare.

Sophie ignored her. "Did you like it?" she asked Agnese.

The girl nodded emphatically.

"It's very famous," Matteo said.

"Infamous," snapped his sister. "A Borghese princess posing nude!"

This reminded Agnese of another question, which had been temporarily banished during her fascination with mechanics. "Why didn't Aunt Paolina have any clothes on?" she demanded.

The carriage was moving now, and Sophie pulled the little girl close to her, thankful that the rumbling wheels would prevent Bettina from hearing this exchange. "She is meant to be an ancient goddess, the goddess Venus. Like the painting on the ceiling of the small dining room at the palace. Venus lived long ago, and she doesn't wear clothing as we do."

Agnese digested this for a moment. "Didn't Uncle Camillo mind that his wife had no clothes on?"

The answer to this question was very complicated, and Sophie chose evasion over explanation. "Well, your great-uncle is the one who asked the artist to make the statue. It was a present for Paolina. He commissioned it right after they were married, as a special surprise."

The girl frowned. "Bettina says he hated her. She says Paolina ruined his life."

"That is not true!" Sophie said fiercely. She pulled her arm out from the little girl's back and swung around to face her. "He loved her. He took care of her when she was ill. He buried her in the family chapel. If he were still alive, he would be going with us right now, to say prayers for her." Sophie touched her chest lightly, where the paper rested, folded in her bosom. She always carried it with her on the anniversary of Pauline's death. "He wrote her a letter about how much he loved her. I read it every year on this day before I go to see her statue."

"Bettina says—"

"Bettina was not there. I was."

Agnese stared up at her, a little frightened at her tone. "Where? Where were you?"

"Everywhere." Sophie leaned back against the velvet pillows. "From the beginning. I was with Paolina when she met your great-uncle. I was at their wedding. I traveled with them from Paris to Rome. I was with them in Turin. I went to Elba with your great-aunt when her brother Napoleon was exiled, and came back to Italy with her after he was defeated at Waterloo. I was with her when she died. Your great-uncle was holding her hand and crying."

"But—" Agnese looked uncertainly at her nurse, then back at Sophie. "Why are there all those terrible stories, then?"

Sophie's voice softened. "They were not happy, Agnese. It was not a fairy tale. The prince married the princess, and everything went wrong, until the very end. But that does not mean they did not love each other."

"Did *you* love Aunt Paolina?"

Sophie smiled. "Yes. At least, most of the time. I was just about your age when I went to live with her, you know. I was ten years old."

"And your mother died, like mine."

"Yes."

Agnese wriggled back under her arm. "And Aunt Paolina offered to be your new mother."

"Well—not precisely," Sophie said dryly. "Paolina's brother decided that she should have me come and live with her. She was a young widow, with a little boy five years younger than I was. I suppose he thought I would be some help to her. He told her to invite me, and he told my father to accept, and that was that. When Napoleon gave orders, everyone listened."

PART I

The Red Rose

Beauty, Romance, Courage

Ventôse 12, Year 11
[March 3, 1803]

Lucien, dearest of brothers, you must help me! Joseph and Napoleon and of course our mother are all in it together, but you will be my ally—won't you? I am a widow and a mother and surely it is right for me to have my own place, and the property is not so very expensive considering that it belonged to a duke and has such elegant receiving rooms, which of course as Napoleon's sister I shall need. In any case I certainly cannot stay with Joseph and Julie much longer; no matter what I do or say Julie always finds fault and Dermide, poor boy, has barely seen me these past few weeks because I am constantly shut up in my room crying.

Please, please come to me right now; I will take you to see it and you will help me persuade the family to let me buy it.

Your loving sister Pauline

Ventôse 14, Year 11

Lucien, it is settled; I am ecstatic. The Hôtel de Charost is mine! Didn't you think the house was beautiful? And the gardens? It is very close to Joseph and Julie, so Mother need not fret about me being on my own. Please send me the name of the young man who did that lovely painting on the ceiling of your friend's dining room, I cannot remember his name (your friend, that is) but we were there for supper just before I left for the West Indies last year and the painting is in gold and blue on a cream background. Julie now very kindly says that she wants to give me some furniture to help me get started, but of course I will buy everything new.

P.

Ventôse 15, Year 11

Lucien, you won't believe this. It is all a trick; Napoleon is only letting me have my house on the condition that I take in some little cousin of Emmanuel's to live with me. She is nine or ten, a horrible age, far too old to be a playmate for Dermide, and I am sure she is a tattletale and that Mother and Napoleon will use her to spy on me. And truly I don't think I can bear it if she looks like Emmanuel—as they say she does. It is bad enough to have lost my husband without having to see his face on some prissy little girl every day. I need your advice; please tell me what I can do.

In haste,
Your Pauline

Ventôse 16, Year 11

Dear Lucien,

Yes, I received your reply. I suppose you were too busy to come in person but of course I would never accuse you of being selfish. Everyone in the family always thinks the worst of me and I should not be surprised when it happens. I would take in a dozen little orphan girls to get away from all of you.

Your sister,
Pauline Leclerc

ONE

Paris, March 1803

There were forty-eight steps from the ground floor, where they had been waiting in an anteroom, up to the first floor, where they would finally be received. So far, they had climbed thirty-six. Sophie was counting, because she was helping her grandfather. Papa Adolphe refused to use a cane; he claimed it was undignified. He had one hand on Sophie's shoulder and the other on the banister, and he would shift his weight from one side to the other as he brought each leg carefully up to the next step. Now they had reached the last landing below the first floor. Twelve more steps.

"You are just the right height, Sophie," her grandfather said, pausing for a moment. "Don't grow any taller." Sophie already topped her grandmother by several centimeters. She was clearly going to be one of the Long Leclercs, like her father.

They climbed six more steps, and now Sophie could see a footman standing by a set of double doors. Her grandfather paused again. "Don't forget," he said, panting slightly. "Curtsey when you are introduced. Speak to Madame Leclerc only when she addresses you directly. And—" He broke off when he saw the footman hurrying over to assist him and hastily levered himself up the remaining stairs.

Sophie finished the list of warnings under her breath. Confine herself when possible to the phrases "Yes, madame" and "No, madame." Look up when speaking. When the adults were speaking with each other, look down at her hands, which should be clasped neatly on her lap. Do not fidget. Do not look out the window. And, the final one, whispered at the last minute by her father: make sure that Papa Adolphe did not drink more than one glass of wine. How this was to be managed when she was looking at her hands and not speaking, Sophie could not imagine.

Her grandfather, waving off the footman, released her shoulder and tucked her arm into his. Sophie walked slowly across the upper hall, giving him time to recover a bit more, while the footman returned to his station and swung both doors wide open.

Sophie's first sight of Pauline Bonaparte Leclerc, therefore, was neatly framed by the doorway. She was sitting at a gate-legged writing table, looking down at a large sheet of drafting paper half-unrolled in front of her. One delicate hand pinned the paper to the table; the other tapped impatiently on the arm of her chair. Her dark hair curled around her face. Her profile was set off by the deep red curtain panels behind her, and her pale skin gleamed above her black dress. Sophie thought Pauline was the most beautiful creature she had ever seen.

"Monsieur Leclerc. Mademoiselle Leclerc," announced the servant, stepping back.

The beautiful creature looked up, exclaimed in surprise, sprang to her feet and hurried over. Sophie remembered her instructions and curtseyed. She kept her eyes rigidly fixed on the floor, but she could smell perfume—something flowery.

"Monsieur Adolphe! How charming of you to come see me," the woman said. Her voice was slightly hoarse, as though she had a touch of catarrh. "And this must be your granddaughter."

"Yes, madame." He bowed over her hand. "May I have the honor of presenting Mademoiselle Sophie Leclerc, your cousin by marriage." Sophie felt herself pushed slightly forward. She looked up, saw a vivid pair of brown eyes regarding her with amusement, then hastily looked down again and made another curtsey.

"Come sit by me, my dear." She felt a warm hand slip around her gloved one; she was being led away from her grandfather and seated on a sofa. To her dismay, the beautiful woman sat down beside her. She could hear her grandfather settling himself in an adjacent chair and orders for refreshment in that strange, husky voice being passed on to a maidservant. Sophie did not see the maidservant; her gaze was now locked on her hands, which, as instructed, were folded in her lap.

"I have not seen you since the funeral," the woman was saying to her grandfather. Her voice had laughter in it. That seemed strange to Sophie, to be laughing when they were talking of funerals. It was Cousin Emmanuel's funeral they meant, she supposed. She had not attended, but her father and grandparents had. Her father and grandfather had come back talking of how lovely Emmanuel's widow was, and her grandmother had come back talking of how dreadful it must have been to sail all the way across the ocean with his coffin.

"A sad business," said her grandfather. "But of course there is my little great-nephew. I am sure he is a consolation to you. How does he go on?"

"You shall see for yourself! Let us have him down to pay his respects." She rang a little bell. "And he must meet his cousin; Dermide likes other children." The door opened, and more orders were given to another unseen maid. Sophie's neck was beginning to hurt from keeping her head bent, and she heard her grandfather shifting in his chair the way he always did when he was nervous.

Suddenly her chin was tilted up and the brown eyes were looking straight into hers. "Are you shy, Sophie?" the woman said, laughing.

How to answer that? "Yes, madame." She could not look down, because the woman was still holding her chin.

"Well, stand up. Let us have a look at you."

Clumsily, Sophie scrambled to her feet. Should she curtsey again?

The woman put her head to one side and studied her. "How tall you are! And only ten years old!"

"Yes, madame."

She jumped up and came over to stand right by Sophie. "Look, Monsieur Leclerc," she said, laughing again. "She is as tall as I am! But so thin! Like a bird!" She laid her plump arm under Sophie's. "We must feed her better!"

Mortified, Sophie looked back down and twisted her skirt in her hands.

"Very pretty hair," the woman said, touching it lightly. "Even fairer than Emmanuel's, and not quite so curly. And a nice complexion." She turned to Sophie and frowned. "What color are your eyes? Are they blue? Green? I cannot tell in this dreadful, dim room."

Sophie's eyes were gray, but they tended to take on the color of her surroundings. She murmured something incoherent.

There was a commotion at the door, and a small blond boy ran in, followed by two maidservants.

"Here he is! Come to Mama, Dermide." She scooped him up and carried him back to the sofa. Now Sophie did not know what to do. Should she sit back down? The little boy was taking up most of her former place. Should she stay where she was? But then she would be in the way. She retreated behind her grandfather's chair, and the boy stared at her solemnly from his mother's lap. "That is your cousin, *caro*," the woman said. She put him down. "Go and greet her. Her name is Sophie. And that is your great-uncle Adolphe."

The little boy took a few steps toward the chair, bowed, and said clearly, "*Bonjour*, Cousin Sophie. *Bonjour*, Uncle."

She was not going to be outdone by a boy who was not even old enough to wear breeches. "*Bonjour*, Cousin Dermide," she answered, stepping out from behind the chair and curtseying.

He took her hand. "Come and meet my Carlotta," he said, pulling her toward the older of the two nursemaids, a woman about her grandmother's age. But Sophie's grandmother was blond and gentle-looking; this woman had black hair and snapping black eyes and thick, fierce black eyebrows. "Carlotta," he said, "Carlotta, *guarda chi si vede; è la mia cugina, Sophia!*" He turned to Sophie and whispered in French: "I told her you were my cousin."

Sophie nodded stiffly and received a grudging bob in response.

The beautiful woman said something in the same language to the maid. Sophie thought she could make out a few words here and there that sounded like oddly pronounced French—"not pretty," and "thin," and "orphan." Both women glanced at her sadly, shaking their heads. When the beautiful woman shook her head, her curls bounced like little springs. Then she turned back to Sophie. "Do you miss your mother, my dear? How long has it been—three years?"

"Yes, madame," she said.

"And shall you like coming to live with me? Here in Paris?"

Sophie thought of the narrow old streets of Pontoise, of the tunnels under the castle where she had played with her brothers, of her quiet, scholarly father, of the apple tree outside her bedroom window, which would be blossoming in a few weeks. She thought of those quizzical dark eyes, which had judged her and had apparently found her lacking. "Yes, madame."

The woman laughed again. "Is that all you can say? 'Yes, madame'?"

"No, madame."

"You must call me Cousin Pauline. I feel like a schoolmistress when you curtsey and call me madame." She smiled at Sophie. Her smile was very different from her laugh. It was a warm smile, not the smile of an adult to a child but the smile of someone who shares a secret with a friend. It lit her eyes.

In Sophie's chest, her heart gave a little jump sideways; she felt suddenly breathless and dizzy and bewildered.

"Can you remember?"

She swallowed. "Yes, Cousin Pauline."

"Carlotta and Dermide will show you the nursery, then, while your grandfather and I have a glass of wine and make the arrangements. No, no"—this to her son, who was trying to climb onto the sofa again—"you must go upstairs with Carlotta. Sophie will come with you, and you may both have meringues. Remember to speak in French so that Sophie will understand. And you must be very kind because she has no papa and no mama."

Sophie did not dare contradict her. After all, her father had agreed to let her go and live with Cousin Emmanuel's widow. Perhaps that meant he would not be her father any longer. She followed the maid and Dermide out of the room, grateful to escape from the woman's terrifying presence.

The moment the door closed behind them, however, she wanted to run back and take one more look, hear her speak once more. How odd that voice was! It had a little catch in it when she laughed. Sophie had never met anyone who laughed so often. Her hand was so soft, too. When she had held Sophie's chin, it had felt as though it was wrapped in velvet. She was the same height as Sophie. Wasn't that odd? Cousin Pauline. She tried it out, under her breath. Cousin Pauline.

Sophie was in love.

She did not recognize the symptoms. This mixture of fascination, guilt, and terror was new to her. All the way back to Pontoise her thoughts flew back and forth like little darting birds: on one side, her father and the apple tree; on the other side, Cousin Pauline and the sound of laughter. When her grandfather asked her if she was feeling unwell, she burst into tears.

Camillo Borghese was also in love. He was in love with Paris, and Paris was in love with him. Ten years earlier, a prince foolish enough to visit France would likely have been ushered straight to the guillotine; now, under the First Consul, Paris was rediscovering the pleasures of privilege and excess. The elegant young Roman with his formal dress and courtly manners reminded the French of the beauty and ceremony they had renounced. Suddenly it seemed appealing, rather than appalling, to hold receptions, to bow, to wear lace and jewelry, to address a young woman as *mademoiselle* again instead of *citoyenne*. Camillo was invited everywhere, introduced to everyone. Frenchmen tried to copy his graceful gestures, his practiced movements on the dance floor, his stylish handling of his horses. Marriageable damsels simpered at him. Matrons wrote him on scented paper, lamenting the cold and indifferent nature of their husbands and hinting that he might be able to comfort them.

The prince found his popularity bewildering and exhilarating. In Rome he had been the shy and unpromising son of a magnetic father; three years after Don Marcantonio's death, Camillo still felt uneasy when addressed by his title and tended to defer to his mother when any important decision confronted him. Here in Paris, with no parents or cousins or uncles or tutors to remind him of past inadequacies, he was reborn. Even his poor French was (at least at first) a blessing in disguise. He often found himself nodding or smiling agreeably in response to something he had barely understood. The result was a revelation: if only he had nodded and smiled more in Rome, instead of trying to consider his response carefully before he spoke! Every reception, every dinner party offered the chance to meet yet another Parisian— usually female—who would say, breathless, eyes shining, "Oh, *Monsieur le Prince*! It is such an honor! I have been hearing so much about you!" He would look at their breasts and smile, and they would chatter, and he would smile, and they would kiss his cheek and invite him to dinner and beg him to take them for rides in his high-sprung two-wheeled carriage.

When Angiolini mentioned the possibility of marriage, therefore, the prince was initially not very receptive. It did not help matters that it was early—not even eleven in the morning—and he had, as usual, been out very late the night before. He was on his third cup of coffee and still felt half-asleep. He was so startled by Angiolini's casual mention of the topic, in fact, that at first he thought he had misunderstood him. But they were speaking Italian, not French, and instead of nodding and smiling, Camillo reverted to his older, less successful practice of staring at something below his interlocutor's eye level—in this case, the floral pattern on his china cup. When that produced no inspiration, he tried scowling and hoped that Angiolini would take the hint.

He did not. "Well?" said the older man. "You look as though I were speaking of a funeral, not a wedding. What do you say to the notion?"

"I—I had not thought about it." This was not strictly true. One of the most enjoyable things about Paris was the temporary respite from his mother's attempts to find him a suitable mate. He thought about marriage every day. *I am still in France, protected from the would-be princesses of Rome. Praise God.*

"Not at all? You will be twenty-eight in a few months."

Camillo shrugged. "My father did not marry until he was almost forty." He took another sip of coffee.

"But you would not object if a match were to be proposed?"

"*Has* one been proposed?"

Angiolini was a veteran diplomat; Camillo did not expect a

straight answer. And he did not get one. "Perhaps I might have heard some rumors that an alliance would be possible," the Tuscan envoy conceded. "Nothing more."

"Alliance" was, of course, the correct term. Borghese princes did not marry for love. Camillo had known since childhood that his bride would require the approval of the pope and would likely be chosen for him rather than by him.

"An alliance with whom?"

Angiolini looked surprised and offended. "With the Bonapartes, of course. Who else is there in France, these days? The young woman is the consul's sister."

Camillo put down his coffee cup. He was suddenly very wide awake. He had met Napoleon—that, after all, was the main point of his visit to Paris. While he had not precisely disliked the man who now ruled France, Belgium, and large chunks of Italy, he had not found him very congenial. In fact, he had found him rather cold and threatening. Someone had told him that the Bonaparte sisters were even more terrifying; as for the mother, she was—according to the same informant—the reincarnation of a pagan fury. He frowned. "But Napoleon's sisters are married. You presented me to Madame Murat yourself, just a fortnight ago. And the other one, Elisa, is the wife of that Corsican fellow, Bocisomething."

"There is a third sister, a widow. She has been living quietly since her husband's death last fall." He paused. "You had not heard of her? Of Pauline?"

Camillo frowned. "I don't believe so." *Had* he heard something? Perhaps there had been some talk of a Pauline or a Paulette. Titters, whispers, French idioms that he did not know. He had not paid much attention. But if this sister was a new widow, still in mourning, the gossip must have been about someone else.

Angiolini smiled and took a small parcel from his pocket. "I will leave this with you, then. Let me know in a day or so if you wish to meet Madame Leclerc. Perhaps a small family gathering, nothing that would give rise to any talk."

Camillo unfolded the brown paper and stared down at the miniature in its silver frame. It showed a young woman with a perfectly shaped oval face, curling brown hair, delicate, slightly rounded features, and mesmerizing dark eyes. He looked at it, twisted it, held it up to the light, rotated it slightly. Nothing changed. The woman was still the most beautiful woman he had ever seen.

"She doesn't really look like this, does she?" he said finally.

As usual, Angiolini did not answer his question. "I shall look forward to hearing from you, Your Excellency." Still smiling, he bowed and left.

"I can't marry a Bonaparte," Camillo said a minute later. His tone was plaintive. "My mother would never approve. The pope would never approve." There was no one there to hear him.

TWO

Cousin Pauline installed Sophie in a beautiful suite of rooms in the mansion she had bought on the rue de Faubourg St. Honoré and allowed her to pick out all the furnishings. Sophie had her own maid and so many new frocks that she could change several times a day. She had tutors—three of them. The music teacher and drawing teacher were both young men; they were meant to come only twice a week but both seemed to find frequent excuses to stop by the Hôtel de Charost and discuss Sophie's progress with her guardian. There was also a governess, who came every morning to oversee Sophie's exercises in Italian, German, arithmetic, grammar, and penmanship. The first incumbent of this position was dismissed when she tactlessly observed that Sophie's spelling and grammar were better than Madame Leclerc's. The replacement, duly warned, concentrated on arithmetic, which Sophie hated.

Sophie's days were very orderly. She would wake up at eight and have hot chocolate in bed. For the first week, this was a thrilling luxury; she thought she would never tire of it. She soon did, but was too shy to ask for anything else, and often threw most of the chocolate surreptitiously out of her window and went hungry all morning. After this, her maid would help her dress, and then she would have lessons in the sitting room adjacent to her bedchamber. At noon, she would have a cold luncheon, followed by an hour in the music room to practice the piano. At two o'clock, she would have either music or drawing; then she would go for a walk in the garden with her maid. At four, she was supposed to lie down in her room; she never wanted to rest, however, and so would usually go up to the nursery and play with Dermide. At six, Sophie changed her gown for supper, which she ate alone in her sitting room, served by a footman named Denis. She knew his name because she asked him; he told her, but then advised her that he was not allowed to speak while serving. After supper, she and Dermide would go downstairs for a brief visit with Pauline; then Dermide was put to bed and Sophie would read or struggle with her embroidery until her maid came to help her get into her nightgown.

She almost never saw Pauline aside from that all-too-short evening ritual. Drawing and music were her favorite lessons because her teachers would often contrive somehow to see their lovely employer while they were there, and then Sophie could see her as well. Sophie also liked Italian because she discovered that Pauline spoke it in preference to French. Her governess told her, with a sniff, that Corsicans did not speak proper Italian at all, but Sophie didn't care. She pestered Carlotta to converse with her and rapidly acquired both a broad accent and a number of

Corsican vulgarities, which resulted in repeated punishments—sometimes merely sentences for her copybook, but more often a stinging blow across her palms or knuckles with a metal-edged ruler.

After one particularly painful morning, Sophie was soaking her throbbing hands in a basin of cold water, provided, with indignant sympathy, by Carlotta, who could always be counted on to take Sophie's side when she was beaten for speaking Corsican. It was raining—again—and when Sophie's maid came clattering up the stairs to the nursery, Sophie thought she was coming to postpone their afternoon walk. But when Nunzia burst into the room, she was bright red with excitement. "The children are to go with the signora to Master Lucien's house," she announced breathlessly. "Right now! In their best things!" She lowered her voice then and spoke in dialect, but Sophie understood her anyway. "It's a new suitor—a real one! A prince!"

Sophie had mixed feelings about the men who haunted the Hôtel de Charost. She was terrified that one of them might succeed in carrying Pauline away; on the other hand, their visits created an extra occasion for Sophie to see her. Pauline liked to show her maternal side to visitors, and after a few weeks, Sophie had become part of the display. Dermide and Sophie were brought in, introduced, and then arranged in a tableau: Dermide on Pauline's lap; Sophie standing just behind her. The gentlemen in attendance would exclaim with pleasure at the sight and offer extravagant compliments, comparing Pauline to the Virgin Mary and Dermide to the Holy Infant. Carlotta would mutter darkly afterward about blasphemy and insist that Dermide pray to the Blessed Virgin for his mother's soul. Sophie, the child of two freethinking Jacobins, did not mind the comparison on religious grounds, but she preferred admiration that included her as well as Dermide.

A few days earlier, Sophie had been standing in her usual position behind the sofa. Pauline was feeding Dermide sweetmeats and teasing him, and Sophie was bored and jealous. The servants had been gossiping about the various suitors and their prospects (or lack thereof) even more openly than usual in the nursery that morning, and Sophie blurted out suddenly: "Cousin Pauline, are you going to marry again?"

There was a shocked silence.

One of the visitors said, with heavy gallantry, "Madame dares not remarry; half the gentlemen in Paris would kill themselves in despair."

Pauline laughed, but the laughter had an edge.

"Who is the girl?" asked another visitor, as though Sophie were not there.

"Mademoiselle Leclerc, Napoleon's ward."

Sophie knew she was in disgrace; usually Pauline presented her as "my late husband's cousin" or even "my foster daughter."

"Well," said the second man, a young man in uniform who had been present several times in the last few weeks when Sophie went downstairs, "what is your answer, Madame Leclerc? Shall you change your name once more?"

"I will do as my brother advises." Pauline's tone was cold.

The young man laughed. "So do we all! And yet, he has advised me not to visit you so frequently, Pauline. If I do not obey, I may find myself posted to the ends of the earth, like your late husband."

Sophie knew from the servants that the West Indies was not one of Pauline's favorite topics. Nor did Pauline permit witticisms at her brother's expense. Her dark eyes flashed. "Then I would recommend that you take his advice. Good day, Colonel." She held out her hand for him to kiss, as though she were a queen dismissing an errant minister.

The young man looked at Pauline in dismay, looked at Sophie, then back at Pauline. It was not a jest; she was not smiling. Chagrined, he bowed over the offered hand and took his leave, although not without giving Sophie a vengeful glare as he went by.

Pauline turned to Sophie after the servants had shown the officer out. "What possessed you, Sophie—my shy little Sophie—to ask such a question!"

"I beg your pardon, Cousin Pauline. I am very sorry," Sophie stammered. But she could see from Pauline's face that her guardian was not angry with her any longer.

"Well, as it happens, I can answer your question. It seems I may be getting married again quite soon." Pauline spoke very loudly and clearly, and although she was looking at Sophie, her reply was obviously directed at the two remaining visitors. One, the portly young Frenchman who had protested at Sophie's question, seemed crestfallen at this announcement. But the other, an older man who had been calling quite frequently for the past two weeks, looked very satisfied.

"Cousin Pauline is not going to marry that Italian man with white hair who was here tonight, is she?" Sophie had asked Carlotta nervously on the way up the back stairs.

"Marry Signor Angiolini! Certainly not!"

Reassured, Sophie had pushed the unsettling topic of Pauline's remarriage to the back of her mind.

Now, at Nunzia's emphatic "It's a new suitor—a real one!"

her anxiety returned, magnified a hundredfold by the maid's vehemence. And Pauline's subsequent behavior only amplified her fear. Pauline was always conscious of her appearance and surroundings when receiving visitors, but Sophie stood (along with half the household) in the front vestibule and watched the normally self-confident Pauline change her mind repeatedly about her dress, her hair, her shoes, Dermide's outfit, Dermide's hair, Dermide's shoes. Even Sophie was sent to change her gloves when one of the welts on her hand broke open and stained the back of her glove with a drop of blood.

After everyone was clothed and coiffed and shod, Pauline fretted about the timing of their arrival. They should arrive early and await the prince at Lucien's. Or perhaps they should make sure he was there first, so that she could make a good impression as she came in. No—the first idea was better: they must be there in time to make sure Lucien used the gold salon and took away the ugly side-table.

At this point, they were now in danger of arriving after the prince, because of all the changes of clothing, and so an express messenger was sent to tell Lucien not to admit anyone save Pauline until she could come in through the terrace in the back. The party was duly received on the terrace by Lucien himself, who seemed rather amused that his elaborately gowned sister was stealing into his garden through a trash-strewn alley. Then Pauline directed her own footmen to rearrange the furniture in the reception room she had selected, banishing all but two chairs and a mahogany daybed. The latter was placed in the center of the room, with Pauline and Dermide posed in a semi-reclining position on its ivory-colored silk cushions. Lucien was sent downstairs to receive the visitors. Sophie was relegated to a spot near the wall, standing behind Lucien's fiancée, Alexandrine, who had one of the chairs. The other, Sophie assumed, was reserved for the prince. She was wrong.

After the chaos in Pauline's front hall, the harried carriage ride, and the furniture-moving, Sophie expected Lucien to throw open the doors of the salon the minute Pauline had settled herself with Dermide. Instead, they all waited in virtual silence for twenty minutes. When Alexandrine made one or two attempts to start a conversation, Pauline simply raised her eyebrows and said nothing in response.

Finally the double doors opened, and Lucien walked in, talking casually with the two men who followed him. Sophie recognized the first man; it was the man with white hair who had looked so complacent a few days earlier when Pauline had answered Sophie's question. Behind him was a taller, much younger man with a wide forehead and curling, light brown hair. He paused just inside the doorway and Sophie saw him take in the charming picture of Pauline and Dermide. He was obviously impressed; he did not even glance at Alexandrine or Sophie.

Pauline was greeting the older man. "Signor Angiolini!" she said. "How lovely to find that you are also visiting Lucien today! Please, do sit down." She gestured toward the only remaining chair. "And who is this you have brought with you?" Sophie heard the low, slightly hoarse timbre of Pauline's voice and her heart sank. That was the voice Pauline used to enchant people.

The young man, looking bemused, stepped forward with Lucien, who bowed slightly to him.

"Your Excellency, may I have the honor of presenting my sister, Madame Leclerc?" He looked down at Pauline and gave a conspiratorial smile before completing his introduction. "My dear, this is His Excellency Prince Borghese. He is visiting us from Rome."

"Oh!" Pauline looked up, dismayed. "I do beg your pardon! This is my son, Dermide, but of course he should not be here when there are visitors. I am afraid I am not the strictest of mothers." She caressed Dermide's hair and then set him on the floor. "Go over to Sophie," she told him in a stage whisper. "She will take you up to play with your little cousins." She then started to rise, blushing, but the prince, also blushing, waved her back to her seat with an embarrassed smile.

"Come sit here by me, then," Sophie heard her say.

And the prince, still smiling, sank down onto the pillows of the daybed.

THREE

Angiolini was all smiles.

"His Holiness favors the match!" he announced, before he had even greeted Camillo or taken the chair the footman held out for him. "Naturally, there will be further negotiations; Napoleon must formally agree to the terms, but I am very optimistic. Indeed, I am more than optimistic. I am confident." He settled himself with a small grunt and waved away the servant, who bowed and withdrew. "I have this from my most trusted man in Rome; it is as good as done." He beamed at the prince. "Congratulations, Your Excellency!"

As he had half-expected, the prince did not smile in return. Over the past few weeks, Angiolini had watched Camillo go through various stages in response to the proposal that he marry Pauline. First, surprise and vague dismay. Next—after the initial meeting with Pauline—fascination.

After a few more meetings, the prince had committed himself to a public pursuit of Napoleon's sister. But it was clear that for all his enjoyment of the rituals of courtship, he was not in any hurry to schedule the wedding itself. He had never expressed any impatience with the lengthy and intricate process of securing papal approval for the match. And, more recently, the diplomat had begun to see occasional signs that the prince was having second thoughts.

Now, for example.

Camillo, who had risen when the older man entered, did not sit down again. His expression was guarded and unhappy. He did not respond directly to Angiolini's announcement but took a turn about the room and then came back to stand in front of his visitor. "I am not certain that we should proceed so quickly," he said.

Quickly! Angiolini kept smiling, but he was gritting his teeth. His correspondence with the pope on behalf of the young couple had been occupying most of his time for the past two months. "Have you heard from your mother?" he asked, temporizing. He knew the answer because he had intercepted the letter and read it before allowing it to be delivered. Princess Anna Maria thought it was high time her son married and produced an heir; she was strongly in favor of this particular match because Pauline had already proved that she could bear sons.

"My mother is hardly an unbiased advisor. She has been urging me to marry for the last five years. Nor has she met my potential bride."

With a graceful gesture, Angiolini acknowledged the point. "Has something happened, then, to discourage you? Has Madame Leclerc hinted that she does not favor your suit?"

Camillo shook his head. "No, she is charming. But . . ." He took another turn around the room, this time remaining by the window, facing away from Angiolini. Abruptly, he changed the subject. "Do you know who spoke with me last week at the reception given by Joseph Bonaparte?" He didn't wait for an answer. "The Contessa di Lanta. You remember her, do you not? My grandfather's cousin? She has been taking the waters somewhere for a few weeks, but recently she has returned to Paris."

Angiolini could not imagine why the prince would care about the comings and goings of a fat old woman, even if she was a distant cousin. Every noblewoman in Rome, after all, was related to the Borghese family in some fashion or another, so that did not distinguish her. And this particular distant cousin was truly distant: she had moved to Paris many years ago. Camillo had never met her in Italy and had barely known her name until arriving in France.

"The Contessa di Lanta, yes," Angiolini said, mystified.

"She, like you, wished to congratulate me on my forthcoming marriage."

And suddenly Angiolini was no longer mystified.

The countess was one of the biggest gossips in Paris. No, in all of Europe. There were many other purveyors of rumor, scandal, venom, and ridicule in the capital, and Camillo had probably chatted with some of them during the endless round of parties marking France's return to frivolity under its new First Consul. But this particular purveyor of poison spoke Italian. The others spoke French. So, for the first time, Camillo had actually understood the innuendos and double entendres in the conversation. In fact, knowing the countess, it had probably been much more than innuendo. He studied the prince's averted face, his folded arms.

He cleared his throat. "Your Excellency, everyone knows the countess is a foolish old woman."

"Not as foolish as I am!" Camillo turned around and glared at Angiolini. "Apparently I am the only one in Paris who did not realize my intended bride is—is—" His face turned red. "I cannot even say the word!"

"And you believed these lurid accusations?" Angiolini's tone was a careful blend of sorrow and incredulity.

Camillo dropped sullenly into a chair. "She wasn't the only one. I've been hearing hints from others as well."

"Those stories have been circulating for years." Angiolini rose and crossed to the bell. "May I? I find I am suddenly thirsty."

The servant appeared, disappeared, returned with a decanter and glasses, and withdrew once more.

Angiolini stole a glance at Camillo as they took up their glasses. The interruption had had its effect; the prince looked more subdued now. "Did you think," the diplomat said gently, "that I would not have heard the tales myself? That I would not have investigated the young woman?" He sipped the wine, set the glass down carefully on the table, leaned back. "What have you heard?"

As he had expected, Camillo was reluctant to make any specific accusations. Eyes fixed on the floor, he mumbled something. The only word Angiolini could be sure of was "wild." Well, that would do.

"Yes, Madame Leclerc was a bit wild as a young girl," he conceded. "There was an older man, a Frenchman. The family had recently arrived here from Corsica; the country was in turmoil; they were treated as foreigners because they spoke French with an accent; her older brothers were away at military academy and her father was dead. This scoundrel took advantage of her fear and unhappiness and persuaded her to elope with him."

"I heard it was Pauline who did the persuading," muttered the prince.

Angiolini raised his eyebrows. "Do you think that is likely?" he asked. "That a lonely fifteen-year-old girl, mocked by her new neighbors for her poor French, would decide to seduce a man of the world three times her age?" As he had hoped, the picture of Pauline as a victim of French snobbery rang true with Camillo. Angiolini was a reader of men, and he had read the adult Camillo as not very different from the reserved, romantic boy who had spent hours in the family's great villa staring at the marble faces of ancient nymphs and avoiding his martinet of a father. The prince could appear at every party in Paris, could talk, laugh, drink, dance, dazzle the new court with his elegant clothes and even more elegant manners—but if he had heard the gossip about Pauline, surely he had also heard the jokes at his own expense: that he danced like an angel but spoke like a dunce, that he could ride any horse in France but could not utter two intelligent sentences in a row. That would sting, would sting all the more because there was nothing he could do to change society's verdict. Of all people, Camillo was most likely to understand why Pauline had been unhappy.

"In any case, it came to nothing. Her family learned of her foolishness and banished the adventurer; shortly afterward she was married to Leclerc and behaved as a good and dutiful wife. She bore him a son. She followed him to the Indies. When he fell ill with a terrible fever, she nursed him day and night with her own hands, and when he died, she was so grief-stricken she cut off all her hair and put it in his coffin. Then she sailed back to France with his remains—months at sea in a tiny cabin with the coffin containing her dead husband. She could not eat or sleep and grew thin and pale." He paused to let this affecting tableau sink in. "At last she arrived in France, and what did the enemies of her brother do? They spread rumors that her hair had fallen out because of some loathsome disease she had contracted! They accused her of having had an affair on the ship!"

At the mention of this last item, Camillo shifted uncomfortably.

So, he had heard the tale of the groaning ghost. It was Angiolini's personal favorite among the current collection of stories about Pauline.

He sighed. "Let me guess what the countess told you. She told you that Pauline not only took a lover during the passage back to France but that she received his carnal embraces on her husband's very casket. That as the sinners reached the height of pleasure, a groan was heard from inside the coffin and the widow fled in terror, screaming to the sailors on deck that her cabin was haunted. That the next morning she found that her back, her legs, her arms, her neck—all the places where her naked flesh had touched the casket—were covered with hideous sores, and when her maid brushed her hair, it all fell out. Thus she was forced to wear a veil and long gloves for the rest of the voyage, in spite of the tropical heat."

Clearly the countess had indeed told this story; the prince was stiff with embarrassment but showed no sign of surprise or shock.

"A very amusing tale," added Angiolini in a dry voice. "And not original. Messer Boccaccio tells one very like it."

The younger man looked up. "Then it is false?"

"Of course it is false! Your Excellency, do you imagine for one moment that I would propose to you an alliance with such a woman? There is not a shred of truth to any of it. You have seen Madame Leclerc for yourself; does she appear to be covered with hideous sores? To be bald?"

At last a suggestion of a smile—the prince sat back in his chair. Absently, he picked up his wine and drained it. They sat in silence for a few moments.

"I can never tell when someone is lying here in France," said Camillo finally. "At home I often can, but here, no. It is a country of deceit and pretense. Everyone is very amiable, but I do not trust them."

"When you are married," Angiolini dared to suggest, "you will return to your own country. To Italy. With the most beautiful woman in Europe as your bride."

"Perhaps." Camillo poured himself more wine. "Perhaps." He still looked troubled.

The most beautiful woman in Europe, at that moment, was sitting in Sophie's room in her oldest dress, with her hair under a sweat-stained kerchief. She had not slept for two days. There were dark hollows under her eyes, and her hands trembled slightly as she held a damp cloth to Sophie's mouth. But her voice was perfectly calm.

"Don't try to talk, Sophie."

She had been saying the same thing over and over again all day yesterday, and all night, and this morning. *Don't try to talk. It will hurt your throat.*

Pauline did not understand how it had happened. None of the servants had been ill, and Sophie did not play with other children. But the previous evening, Sophie had not come downstairs with her cousin to say good-night. Since Pauline was going to a supper hosted by Joseph—yet another group of dignitaries paying homage to the new First Consul—she had been preoccupied and had not questioned the servants about Sophie's unusual absence.

When she had returned home a few hours after midnight, Carlotta had been waiting for her, half-asleep on a chair in the anteroom to her bedchamber.

"Signora—" she started to say as she scrambled to her feet.

"What is it? Is it Dermide?" Pauline glared at her. "Why are you here? You should be with him! One of the other servants could have waited for me! You should have sent to my brother's house at once!" While she was speaking—or rather, nearly shouting—she was running up the stairs to the nursery, followed by the panting servant, who called after her plaintively:

"Signora, signora, no!"

Carlotta did not catch up with her until she was kneeling by Dermide. He was sleeping peacefully, curled up in his usual position facing the wall with his thumb in his mouth. She ripped off her right glove and felt his forehead. It was cool, a little damp. He looked angelic.

"It is not Dermide," gasped Carlotta. "It is Sophie."

Pauline frowned. "She did not come to the drawing room after supper with Dermide to bid me good-night," she said slowly, remembering.

"No, signora, she told Nunzia that she had a sore throat and went to bed early." Carlotta wrung her hands. "The stupid girl did not think to tell anyone that her mistress was not feeling well. But when she came upstairs to turn down the lamps,

Sophie was very ill. She fetched me, and I thought you would be back shortly and would know what to do."

Pauline got up and headed back down to the third floor. "Who is with her now?" she said, looking over her shoulder. "Nunzia or Margot?"

"Nunzia, of course." Carlotta patronized and bullied the younger servant but defended her to the death against the French-speaking members of the staff.

"What is wrong with her?"

"I don't know, signora." Carlotta, hastening down the stairs behind her, was still trying to catch her breath. "She has a fever, I think."

Sophie's door was ajar, and lamps were burning in her bedroom and in the sitting room. Pauline swept in, ignoring the young maidservant seated by the bed. She bent over the thin face on the pillow. "Sophie!"

The girl's cheeks were flushed, and her breath had an odd, staccato catch. The skin on her wrist was like heated parchment. Beside her, Carlotta laid her seamed brown hand on Sophie's brow. "Blessed Virgin, save me, she is burning up!" she muttered.

"Go get a pitcher of water, a basin, and some cloths," Pauline snapped at the younger maid. "And have someone in the kitchen put a kettle on to boil." She turned back to the girl and shook her gently. "Sophie! Can you hear me?"

Sophie's eyelids quivered but did not open.

"It's Cousin Pauline," Pauline said crisply. "Please try to wake up. You are ill, and we need to give you some medicine." In an undertone, to Carlotta, "Fetch the small green bottle from my traveling case, and a spoon." After her husband's death from fever six months earlier, she was never without that bottle, a tincture of Peruvian bark. She tugged the bolster forward and lifted Sophie onto it so that she was almost sitting up. Her head lolled over to one side. Pauline had seen this before, when Emmanuel was dying. Panicking, she grabbed Sophie's head and held it up, pushing at the bolster with her other hand to wedge it more firmly upright.

The gray eyes opened, closed, opened again, inches away from her own.

"You're awake!" Pauline was so relieved that she almost let go. She lowered the girl's head back down to the pillow.

Sophie's mouth moved. She was trying to say something, but only a croak emerged.

"Here, this will make you feel better." Carlotta had reappeared with the bottle and spoon, and Pauline poured out half a measure and lifted the spoon toward Sophie.

Looking terrified, the girl shook her head.

"Come now, you're not a baby like Dermide! You're not afraid of a little medicine!"

Sophie tried to talk again, and again nothing came out. Tears were running down her face. She pointed to her throat.

"Your throat hurts?"

A weak nod.

"The medicine will help," Pauline said firmly, tilting the spoon between the cracked lips. "It will taste bitter, but only for a moment."

Sophie tried to swallow. Pauline could see the muscles in her throat working. But something was wrong. The brown liquid dribbled back out, running down her chin to mix with the tears.

"God," whispered Pauline. "First Emmanuel and now this

poor girl! Heaven is punishing me for neglecting her." She could feel tears welling up and blinked them away.

"Shall I send for the doctor, signora?" It was the maid, nervously holding the pitcher and basin out in front of her like a shield. Behind her were two of the kitchen staff; in the hall below more lamps were being lit and she could hear the voice of her chamberlain giving orders.

Pauline straightened her shoulders. "Send for the doctor, yes. Heat some barley water with honey. And bring me some wine."

The servants scattered, but Carlotta turned back at the doorway. "If she dies, she will go to hell," she said gruffly. "Her father is a godless heathen. We must send for a priest and have her baptized at once."

For two hours, until the doctor arrived, Pauline sat by Sophie, bathing her face and trying to coax her to swallow the barley water and honey. Carlotta was barred from the room lest she carry the disease to Dermide, and when Nunzia tried to help, Pauline called her a clumsy fool and banished her as well.

The doctor came and went; Pauline did not call him a clumsy fool to his face but thought him even more useless than the maid. He felt Sophie's pulse and bled her a little. Then he took a small mirror from his bag and reflected a lamp into Sophie's mouth, opening her jaw as though he were examining a horse or a cow and peering at the back of her throat. He shook his head. "I am afraid that she has the strangling sickness, Madame Leclerc," he said. "I can do very little. Already she cannot speak; if her throat swells any more, she will be unable to breathe."

Nunzia, hovering in the doorway, came in as the doctor bowed himself out. She whispered to Pauline, "Signora, I can send for the priest. Father Laurent will be done with the morning service by now."

"Get out!" screamed Pauline. "Get out, you stupid bitch! We do not need a priest!"

The maid fled.

Sophie couldn't swallow the barley water, not even in small spoonfuls. Pauline dipped a napkin into the beaker and trickled drops into the corner of Sophie's mouth. Sophie would doze and wake, and every time she woke, Pauline would jerk herself out of her anxious stupor and hold the warm, sweet cloth at the edge of her lips, squeezing until a thin thread of liquid ran back through her teeth.

"Don't try to talk," she said every time Sophie woke up. "It will hurt your throat."

But the sick girl did try, over and over again; there was something she wanted to say. No sound came out.

The servants tiptoed in and out, bringing Pauline food. At some point—she did not remember when—she had left the room briefly to change out of her evening dress. It was ruined; there were rust-colored stains all down the bodice. She left it crumpled on the floor, pulled the jet beads out of her hair and grabbed an old gown and shawl. Halfway up the staircase, she realized that she still had on her black satin shoes. She stepped out of them, leaving them on the landing, and continued in her stocking feet.

Back to Sophie's bedchamber, where the shutters and curtains were closed against the infectious outside air, and it was always dim and stuffy—never quite day and never quite night. The timeless twilight of the sickroom was terrifyingly familiar.

Sophie even looked like Emmanuel—the same fair hair and long, gentle face.

Not this time, Pauline said to herself over and over again. Not this time. I am in Paris, not the West Indies.

Should he marry Pauline Bonaparte? Camillo paced back and forth in front of the chair where Angiolini had been earlier. One thing was clear to him: if he did nothing, he would soon find himself wed to Napoleon's sister. Gigantic forces were pushing him toward the altar: Angiolini, the Bonaparte brothers, his own family, and, above all, the pope's desire to protect his land from the French army. Now was the time to take a stand; no public declaration had been made; it was all still couched in elaborate conditional queries sealed inside confidential dispatches. He had said nothing to Pauline; she had said nothing to him and treated him no differently than her other admirers. If he went to Joseph Bonaparte today and told him firmly, resolutely, that he had decided against the match, he could stop the proceedings before it was too late. Joseph, he had decided, was a safer choice than Angiolini, for this purpose. Angiolini was too glib and persuasive.

Should he marry Pauline Bonaparte? Did he want to marry her? Did he want to marry anyone?

Camillo considered the last question first. He knew that he was obligated to marry. He had been avoiding it for years. Now he admitted to himself that it was time to marry. A prince required an heir. More: a prince required a princess—a hostess, a governess of his households. As for wanting . . . Yes, he wanted a companion, a helpmate, a loving woman bound to him by vows and loyalty rather than by gifts of jewelry (his last mistress in Rome) or boredom with her husband (his next-to-last mistress in Rome). His reluctance to marry was rapidly diminishing now that his mother was so far away. In fact, yet another advantage of marriage: his mother would have to relinquish her place as the highest-ranking female in the Borghese family.

Next he considered the first question. Was marriage to a Bonaparte useful to his family? Unquestionably. Every single political consideration argued strongly for this alliance. Seven years ago, Napoleon had marched into northern Italy; it had taken him little more than a year to evict the "invincible" Austrians from their holdings and gobble them up for France, along with the papal states, only recently restored. Anything that a Borghese could do to dissuade France from once again invading the papal territories was a sacred duty.

That left the most difficult question: Did he want to marry *her?* Pauline. Beautiful, flirtatious, charming, capricious Pauline. He could picture her in every room of his enormous palace, making its gloomy, Tiber-damp chambers suddenly brighter. He could picture her in the tree-lined walkways of the Borghese villa just outside the city, admiring the decorative flocks of sheep and trailing her fingers in the fountains. He could picture her dancing and sparkling in the villa's elegant reception rooms. He could picture her in his bed.

He could definitely picture her in his bed. But who would be in bed with her?

For all Angiolini's reassurances, Camillo was inclined to believe at least some of the stories about Pauline. He had seen the shiny pink circle of the healed ulcer on her left hand himself. Her hair was very short. Too short to be explained as a fash-

ionable whim. Even if she had not copulated on her husband's
coffin, there was something about her that suggested that she
had copulated in other exotic locations.

He remembered watching her with one of Napoleon's young
officers a few weeks earlier. The lieutenant had been turning away after bidding her farewell, and Pauline had evidently
decided that she did not want him to leave just yet. She had
stretched her shoulders back like a cat, pushing up her breasts,
tilting her chin, drawing in her breath—for one small moment,
a woman on her back in bed, although she was standing fully
clothed in a crowded receiving room in the Tuileries. The young
officer had been frozen in place.

So had every other man in the room.

She *was* wild. Too wild.

The following morning, he presented himself at the Hôtel Mar-
boeuf, Joseph's mansion, and was ushered at once into the same
large salon where Joseph and his wife, Julie, had received him six
weeks earlier on his first afternoon in Paris. Then the room had
seemed bright and hospitable; now the tall windows and heavy
furniture loomed over him and made him feel nervous. When
Joseph bustled in, friendly and eager, a few moments later, Camillo could barely pull himself out of his chair.

How on earth had he believed he could tell Pauline's brother
that he found his sister unacceptable? Yes, he and Joseph had
become friendly, had talked of horses and travel and music, and
even, in one slightly drunken conversation, of their overbearing
mothers. But this was no casual conversation about common in-
terests or family foibles. Camillo could hardly pretend that he
thought Pauline unattractive or socially awkward.

Joseph would know the truth: Camillo thought his sister was a slut. The man would be outraged, perhaps even outraged enough to issue a challenge. Camillo was quite proficient with the small sword; it was possible he would kill Joseph . . . kill the brother of Napoleon . . . this was a disaster.

"My dear fellow!" Joseph, like Angiolini the day before, was ebullient. "Everything is all but settled, I hear. No, no, sit down." He waved Camillo, who was standing frozen in dismay, back to his seat. "I have sent for some champagne. We will toast your nuptials."

"Well. Yes. About this marriage—" Camillo looked helplessly at his host. Joseph's face, in the gentle sunlight, suddenly bore a remarkable resemblance to Pauline's—a perfect, delicate cameo of a face. "I—I do not think your sister cares for me," he stammered.

Joseph looked surprised. "But she likes you very well! She has told me so herself, in fact."

He was floundering. "I called yesterday and was turned away."

This was not entirely true. He had not visited in person, but one of his servants, sent over to the Hôtel de Charost with a note, had reported that Madame Leclerc was not receiving visitors.

Joseph laughed. "Ah! Now you show me that you are a lover, to read so much into so little! Well, Pauline does not wish it generally known, but her little cousin, Mademoiselle Leclerc, has been ill for the past few days."

It took Camillo a moment to recall Sophie; so much fuss had been made over Dermide on his previous visits that the other child had faded into the background. He remembered her now: an awkward, pale girl who never smiled and in fact had seemed to glare at him once or twice. He had thought her rather unappealing and far preferred the exuberant and cheerful Dermide, whose blond curls set off his mother's dark elegance beautifully. Nor did he have much sympathy for the sick; he was rarely ill and had never paid much attention to discussions of disease or infirmity, which seemed to him slightly distasteful. If it was taboo for polite men and women to discuss the normal functions of their bodies—sex and defecation, for example, two of the most pleasurable activities, being entirely forbidden—then why was it acceptable to dwell endlessly on the malfunctions of those same bodies?

"I hope she is better now?" he said politely.

"Yes, I sent a boy this morning to inquire and he reports that she is improving. In fact, I am going over there shortly to see Pauline, now that the child is out of danger. Perhaps you could accompany me, let her make her own excuses for her discourtesy yesterday?"

Camillo was saved from answering by the appearance of the champagne, which was duly poured.

"To Mademoiselle Leclerc's recovery," he said hastily, before Joseph could propose a toast to his marriage.

"Indeed." Joseph eyed him narrowly and turned the conversation to the unseasonably cool weather.

By the third day of Sophie's illness, Pauline began to hope, cautiously, that she had won the battle. The fever had gone down—not entirely but enough. The rattle had disappeared from the halting breaths. The drops squeezed from the endless supply of napkins seemed to be making their way somehow down Sophie's throat. Pauline allowed herself to sleep for a few hours at a time on a cot instead of on the chair next to Sophie's bed. When

Nunzia came to tend the fire, signaling the arrival of yet another dawn, she let her open the curtains and bring up some chocolate. She had finished half the pot and was nodding off in her chair when she heard a rustle from the bed beside her.

Sophie was awake. Truly awake, blinking. And as Pauline hastily brought over a fresh cloth and squeezed it between her lips, she swallowed, very carefully, wincing but triumphant.

What a miracle, thought Pauline, watching the slender throat contract and relax again. From the lips, to the tongue, to the back of the mouth, to the throat, to the stomach. Impossible without those tiny muscles in our neck, without that opening sloping down behind our tongue. *How frail our bodies are.*

Sophie clearly thought one swallow was enough for the moment. Pauline disagreed. Quickly, she tipped a little bit of the liquid into a glass and held it to Sophie's mouth.

"Ah," said Sophie, indistinctly after the second swallow. It was more of a croak than anything else.

"Don't talk," said Pauline automatically, offering her more barley water.

"Ah, ah." She looked determined to speak.

"Here." Pauline set down the glass and propped Sophie higher on the pillows. She tried to guess what Sophie was trying to say. "Do you want something else to drink? Something hot? Or some cherry cordial?" The cherry cordial was Dermide's favorite, although Pauline diluted it so much that it was more like cherry-flavored water.

"Sorra," whispered Sophie.

Pauline bent over her. "Hush."

"I'm sorry." This time it came out more clearly.

"You can talk again; that is wonderful," said Pauline, patting her hand. "And swallow properly. The doctor will be very pleased. Can you drink more?"

Sophie nodded.

Pauline slipped her arm behind Sophie's shoulder and helped her sit up and take small sips of the barley water. Every swallow made Sophie wince. "That's it, that's my brave girl," she said after each sip. She made her drink half a glass, then said, remembering, "Why are you sorry?"

"For getting sick," mumbled Sophie. "For being such a trouble."

Pauline laughed. "As if you had any say in the matter! No one chooses to be sick!"

Later, Sophie would remind her of that comment, but now she just gave a little smile and closed her eyes again.

Pauline stepped into the sitting room and beckoned to Nunzia, who had been keeping her own vigil.

"Broth, tea, watered wine," she ordered. "And perhaps some grapes, if Madame Golet can obtain them. Beef jelly." Her mental inventory of food for convalescents failed her temporarily. "Whatever else Carlotta thinks a sick child should eat. We'll let her sleep for two hours, and then see what she can get down."

Nunzia looked at the sleeping Sophie, then at Pauline. "She is getting better, then? It is true? God be praised!" She had tears in her eyes.

"The kitchen. And Carlotta," Pauline said, prompting her.

"Yes, signora." Nunzia danced out the door, calling out in Corsican as she reached the back stairs, "She is better! She is better! I need Carlotta in the kitchen right away!"

Pauline sank back into her chair, exhausted. It was probably safe to leave Sophie with someone else now. She could take a break from the sickroom. Her stomach grumbled; she had barely eaten for three days—the servants had brought her food, but terror had killed her appetite. She should eat. She should summon her chamberlain and see if the household was still functioning after three days of neglect. She should have a bath and wash her hair, which was so stiff with dried sweat that it felt like a wig glued to her scalp.

Instead, she fell asleep, her feet tucked up beneath her and her head resting on the curved back of the chair.

"My sister is expecting me," said Joseph, handing his hat and coat to the nervous footman who had finally answered the door. "Is she with Mademoiselle Sophie?" He looked around. The household seemed to be in a state of chaos. None of the old retainers he knew were visible anywhere; strange servants were peering rudely from the side room at the two men without offering to help the footman, and he could hear some sort of commotion floating up from the kitchen, which was underneath the back hallway.

"I believe so, monsieur." The footman looked around desperately for a more senior member of the household staff.

"Never mind," said Joseph, adding Camillo's coat to the pile on the man's arm. "I know the way." He led Camillo toward the stairs. "This place was a mausoleum when Pauline bought it," he confided as they began climbing. "She was living with me and Julie when she returned from the West Indies, and she wanted a house of her own, but we thought she was mad to buy something this size. At any rate, she wanted to show me every room in this cursed house at every stage of the redecoration. And when the little girl came to live with her, she redecorated that suite *again*.

Now Julie wants to buy new furniture for the first-floor rooms in our house. A chair is a chair, I said, but she tells me I have no notion of fashion." He paused for breath at the second landing. "One more flight, Sophie's rooms are right over Pauline's."

Camillo had never been beyond the public rooms on the first floor of Pauline's house; he was surprised to see that the carpeting and paneling continued all the way up to the second and third floors. Lamps in the halls, some still lit, silk hangings, elaborate plasterwork. Pauline had expensive taste.

"Just down here," Joseph was saying. He knocked gently and pushed open the doors. "Pauline?" He motioned for Camillo to follow him and went in.

They were in a small sitting room whose furnishings had clearly been chosen by a young girl: pink and white walls, pink damask curtains, flowered cushions, small china animals on every available surface. The room was empty, but the door to the adjacent bedchamber was open. They walked toward it, suddenly quiet, remembering that this was a sickroom.

Camillo could see over Joseph easily; he was nearly five inches taller. The girl was asleep in the bed. Next to her, curled up in a chair, was Pauline. She was wearing a faded yellow cotton dress and her hair was tied up under a kerchief. It was the first time Camillo had seen her wearing any color but black. It was the first time he had seen her without jewels and cosmetics. It was the first time he had seen her asleep.

She looked terrible. There were dark circles under her eyes, and her lips were pale and dry. Her hair, what little could be seen underneath the kerchief, was plastered to her forehead. Scattered around her was all the evidence of the recent ordeal: basins, glasses, pitchers, spoons, droppers, bottles of medicine. Below her chair on the floor was a pile of discarded napkins, each with one wrinkled, stiff corner.

As quietly as possible, Camillo backed away. He tiptoed through the sitting room with its menagerie of china animals, tiptoed down the three flights of carpeted stairs, tiptoed through the entrance hall, and let himself out the front door. He didn't try to find a servant to bring him his hat and coat. He would be back later. He would send her a note, and she would bathe and dress and put on jewelry and curl her hair and arrange herself on her chaise with Dermide like a goddess with an attendant cherub.

And then he would ask her to marry him, because he had seen her when she thought no one was looking.

FOUR

Two days later, Camillo returned to the Hôtel de Charost. Forty-eight hours of reflection had not banished the oddly magnetic image of the haggard, sleeping Pauline. Part of him wanted to be cautious, to consider, to delay. He had tried to summon up the doubts and misgivings that had prompted his visit to Joseph. They were still there but misted over, like faded ink on an old sheet of paper. Part of him wanted to rush back to Pauline and throw himself on his knees now, at once, before his more cowardly self could stop him. In the end, he did go back—he could not stay away. But he did not commit himself yet; he sent no word of his visit in advance and announced, as he handed his hat and gloves to the footman, that he had come to inquire after Mademoiselle Sophie. He assumed that he would be taken to one of the formal drawing rooms and that Pauline would receive him. He expected to wait; he had come without warning, after all, and he knew that Pauline would want to look her best. He expected to be dazzled, as always, by Pauline's beauty. He expected to be given some sign—a word, a gesture—that Pauline wanted him to propose to her.

He did not expect that he would actually be taken to see Sophie, and so he paid no attention to where he was going until it was too late.

The young Corsican maid who escorted him upstairs noticed the flat box under his arm just as she opened the door into the pink sitting room.

"Oh, Your Excellency, I should have taken that from you!" she said, horrified. Before Camillo could say anything, she had it firmly in both hands and was stepping into the suite ahead of him, holding out the box.

"Sophie! Signorina Sophie! You have a visitor!"

The sick girl was sitting on the sofa, swathed in shawls, paging listlessly through a magazine. There was a pile of half-open books and magazines on the table beside her, pushing the ranks of china animals into a multicolored herd in one corner. At the sound of her name, she looked up, suddenly flushed and eager—until she saw who it was.

"Look," said the maid triumphantly. "His Excellency has brought you a present!"

Camillo watched in horror as the maid laid the box on Sophie's lap. He had thought for hours about what he could give Pauline today. Not jewelry; that was for when he made his formal proposal of marriage. Not flowers; that would say that today's visit was an ordinary call. Something in between. Something that signaled his intention to propose marriage. A voucher. A pledge of alliance.

He had settled on one of the family heirlooms he had brought with him from Rome, a large cameo medallion set in gold. The medallion showed a dragon—one of the emblems of the Borghese house—in high relief, green against a white background. The scales were edged in gold leaf; the eyes were tiny rubies. It had been made as one of a set of six for his great-grandfather, but the others had been lost or broken.

"That is very kind of you," said Sophie woodenly. She did not smile or look at him, and she made no move to open the gift.

"How—how are you feeling?" said Camillo, wrenching his eyes away from the box.

"Better." She added after a moment, "Thank you." Then, in response to an urgent gesture from the maid, "Won't you sit down, Your Excellency?"

"Thank you." Camillo sat, his eyes returning to the box.

There was an awkward silence, and then Camillo took a deep breath. It was just a piece of glass. Let it go. "It is for your collection," he said.

"My collection?" She looked up for the first time, puzzled.

He gestured toward the crowded jumble of china and crystal fauna on the table. "You don't have a dragon."

"Oh." She looked down again, then slowly untied the ribbons and opened the box. The maid gave an audible gasp when Sophie lifted out the medallion. "It is very nice," Sophie said politely. She held it on her lap, studying it for a moment, then set it on the table on top of one of the open books. "Thank you."

"Your Italian is quite good," he offered.

"Thank you," she said again, eyes still lowered.

Camillo wondered if they were going to sit here saying "thank you" to each other for the rest of the visit. And if the girl ever looked at anyone when she talked to them. Of course, she had been ill. She was tired.

"How is your cousin?" he tried, after another short silence.

"Oh, Dermide is fine. He did not get infected."

"Ah, that is good." He cleared his throat. "I meant Madame Leclerc, actually."

"I don't know." Sophie's head was bent so low that he could not see her eyes any longer. All he could see was the neatly parted fair hair and the tops of two blond eyebrows. "I haven't seen her today. Or yesterday. I think she is resting." There was a slight quiver in her voice. Then, more firmly, "She nursed me, you know. For days. She slept in here, with me." There was almost a challenge in her tone.

How long had he been here? Three minutes? Five? It seemed like an eternity.

It all happened at once: quick footsteps, a rustle of skirts, Sophie's pale, drooping face suddenly alight, turned toward the door, eyes shining. Pauline was here, and the dead space had come alive. She was dressed in black once more, but it didn't matter; she was still the most colorful, vibrant thing in the room.

"Prince Camillo!" She swept him a sketch of a curtsey, smiling. "I see I have a rival for your affections! You slight me for Sophie!"

He would have protested, but Sophie jumped in first. "No, no," she said, trying to stand up and struggling with the shawls. "He asked about you! He was just being polite!"

Pauline gave him an amused glance. "Do sit down, Sophie, you're still not well," she said, without really looking at the girl. She was surveying Camillo and evidently liked what she saw; her smile took on a hint of possessiveness.

"I'm better," said Sophie, breathless.

"Nonsense." Pauline finally looked at her. "You're flushed, and I can see you trembling from here. Nunzia, get her something to drink. And some wine for His Excellency." She pushed Sophie back onto the sofa. "Don't you know how to entertain callers? You should have rung for refreshments at once." The maid bobbed her head and vanished.

"I beg your pardon," said Sophie, looking mortified.

"I don't think Sophie has ever had any callers before," Pauline said to Camillo, gesturing him back to his chair as she sat down by Sophie. Her eye fell on the box and ribbon, which had slid to the floor. "What's this? Did His Excellency bring you a present, Sophie? How very thoughtful of him!"

As Pauline's eye went from the ribbon to the empty box to the glittering cameo on its precarious perch on the table, Camillo felt as though time had stopped, allowing his mind to see, in detail, all the hideous possibilities. Pauline might think he had brought a fantastically expensive and inappropriate gift for Sophie, marking him as a fool. She might think he had given the dragon to Sophie to win her over to his side, marking him as a schemer. Or she might deduce the truth: that he was so socially inept that he had allowed a maid to take Pauline's gift and give it to her ten-year-old ward.

In that frozen moment, Camillo saw Sophie's expression and knew that the panicked indecision he saw there was a precise mirror of his own face.

Luckily, Pauline was staring at the medallion. She picked it up. "You shouldn't leave it on top of something else, Sophie. It's breakable. And very valuable." Her finger traced the outline of the dragon's neck. "Lovely," she said, setting it back down, carefully, in a clear space away from the edge. Was Camillo imagining it, or had there been a wistful undertone to that "lovely"?

His eyes met Sophie's again.

"It isn't for me," Sophie said suddenly, just a little bit too loud. "It's for you." Her chin tilted up, and for an instant she didn't look like a child at all. "The prince wanted to show it to me, to see if you would like it."

"It's for me?" Pauline turned to Camillo.

He nodded.

Pauline gave Sophie a quizzical look. "Well, what did you tell him, Sophie? Did you think I would like it?"

"I said it was very nice. But—but you were not supposed to see it yet."

"Very nice! Sophie, you goose, it is a treasure!" Pauline snatched the medallion and held it up. "Look, the eyes are little jewels!" She turned to Camillo. "It is beautiful; thank you."

"You should thank me, too," said Sophie. "I told him to give it to you."

Pauline tilted her head to one side and looked at Sophie, at Camillo, and finally down at the dragon. She knew, Camillo realized. She knew exactly what had happened. "Well, I do thank you, Sophie." She tapped the medallion lightly. "You have very good taste."

He did not stay long; Sophie was a convalescent. The maid came back with wine and candied nuts and dutifully admired Pauline's gift with no apparent surprise at the change of recipient. Sophie drank a tonic and was sent off to bed, bribed with the promise that Pauline would return to check on her after seeing Camillo out.

They walked downstairs side by side, Camillo's hand just touching the inside of her elbow.

"So," she said, just as they reached the front door. "Are you going to ask me to marry you?"

"Yes," he heard himself say. Calmly. Without a second thought. "Are you going to say yes?"

"I suppose so." She looked up at him, her dark eyes serious for once.

"You don't mind that I almost gave the last Borghese dragon medallion to a ten-year-old girl?"

She gave a little smile. "No. Poor Sophie, I will have to give her something to make up for it."

"You do like it, don't you?"

"Oh, yes." She reached up and touched the side of his face, a slight caress, like the way she had stroked the dragon's neck. "I am very fond of rubies."

A servant appeared with his hat and coat.

"Tomorrow?" he said.

"Tomorrow, at three."

Pauline had the whole story from Nunzia ten minutes later. The maid kept trying to apologize, but Pauline was laughing so hard she had to sit down and fan herself before she could speak.

"It's all just a misunderstanding; there's no harm done," she finally said, still breathless. "Just imagine, though—that thing must be worth ten thousand francs if it's worth a sou! Thank heavens for my wise little Sophie!"

"Oh," said Nunzia, remembering. "She is asking for you."

"I'll go and see her later." Pauline dabbed her eyes and stood up. "I have to go and decide what I am wearing tomorrow. The prince is coming to ask me to marry him."

Nunzia gave a little shriek and started to dart away to spread the news.

"Nunzia!"

The maid turned back.

"Not one word," Pauline said sternly.

"About the marriage?"

"About this afternoon. The prince's gift. Swear on the Blessed Virgin. And warn Sophie, too."

The girl nodded solemnly and crossed herself.

It was a delicious tale, but there was no point embarrassing the prince by letting it be known. Her brothers, for example, would never let Camillo hear the end of it. Although she wondered what Joseph would have done, or Napoleon, if they had found themselves in Camillo's shoes this afternoon.

She stopped, her hand resting absently on the banister. She knew exactly what they would have done. They would have slapped Nunzia, grabbed the box back, left Sophie in tears, and stormed away in a temper.

Maybe the story wasn't so funny after all.

Camillo proposed—very formally, with a gift of a pair of ruby ear-drops, purchased in great haste after his visit to Sophie. Pauline accepted—equally formally, with a gift of a portrait of herself *à la bergère*. She thought she looked quite fetching as a shepherdess, and scowled at her brother Lucien when he made pointed remarks about Versailles and Marie Antoinette. Lucien was the exception, however. Everyone else in the family seemed quite pleased that Pauline was soon to be Princess Borghese. Even Pauline's mother smiled benignly at her willful daughter and dreamed of audiences with the Holy Father in Rome.

Pauline's dreams were different and did not include the pope.

When Pauline thought about her first marriage now, it was to marvel at how young and naive she had been. Seventeen. A child. Leclerc was hardly much older, in his mid-twenties. He was slender and short—she called him her little Leclerc—and the two of them looked like china miniatures when they appeared together on formal occasions. Her world had been changing so rapidly in those days. At thirteen, she had fled Corsica in the middle of the night. Pauline could still remember the three flea-infested rooms in the worst quarter of Marseilles that had housed her whole family. At fifteen, she was writing passionate love letters to the forty-year-old adventurer Fréron. Two years later, she was in Italy, where her brother was conquering Austrians one week and granting fairy-tale wishes the next. Pauline was to be married? Very well, her husband would now be a general. Josephine found Milan was too noisy and crowded? The Crivelli family would be delighted to offer the Bonaparte family their summer palazzo at Mombello. So Pauline had married Victor Emmanuel Leclerc in an elegant mansion overlooking a poplar-studded valley. Her dowry of forty thousand francs had seemed a small fortune.

Her dowry now was to be half a million francs, and Napoleon's personal gift to her, in addition to the dowry, would be a set of diamonds worth several hundred thousand more. Camillo was showering her with jewels, fans, and gloves. She was young and wealthy and beautiful and she was going to be a princess.

* * *

There was only one problem: Napoleon.

The bride and groom had obtained the First Consul's approval for the match; the contract was drawn up; the dowry established; Pauline's jointure duly recorded. Unfortunately, no one had consulted Napoleon about the date of the wedding.

"Too soon," he said curtly when his mother traveled out to St. Cloud with Pauline to announce that the ceremony would take place at the end of the summer. "I will not authorize it." He returned his attention to a pile of letters on the desk in front of him, dipped his pen into the inkwell, and made a notation in the margin of one sheet.

"Too soon!" Pauline's eyes flashed. "Just three weeks ago you were kissing me on both cheeks and congratulating me! We propose a date six weeks away, and you say 'too soon'?"

Every day since Camillo's proposal, she had seen more to like. He was tall and athletic; he had a delightful low voice and musical laugh; he read poetry to her in Italian and paused in mid-sonnet to kiss her hand. Yet for all his polish, he could be shy—he had blushed like a boy one afternoon when his hand had inadvertently nudged her breast. She found this appealing. It made her feel innocent and desirable. When Camillo took her arm, she felt a warmth and eagerness passing from his body to hers. The weeks of waiting for the pope's official endorsement of the match had seemed very long, and there were still the banns to call. Flirting was all very well, but as a steady diet it lacked substance. Pauline wanted a husband.

"It is too soon," repeated her brother, unmoved by her stormy expression. He pointed with his pen at her dress. Her black dress. "You are still in mourning. The customary period of mourning for a widow, as prescribed by the regulations, is one year. In fact, I believe it may be a bit longer than that. But certainly a minimum of one year. You may not be married for another four months."

"Four more months!" She jumped up. "Are you mad? By then I will be a nervous wreck! Camillo will forget me! He will take a mistress!" She leaned over the side of the desk and changed to a coaxing tone. "Napoleon, this is me, your little Pauline. Think how ill I have been, how terrible it was to sail home from the West Indies with Emmanuel's body. As a personal favor, could we not make an exception?" She ran one hand down his arm in a tentative caress.

He stared down at the pile of correspondence, shoulders rigid. "No."

"Please?"

"No."

"I am not some peasant woman," she said angrily, jerking her hand away and stalking around to the front of the desk. Her mother was frowning at her, but she ignored her. "I am *your sister.* This is a marriage of state. What do I care what the rule is in some silly book?"

"That silly book is the *Almanac National de France!*" her brother roared, throwing down his pen. "You are *my sister,* yes. I am the leader of France. You must be more careful than a 'peasant woman,' not less. You will abide by the regulations prescribed for a widow, or there will be no dowry and no diamonds. You will wear black. You will not dance. You will not attend the theater. And you will not be married until November at the earliest. That is final."

Pauline stalked out of the room in a rage, leaving her mother to placate Napoleon. In the carriage on the way back into town, she stared defiantly ahead, daring Letizia to scold her. But it was her mother, in fact, who came to her a few days later with a proposal: Napoleon and the *Almanac National* governed the civil ceremony that had been the state's lawful marriage rite since the revolution. But the Catholic ceremony, which Pauline and Camillo had planned to celebrate in conjunction with the state license, was not subject to Napoleon's rules. Why not publish the banns at once and have the church wedding as planned? If the banns were called in some small, obscure parish—say, Mortefontaine, where Joseph had a country home—Napoleon would never know. The wedding would have to be a quiet family affair, but surely that was better than waiting four more months?

Her first wedding had been a quiet family affair, and she had hoped, as a princess-to-be, for something more public and festive. But the thought of tricking her priggish older brother was almost as satisfying as the thought of a glamorous wedding feast. The banns were called. The papal legate, Cardinal Caprara, was invited to perform the ceremony. On the twenty-eighth of August, still wearing black, Pauline Bonaparte was married to Prince Camillo Borghese in the eyes of the church and, more important, in the eyes of her mother.

FIVE

Nothing in Camillo's life had prepared him for his wedding night.

He was not a complete innocent. True, for a time in his mid-teens he had harbored secret longings for the priesthood and had backed out of several engagements where older boys promised to "make a man of him." But flesh had eventually triumphed over spirit. A few weeks after his sixteenth birthday, two friends had dosed him with brandy and pushed him into the best bedroom of a local brothel. The whore's name was Marietta. She was probably about twenty but looked twice that. Her teeth were brown and cracked. Her hair, an odd reddish color that was contradicted by the dark thatch between her legs, was already thinning. Still, he was a bit drunk, and she smiled cheerfully at him and let him take his time. The fascination of touching things he had only glimpsed—breasts, nipples, buttocks—made more of an impression than the act itself.

The next morning he had a monumental hangover, which he interpreted as a punishment from God for fornication. For two days he stayed in bed with the curtains drawn, feigning illness. He was sure that anyone who saw him would know instantly what he had done and denounce him to his father. On the third day, he slipped out of the house late in the afternoon and went back to Marietta, where he discovered that the process was much more enjoyable when he was sober. On the fifth day, he went again. Marietta told him he was coming along very nicely and even let him sleep next to her for an hour afterward and have a second round before leaving. On the eighth day, he arrived at the brothel only to be told that Marietta had another visitor. Would he like a different girl, or would he prefer to wait for Marietta? She would not be much longer. Horrified, he fled. It had never occurred to him that Marietta did to anyone else the moist, dark things she did to him. He swore himself to abstinence and kept the vow for four agonizing months.

He grew up. He learned what was expected and did it. Young men had mistresses; Camillo acquired a plump little Venetian who claimed to be a singer. Young men had occasional affairs with married women; Camillo courted a neglected matron and visited her discreetly. None of these liaisons had ever been very satisfying. He found adultery distasteful and often fantasized about dying nobly in a duel, redeeming his honor by refusing to fire at the wronged husband. (Ironically, these daydreams left a morbid, erotic aftertaste that often drove him back to the wife's bed.) Courtesans were at least fair game, but his Venetian singer intimidated him, and he was happy to relinquish her to a rival after a year. He knew she was vulgar and greedy, and he wanted to despise her. But her expertise in bed made him worry that instead she would despise him—a man who still, after all her coaxing and instruction, preferred to make love with his shirt on, in the dark, in silence.

Camillo had occasionally pictured his wedding night. His bride would be a virgin; he would perform the sacrament of marriage upon her body as gently as possible, with modesty and dignity. Then he would retire to his own bed, and the next morning, after she had bathed and been tended by her maids, they would go to church and pray for a blessing on the consummated union. His bride would wear a veil to church so that no one could see her blushes. And in bed, Camillo would (for the first time) be the teacher instead of the student.

Once he decided to marry Pauline, the picture had to be revised slightly. Obviously, Pauline was not a virgin, and when the young officers who surrounded her at every public occasion stepped well over the line of what was proper, in their crude attempts at flirtation, she was more likely to laugh than to blush. He still envisioned himself carrying her reverently to bed, however. He still planned to sleep in his own room afterward and to escort his new bride to church in the morning. He still believed—and this, he admitted to himself later, was the most ridiculous idea of all—he still believed that he would take the lead in bed. Masterful and dignified. Those were his watchwords. Pauline was a butterfly, a tease, a party girl. He would show her the power and solemnity of married love.

The odd circumstances of the wedding created more deviations from the ideal in his imagination. For example, he had not anticipated spending his first night with his bride surrounded by her family. It was, frankly, a bit embarrassing to follow Pauline up to bed in her brother's house, under the eyes of his mother-in-law. His own younger brother, Francesco, had come to Paris from Rome for the occasion. After one look at Letizia Bonaparte's stern face and fiercely clasped rosary, Francesco had prudently abandoned the traditional toasts and songs he had prepared as his brother's best man. Instead, he whispered as Camillo rose from the table, "Good luck, brother! Your bride looks well worth taming, but the ride may be rough!"

Pauline was waiting for him just inside their suite of rooms, looking demure. His spirits rose as he saw her expression, and he gave her a reassuring smile.

"Where are you going?" she said, puzzled, as he turned toward his own bedchamber.

"To get undressed. My valet is waiting for me." He looked around. "Where is your maid?"

"I sent her away. And I sent away your man as well. We can undress each other." Her demure expression suddenly did not look so innocent. A little flutter of panic rose in Camillo's throat. No one had ever seen him completely nude. Nudity was for pagan statues. Nudity was for animals. Men wore clothing.

"Why don't you get into bed," he said, his voice a bit hoarse. "I will just be a minute." He stepped into the adjacent room, trying not to look as though he was hurrying, and closed the door. She had indeed sent away his valet; the man was nowhere to be seen. Camillo thought of ringing for him, took a step toward the bell, then stopped. No, that would take too long. His hands were shaking slightly as he took off his jacket and waistcoat. His skin was cold, too, even though it was a warm August night. When his clammy palms brushed his belly and groin, he flinched.

Breeches, hose, and shirt were tossed onto the floor. His dressing gown was neatly folded on the bed; he wrapped himself in it gratefully and moved back toward the connecting door.

Then he stopped, paralyzed. What if he went in and she was still undressing? Should he knock? Would she expect him to knock? It was so much easier with a mistress! The married ones led you hastily into some dark room and pulled up their skirts; the kept ones played by your rules. Now he was wondering just what the rules were for a bridegroom whose wife was rumored to have made love atop a lead coffin.

Taking a deep breath, he knocked.

He heard her giggle. "Come in!"

His own room was nearly dark; only one lamp was burning by the fireplace. Her room was blazing with light. She had kindled every lamp and every candle in the place—sconces, candelabras, candlesticks, everything.

On the bed, on top of the coverlet, Pauline lay stark naked. She was on her side, facing him, one arm draped over her hip, the other propped underneath her head. Her breasts stood out like little round marzipan cakes, tipped with cherries.

"Welcome, prince husband!" she said gaily.

He froze.

Dignity, he reminded himself. But he could feel his face growing hot. Other parts, too.

Pauline hopped off the bed and danced over to where he stood paralyzed with embarrassment. Without any self-consciousness at all, she untied the sash of his dressing gown and pulled it off.

"You're so tall!" she said, delighted. She squeezed his arm. "And rounded! Napoleon is like a stick, you know. He has the shoulders of his coats padded."

Hastily, he grabbed back the dressing gown but then found himself torn: Who to cover, himself or her? Chivalry won; he wrapped the silk around her shoulders. The hem trailed on the floor.

"Why did you do that?" She wriggled impatiently, and the garment slithered to the floor.

"I—I thought you might be cold," he stammered.

"Cold?" She gave him an incredulous stare. "If anything, it is a bit stuffy in here." She looked down at her breasts. "See, I am sweating."

Camillo was sweating now, too.

"Perhaps we could snuff some of the candles and lamps," he ventured. "If you are warm, that is." She had taken his hand and was tugging him toward the bed, kicking aside the crumpled dressing gown on the floor.

At this, she stopped and turned around to face him. "Don't you want to see me?" she asked, her dark eyes open wide, lips pouting slightly.

Was she surprised? Offended? Teasing? He couldn't tell. It would be cruel to insist on modesty now, he thought. They would consummate the marriage, he would retire to his own room, and in the morning, before church, he would explain that married women in Rome did not permit themselves this sort of license, even with their husbands. It was understandable that Pauline, a young and unworldly bride, might have unwittingly taken the customs of the West Indies as the norm. But here in Europe, she must conduct herself differently.

For example, she should not touch him there. Or squeeze it. Or move her hand underneath—

He closed his eyes and groaned.

"That's better," she whispered, feeling him grow hard. Her fingers were doing something outrageous and exquisite with his balls while she pulled his head down and kissed him, flicking her tongue deeper and deeper into his mouth. They stumbled up against the bed and collapsed across it, with Pauline on top. She wriggled provocatively against him and then pushed up on her elbows and surveyed him.

"My tasty prince," she murmured happily. With a mixture of horror and delight, he watched her dot wet kisses down his stomach, down, farther down, surely she did not mean . . . only whores . . . a spasm of blissful agony shot through him as she took him in her mouth.

"No," he gasped.

But his hands floated down to the top of her head, pressed the fine curls more and more urgently as she licked and sucked. He felt as though he was going to explode. With a superhuman effort, he pushed her away.

"Mmmmm; too fast," she said judiciously. "Your turn, then." She stretched out next to him, hands behind her head, and smiled invitingly.

His turn! Oh, God, all he wanted to do was throw himself on top of her and pound into her until they were both senseless. But there were her breasts, right next to his hand. Her beautiful, soft, pale pink breasts, with their delicious nipples. Hesitantly, he reached out and cupped one breast. It felt wonderful. He slid the nipple through his fingers and watched it spring to attention.

"Mmmmmm," she said again, in a very different tone.

Encouraged, he lowered his head and kissed it. Just a quick, gentle kiss. But when he pulled his head back, she arched her breast up toward him, asking for more. He lost himself for a long time nuzzling and licking and kissing—her breasts, her nipples, the delicate boned valley in between, the hollow of her neck, even her armpits. She was not touching him at all, but the sound of his own kisses and the taste of her sweat were sending pulses of heat through him.

He was losing the battle against temptation. In fact, he was on the verge of complete surrender. His body was not interested in dignity or the church's teachings on marital duties. It had been waiting for its chance to try all the things that schoolboys whispered to each other in feigned disgust, all the fascinating poses in the Raimondi engravings. Just this once. Just once. He could confess when he went to mass tomorrow.

His kisses went lower, and lower still, and then his mouth was fastened on the most forbidden of female places.

Part of him was horrified, but that only added to the plea-sure. He started out slowly, then licked harder and harder, pushing into her with his tongue and feeling her quiver at each touch. The pulses in his groin became flames, and then ago-nized, swollen, delicious torture. Gradually he went faster and deeper, until Pauline had her hands twined in his hair and was rocking furiously.

"Camillo! Oh, Camillo! Camillo!" she gasped.

He was the master now, and he knew it. He waited until she was nearly sobbing, and then, in one movement, pulled himself up, squared her hips, and thrust deep inside her.

She came almost immediately, with a trilling cry of delight that sounded like birdsong. As she shuddered beneath him, he rose up on his elbows and pumped into her, so forcefully that he shoved her up against the pillows and slammed the bed into the wall. She felt unbelievably good—every part of her, inside and out, so smooth and moist and curved. It was his turn to gasp and call her name. He forced himself to slow down, to move more gently, to try to make it last a bit longer.

Then, incredulous, he felt her quicken again beneath him. She began to moan and strain herself against his thrusts. As he lost himself in a final shower of delirious pumping, he heard the birdsong again, like applause.

They both lay there, panting, for several minutes. Pauline got up first.

"Would you like some wine?" she said, going over to the side table and pouring herself a glass. She seemed not at all disconcerted by what had happened.

Would he like some wine! Camillo was still trying to persuade himself that this was not some bizarre dream. Had he really licked her *there* and let her suck and kiss *that*? Had he really been as hard as an oak tree for nearly an hour? Had he, Camillo, really made the most beautiful woman in Europe come not once but twice?

She poured a glass for him without waiting for an answer and brought it back to the bed.

"You know," she said, pushing the tangled covers aside and sitting down. "I always thought you were a bit of a prude. You certainly proved me wrong."

Now, thought Camillo. *Tell her now. I am a prude. No, that is the wrong way to think about it. I am simply a civilized man. And she is my wife and must behave like a civilized woman. This cannot happen again.* He propped himself up on one elbow and took his glass. The wine tasted like honey. The whole world tasted like honey. He was floating on a tide of sated lust.

Pauline curled up next to him and laid her head on his chest.

She dipped one finger into her wineglass and began sucking wine off her finger, drop by drop. Through his half-closed eyes he could see her head and shoulder, resting in the circle of his arm. He felt tender and protective and deeply content.

"I should go back to my own bed," Camillo said drowsily.

"Why?" Pauline dipped her finger again, touched it to her lip, inhaled the drops of wine.

He dozed for a few minutes, with the faint sound of sucking in the background. Then he felt something cool on his skin and opened his eyes again. Pauline was painting lines of wine down the middle of his chest.

"Hey!" He started to sit up.

"Lie still, you'll spill it." She bent over and licked up the bits that were starting to run down his side.

"I should go back to my own bed," he said again. But he didn't move.

She smiled at him. "Don't be silly." She traced patterns in the little puddle of wine, pushing it out of the hollow of his breastbone and then letting it dribble back in.

He couldn't possibly be here, in the light of a dozen lamps and candles, watching a naked woman paint wine on his chest.

She eyed the puddle of wine, considered, shook her head. Then she leaned over and licked it up. Slowly. He could feel himself harden at the first touch of her tongue.

"You must be tired," he said.

"I'm not tired." Her eyes rested on his returning erection. "I don't think you are, either. Would you like to try doggy-style this time?"

"No," he whispered. But he was already picturing her, head

down, with her lovely white cheeks and white thighs pushed up behind her, waiting for him.

He never returned to his own bedroom.

They did not go to church.

Every few days, Camillo resolved to speak firmly with Pauline about her behavior. He said nothing. The weeks of September and October passed in a lust-filled haze, with the necessity of keeping the marriage secret from Napoleon adding a furtive thrill to their encounters. Each evening, he would escort Pauline to yet another glittering assembly. Paris throbbed with money, energy, and ambition, and Pauline—even in black—was the sparkling heart of every crowd. Each night, he would dutifully escort Pauline back to the Hôtel de Charost, kiss her hand, climb into his carriage, and return to his rented townhouse, the Hôtel d'Oigny, a few streets away. An hour later, he would return on foot, alone, slip into Pauline's house through a side entrance, and stay until just before dawn.

At least now they were spending more time under the bed-clothes; the nights had grown chilly. But Pauline still wanted to make love in the bright halo of two dozen candles.

"Don't you want to see me?" she would say when Camillo started to pinch them out. She didn't like it when he closed his eyes, either. "Look at me, look, look," she panted, putting her hands on his face and trying to push his eyelids up. Or she would coax him. "Please, open your eyes. I love your eyes; they are such a beautiful brown, like polished wood, with a little green showing through." He couldn't help it; he would smile and open his eyes and see her laughing up at him. He had never before made love to a woman who was laughing.

They spent every moment together and would sometimes send regrets to state occasions, pleading illness, and escape in a hired carriage to one of the great parks or estates on the outskirts of Paris. Fondly imagining that no one recognized them, they would walk through the formal flower gardens or lose themselves on woodland paths. On one sunny October day, Camillo rented a little boat at Tivoli and rowed in lazy circles on the artificial lake, watching the leaves drift away from his oars. Pauline had taken off her bonnet and was curled up with her head against the bow of the boat.

"You'll turn brown," Camillo said, twisting around to look at her.

"No, I won't," she said. "I did in the West Indies, but the sun here is not strong enough." She trailed one finger in the water, frowning. "Can't you row facing me?"

"Not in this boat."

"Let it drift, then."

He sighed, shipped the oars, and turned himself around. "We're heading for a stone wall," he pointed out.

She turned her face up to the sun and closed her eyes. "You'll stop us in time," she said, yawning.

"You're not even looking at me; why can't I go back to rowing?"

"I'm looking at you through my eyelids."

"Don't be absurd."

She sat up suddenly and smiled at him. "Do you know what I like best about you?"

"What?" he said warily.

"It's so easy to tease you!" She burst out laughing.

That night, as he caressed her, he whispered, "Could you really see me through your eyelids?"

"I see you every time I close my eyes," she said. "Whether you are there or not."

The idyll came to an abrupt end on the sixth of November. On that day, Camillo and Pauline were married again, this time according to the laws of France. This wedding, too, was a small family affair. Napoleon had finally heard about the church wedding and stalked out of Paris in a huff, leaving Pauline and his mother to arrange the civil ceremony without him. Camillo was secretly relieved that the second wedding would not be an elaborate display; the engagement party hosted by Napoleon had been more than enough for him—a formal banquet for two hundred guests at the Tuileries. Pauline, however, was clearly out of sorts, pursing her lips during the ceremony and toying with her food at the meal that followed.

When she and Camillo at last retired to their room, she flung herself into a chair.

"I hate my brother," she said, scowling. "Everything must be just as *he* says, just as *he* wants. His absence today is an insult to you and to me and to both of our families."

"He is a general; there is a war underway. He was summoned to Boulogne," Camillo said mildly.

Pauline glared. "No one 'summons' him these days. He 'summoned' himself to inspect that camp, just to spite me. We were to be married in Paris, with a grand ball afterward, and instead here we are back in Mortefontaine with my mother and my sister-in-law."

"We will have a ball in Rome, to introduce you to everyone there," he said, moving behind her chair and caressing her curls. He loved the feel of them, like little feathered arcs under his hand.

She twisted around to look at him. "Really? A ball?"

"More than one, in fact. We will give a formal ball soon after we arrive, and then during Carnival there is a masked ball at our villa, just outside the city."

Now she was smiling. "Masks? And costumes, as well? Oh, I have always wanted to go to a masquerade! May I have any costume I please?"

"Certainly." He ran his hands down the side of her neck. "What would you like to be?"

She sighed with pleasure and leaned her head against his arm. "A bacchante."

His hand stopped moving. "A bacchante?" Surely she did not mean that. Pauline's education had been somewhat haphazard. Presumably she had heard the word or seen a painting and did not really know what she was saying.

"Yes, one of those wild women who follow Bacchus, with vines in their hair, and animal skins, and their breasts bare." She sprang up and crossed over to the mirror, pulling her dress off her shoulders and tousling her hair. "I would look very well, I think. And you could be a satyr."

Camillo pictured his mother's reaction to the news that the Prince and Princess Borghese had hosted the family's carnival ball dressed as a priapic goat-man and drunken slut, respectively. And he realized, with a heavy, sick feeling in his stomach, that he could no longer put off talking to Pauline about her duties as his wife.

They were married now in the eyes of the world. Her flirting, her disregard for convention, her brazen physicality, were now a danger to his own reputation. There could be no more nude chases through the bedroom, no more crescendos lit by a myriad of candles, no more frantic couplings in the carriage. This woman would be the mother of his children. It was time to stop pretending she was his mistress.

"Pauline," he said, speaking to her in the mirror, over her shoulder. "You know, as my wife—that is—" He stopped.

She turned and looked at him. "Well?"

He took a deep breath. "Yes, that is, now that we are publicly known as man and wife, there are a few matters—" He stopped again.

"You're going to preach at me, aren't you?" she said, folding her arms. One bare nipple peeked out from the crook of her elbow. "Go ahead. I'm used to it. My mother does it, my brothers do it, my uncle does it. I thought you were different." Her eyes were dark with anger. "You are not different. You are just like Napoleon. *My* sister must not do this! *My* sister must not do that! Only now it will be *my* wife must not wear such a costume, or dance with such a man, or do anything else amusing!"

"It is not fitting," he said, exasperated.

"*What* is not fitting?"

He pointed at her nipple. "Well, that, for example."

"Oh? And what else?"

"You should wear a nightdress." He would get this over with quickly. "Always. Even when we are, well, together. No candles. No mirrors." He closed his eyes, remembering how the mirrors had made her skin shimmer with reflections. And he brought out the carefully constructed sentence he had been practicing for the past six weeks. "Marital relations should be conducted with dignity and discretion in the bedchamber of the wife."

"Now you sound worse than Napoleon," she said, pulling up her dress with an angry jerk. "You sound like that damned *Almanac National*. Did my brother give you a copy, with the passages about wifely behavior specially marked?"

"He did not have to give me a book," Camillo snapped. "I know what is due to my name and my dignity."

"You and your name and your dignity can go to hell," she said, furious. And before he could stop her, she had slammed out of the room.

He searched the whole house for her. At first, he was quiet and careful, so that no one else would know they had quarreled. As it grew later and later, he became worried and called in the servants.

No one had seen her.

Just before dawn, he thought to try the children's rooms. Dermide was asleep next to his nurse, a Corsican virago who terrified Camillo. Hastily, he closed the door. The next room was Sophie's.

Pauline was curled up next to the girl, her arm carelessly lying across Sophie's chest. She was sleeping heavily and did not even stir as the door opened and Camillo peered in, holding up his candle. But Sophie was not asleep. She was lying very still, wedged against the headboard of the narrow bed, her arms pinned to her sides by Pauline's weight. Her eyes were open, and as she looked up at Camillo, she gave a little smile of triumph.

SIX

Rome, February 1804

Sophie was sitting by her window looking out at the dawn and thinking about Camillo. Today was the first day of Lent, when Catholics began forty days of penance. Sophie was not Catholic; nevertheless, she decided gloomily that Lent had come to her and assigned her a penance anyway. Her penance was thinking about Camillo. She did not particularly want to think about him. She hated him—or, at least, that was what she told herself. It had started to take on the character of a reminder rather than a fact.

It had not been hard to dislike him initially. All suitors of Pauline were suspect in Sophie's eyes: if they ignored her, they were rude boors; if they courted and flattered her in the mistaken belief that she had any influence with Pauline, they were fools. Camillo was doubly damned—he had the warm, open smile of the fools and the glazed focus on Pauline of the boors.

Then had come the rumors, the family meetings, the consultations with the oily and sinister Angiolini. Suddenly Camillo was no longer *a* suitor; he was *the* suitor. Which meant, in Sophie's eyes, that he had graduated to the status of declared enemy. And when he and Pauline fell in love, Sophie was engulfed in rage, the black, bitter rage of someone who has been betrayed and discarded.

After the first wedding, she had lain awake every night, listening for the sounds in the room beneath hers that told her that the prince had crept back into the *hôtel* and was with Pauline. In Pauline's room. In Pauline's bed.

She was not quite sure what they did in the bed, although she knew several different coarse terms for it, and Nunzia kept trying to describe it to her. But her imagination refused to connect scenes of dogs and horses with Pauline or any other rational human being. Whatever it was, it involved a great deal of giggling by Pauline and episodes of furniture-thumping that made Sophie burrow down in her bed with her hands over her ears in an agony of jealousy and embarrassment. Whatever it was could also apparently happen in their carriage, or in the garden, or, if she could believe the cook's shocked account, in the wine cellar of Pauline's *hôtel* while guests were waiting for dinner.

The entire household was caught up in the delicious secret of the hidden marriage. All the servants were delighted to be coconspirators, and when Pauline and Camillo smiled meaningfully at each other in public, their friends and attendants exchanged echoing smiles—except for Sophie, who clamped her teeth together and wished furiously for something terrible to happen to the oh-so-charming prince. She was the only one, the sole island of resistance. Even Dermide liked him.

"Don't you remember your own father?" Sophie had asked him one morning, exasperated. "Do you really want a new father, a stepfather, who won't love you?"

"But he does love me," Dermide had said placidly. "Everyone loves me."

It was true. Everyone did love Dermide.

No one loved Sophie.

Pauline, never an attentive guardian at the best of times, had ignored Sophie completely in those early, heady days of the marriage. When Camillo was not with her, she flitted from room to room with a dreamy expression on her face or stood for hours in front of the cheval glass in her boudoir, holding up dresses and jewels and asking anyone nearby whether they became her and would Camillo like them.

So Sophie had ground her teeth until her jaw ached and looked so sour that Nunzia started giving her dandelion tea and asking pointed questions about her bowel movements. She did her lessons and practiced her music every morning; she played with Dermide in the afternoon; but she was not really there. Her real existence began at night, when she lay awake and concocted ever more elaborate fantasies involving herself, Pauline, and the prince.

In her favorite one, she was dying—yes, dying—poisoned by the prince. She lay pale and lovely in her bed, surrounded by vases of flowers. The whole household stood outside her bedroom door, weeping. Pauline would nurse her, but it would be too late, and as Sophie drew her last breath, Pauline would beg her forgiveness and curse the name of Camillo Borghese.

On nights when she did not feel like dying, she produced slightly more realistic visions. For example, Pauline would quarrel with the prince over money (Sophie had overheard many such quarrels between Pauline and her brothers). Or a mysterious letter would come from Rome, heavy with seals, and the prince would open it and turn pale and leave Paris, never to return.

The prince did not poison her. No mysterious messages arrived from Rome. Sophie grew heavy-eyed from lack of sleep, but the calendar marched on inexorably through September and October and the first week of November. She stood in a new silk gown and matching silk slippers at the second, official wedding, still wishing with every atom of her will for some blight to strike down the prince. And when it did—when Pauline burst into her room, flushed with anger, late that same night, crying and cursing and imploring Sophie to hide her—she was so astonished and thankful that for the first time in her life she considered the possibility that there might be a divine being. Her prayers for help in the battle for Pauline's love were not directed at anything or anyone more specific than the cosmos; freethinkers did not pray, in the conventional sense of that word. But if there was no God, then who had answered her prayer?

She had still hated the prince when they left for Italy ten days later.

The prince had clearly hoped to have Pauline to himself during the journey. There was ample space in the other vehicles for Pauline's attendants (ten, not including Dermide's nurse and governess) and Camillo's (a mere three). But the enormous berlin conveying the newlyweds was certainly wide enough to hold more than two passengers. And while Pauline's other attendants took Camillo's hints and excused themselves tactfully to ride with the senior servants or with the nursery party, Sophie clung tenaciously to her spot next to Pauline.

In part, this was because the prince had made a very bad blunder the first time he tried to hint Sophie away.

"Perhaps you would like to ride with Dermide?" he had said, smiling at Sophie. It was a patronizing smile, an I-am-an-adult-and-you-are-a-child smile. Any self-respecting eleven-year-old would at that moment have resolved to be carried from the carriage kicking and screaming before ever voluntarily accepting a place in the children's vehicle.

But that was not the only reason. Sophie considered it her duty to safeguard Pauline from her own infatuation. As painful as it was to watch the sickening displays of affection in the carriage, it would be even more painful to leave Pauline and Camillo alone and ride in another vehicle, imagining what was happening in her absence. Without wanting to, she kept remembering the coachman's account of meandering late-night rides around Paris during the "secret" phase of the marriage. "The whole carriage would shake!" he told the servants, enjoying himself hugely. "Like an earthquake! I could barely steer, the chassis was bouncing so hard!"

There would be no bouncing carriages on this trip, not if Sophie could prevent it. She was willing to endure Camillo's odious presence, and his increasingly open hints that she was unwelcome, so long as it kept her out of the nursery carriage and at Pauline's side.

What Sophie had not anticipated was that Pauline would turn into a monster. The princess loved the idea of travel but hated the actual traveling. She was cold. She was hot. She could eat nothing. She was famished. It was too bright; draw the shades. It was too dim; open them.

"I need to walk—stop the carriage!" she would say suddenly. The entire cavalcade would stop, the couriers would run back and forth advising all the coachmen and servants of the delay, and Pauline would emerge, walk a few dozen steps, complain of the mud and the cold, and return to the carriage.

"I have a headache. I must have the carriage to myself," she announced at another time. Even Sophie was evicted on that occasion. Servants were constantly being sent ahead to order special food or arrange for hot baths with mineral salts to be waiting at the next inn. When Pauline was cold, she would hold out her hands and feet and demand that Camillo or Sophie or one of her ladies warm them; when she was hot, all the carriage windows were lowered, in spite of the rain and wind of the mountain passes.

Sophie, determined not to be banished, had made herself indispensable. She put all of Pauline's favorite medicines in a basket that she kept under her skirt between her feet. It was very uncomfortable—the basket bruised her shins even through her stockings—but they did not have to stop the carriage and fetch cases from the luggage coach every time Pauline's symptoms changed.

The princess took Sophie's ministrations for granted. It was the prince who thanked her, very courteously, every time she handed Pauline a handkerchief soaked in cologne or excavated a box of pastilles from the basket at her feet. He never lost his temper or gave any sign that he noticed the wild and illogical variety in his wife's complaints.

"Her Excellency needs fresh air," he would say, beckoning one of the outriders over to the carriage. And then, a few minutes later, "The princess is fatigued from walking and must lie down and have complete quiet." Then he would assist her very gently back into the carriage, arrange all the cushions and covers, close the window shades, and sit across from her, looking as anxious and affectionate as though this were the first such episode that day instead of the tenth.

Reluctantly, Sophie found herself his ally—two nursemaids trying to coax an ill-tempered princess across the Alps. When she went to bed each evening, usually with Dermide and Carlotta, she no longer lay awake plotting disasters for the prince. She was too tired and stiff. And she heard plenty of good-humored but uncomplimentary descriptions of Pauline from the servants.

"Our Paolina was certainly not at her best this evening," Carlotta had said one night. They were in a small mountain village, and earlier that evening Pauline had suddenly declared that her throat was sore; she required blackcurrant brandy. The inn was turned upside down; villagers came forward with various alternatives—cherry brandy, apple brandy, even a treasured local recipe made from sour pears. Pauline rejected them all and appealed to the heavens for mercy; this trip would kill her; no one could imagine what she was suffering; why had they not stopped earlier/later in village X/town Y, where there would certainly have been a supply of the stuff.

"She was not feeling well," said Sophie.

"When does she feel well, these days?" Carlotta tucked Dermide in more firmly next to Sophie and climbed onto her own trundle bed.

"It isn't her fault," said Sophie defensively. "Travel doesn't agree with her."

"Travel doesn't agree with anyone! The rest of us are just as jostled and tired as she is, but you don't see anyone else complaining of something new every two hours! The blessed saints only know what she will decide is wrong next. I swear, if she could feel pain in her fingernails, she would be demanding a fingernail doctor."

Sophie couldn't help it—she snorted with laughter.

"Don't put it past her." The nursemaid pinched out the candle. "How you endure it, Sophie, is beyond me. And His Excellency—he is so patient with her! If I were her husband, I would beat her."

He *was* patient, thought Sophie. And just for one moment she felt sorry for him.

"I wonder what it will be tomorrow," said Carlotta drowsily. "We'll be sent to find mare's milk, maybe."

"Or fresh peaches," Sophie ventured. "Peaches in November in the mountains." She gave a nervous giggle, half-amused, half-dismayed at her own treachery. She waited to see if Carlotta would laugh in response. But Carlotta was asleep.

Once they had reached Rome, Sophie had seen very little of the prince or princess. At first she was glad, grateful for her own room, for time to read and walk, for a respite from Pauline's complaints and demands. But within a few days, she was bored and lonely and homesick for her well-ordered life in Paris and the evening ritual of bidding her goddess good-night. Rome was noisy and foreign; the Borghese palace was an enormous warren of cold, echoing rooms that led endlessly into one another. Sophie regularly got lost on her way from her bedchamber to the kitchen. Anything or anyone familiar began to seem very appealing—even Camillo. And that was before the battle with Camillo's widowed mother over Sophie's heresy.

The third morning after their arrival was Sunday, and the dowager princess was getting ready to display her son and new daughter-in-law at mass. The palace had its own exquisite little chapel, but this was to be a grand excursion to Santa Maria Maggiore. Sophie was helping Dermide put on his gloves when Donna Anna noticed that she was not dressed to go out.

"Why is the little cousin not ready?" she demanded, turning to Camillo. "We will be late! She must follow after us; one of the servants can bring her."

"Oh, Sophie is not coming," Camillo said hastily. He took his mother's arm and tried to shepherd her toward the doorway, but she frowned and turned back.

"Sophia," she said loudly and very slowly, in Italian, "are you ill?"

Sophie looked up, startled. "No, Your Excellency."

"Why are you not dressed to go to mass?"

Pauline intervened. "Sophie is a freethinker, Donna Anna." There was no Italian word for it, so she used the French.

"What!" Donna Anna crossed herself, horrified. "Not even a league from the seat of the Holy Father! In my own house!"

"*Our* house, Mama." Camillo's tone was gentle, but he looked stern.

"I cannot allow it—this poor, innocent child—" Although she had described Sophie as a poor, innocent child, she had taken a step back and was looking at her as though Sophie had turned into a venomous snake.

"We must leave now; the carriage is waiting," Camillo reminded her, taking her arm once again and steering her firmly away from Sophie.

"Is she even baptized?" Donna Anna asked, twisting around as Camillo tugged her along. "I won't have her here if she isn't baptized!"

Sophie stood frozen in the center of the marble floor, still clutching one of Dermide's gloves.

"Yes, you really should be baptized, Sophie," Pauline said carelessly, taking the glove and pushing Dermide toward the door. "That sort of thing was all very well ten years ago in France, but we are more civilized now."

The dowager princess and Pauline had persisted on this theme for about a week, but Camillo held firm: Sophie was Napoleon's ward, and without his express command, they had no right to interfere in her religious education. Grudgingly, Sophie found herself grateful. Her free thought was the only thing she had left of her own family. Everything else—her clothing, her books, her maid, even the Italian she now spoke in place of French—had come from Pauline. She had clung to this last link to her father with a kind of stubborn desperation, in the face of numerous attempts by Pauline and Carlotta and Nunzia to bring her into the church.

She was too young to appreciate the irony of a papal prince defending her agnosticism from a daughter of the French revolution.

As if to make up for her tantrums and megrims during the journey, Pauline had behaved perfectly for nearly a month after arriving in Rome: charming, elegant, deferential. She received dozens of elderly noblewomen in the drafty salons of the Borghese palace. She attended church with her mother-in-law. She walked out with Camillo to see the great ruins in the center of the city or went driving with Sophie and Dermide, the picture of lovely motherhood. Camillo and his mother held a grand reception at the palace in Pauline's honor and began to plan an even more elaborate affair at the villa for the last night of Carnival.

Then the German had arrived, seemingly out of nowhere, and Pauline had forgotten all about Camillo and Donna Anna and her obligations as a princess.

Georg was the heir to a northern duchy and came made-to-order for anyone who wanted someone completely different from Camillo. Prince Borghese had a lofty, square brow, hazel eyes, and curly, thick hair; he loved the outdoors; he knew everything about dogs and horses; he liked to dance and eat and laugh. He rarely read books; his French was execrable. The German prince had a long, narrow face. His hair was blond and fine and straight, his eyes a pale blue. He prided himself on his learning. He detested all forms of sport. He spoke fluent French. He rarely smiled.

Sophie at first had heard only the rumors. Pauline was not interested in looking maternal for this visitor, so Dermide and Sophie were not invited to appear when she received the northerner.

"*She* is at it again," Carlotta whispered to Nunzia one morning. She had found some pretext to come to Sophie's room, hoping to find her countrywoman there. "And if the family hears of it, there will be trouble."

Sophie was over by the window, working on her drawing—an accomplishment she despaired of ever mastering. Carlotta's vehement "she" could only mean Pauline; Sophie's pencil fell from her hand and bounced from the table to the floor. At once both maids looked over at her, startled, and she dove under the table after her pencil. When she reemerged, she studiously resumed her sketch, trying not to look as though she had heard anything.

"I think the cardinal knows" was Nunzia's low-voiced response. "I saw him with her yesterday, and he looked very grim."

Cardinal Fesch was Pauline's uncle, Letizia's brother. Sophie had met him a few times and found him nearly as frightening as Pauline's mother. He, too, was constantly urging Pauline to have Sophie baptized.

What did he know? Sophie wanted to ask. But the intimacy of the voyage had receded now that Sophie was a young lady again, in her own room, with a new and very dignified Roman governess. Carlotta no longer confided in her.

"I can't imagine what she sees in that German." Carlotta glanced over at Sophie and apparently was reassured because she continued, "Never a *mancia* for the boy who holds his horse, never a thank-you or please to anyone. Stiff as a poker, and so pale you wonder if he ever sees daylight."

"General Leclerc was blond," Nunzia said thoughtfully. "Perhaps she likes blonds. And he *is* a prince."

So, thought Sophie. It was another prince. A mean, blond, German prince. She tried to think of who it could be, but her knowledge of Roman society was very limited. Rome was far more conservative than Paris about admitting children to adult events; she and Dermide rarely came downstairs in the evenings now, even to say good-night. The only people Sophie saw regularly were the servants, her governess, and Dermide.

Carlotta sniffed. "I like the prince she already has better."

They had left, still whispering, and Sophie had stared down at her drawing. How could she fight an enemy she had never seen? How could she somehow gain access to the salons downstairs, where guests were entertained? Sophie had meekly accepted her isolation for six weeks; now her misery and loneliness stood plainly exposed and she was determined to do something. Pauline had a page, not much older than Sophie, who accompanied her nearly everywhere. Why could Sophie not be something like a page? Pauline's other attendants were young women from influential families, who had been chosen either by Napoleon or her new mother-in-law; no doubt Pauline would like having another companion who was loyal only to her.

Thus had begun Sophie's campaign to transform herself into a junior lady-in-waiting. She suborned one of Pauline's young maidservants, who stole some of Pauline's cosmetics. Nunzia cut and curled Sophie's hair and helped Sophie alter one of her dresses, lowering the neckline and shortening the sleeves. Sophie sacrificed half of her small store of pocket money for a pair of long gloves. Her governess's lessons on posture and deportment were suddenly of the greatest interest to Sophie, and she practiced walking with a book on her head for hours at a time every day.

When to approach Pauline? Sophie did not dare wait for the now-infrequent summons to come down with Dermide before preparing for bed. Instead, she spent more of her coins to bribe the page, Paolo, and was waiting one evening in the front entrance hall of the palace when Pauline, Donna Anna, and Camillo returned from an outing to visit Camillo's younger brother.

Pauline swept in first, shedding her bonnet, muff, pelisse, and gloves into whatever hands would receive them. "I do not understand why Francesco prefers to stay in Frascati, so far from

Rome," she announced loudly. "In the summer I am sure it is all very well, but at this time of year—" She broke off, as Sophie advanced and made her very best curtsey.

"But who is this?" She turned to Camillo, who had come up behind her. "Is this one of your young cousins, husband? She is charming!"

Sophie had hardly dared to raise her eyes, but now she did. Pauline, in her usual careless fashion, was already turning away. So Sophie's beseeching glance caught Camillo's instead.

He touched Pauline's elbow. "Dearest, look again," he said, with a hint of laughter in his voice. "It is not my cousin but yours."

Pauline stopped, turned, and peered at Sophie, who stood in her very best book-on-the-head manner. "Sophie?" She stepped closer, then burst into peals of laughter. "It *is* Sophie! Mother of God, look how grown-up she is! And tall! She towers over me!" This was an exaggeration, but Sophie was now several inches taller than Pauline. "Sophie, how old are you now? I thought you still a child!"

"Thirteen, Cousin," said Sophie, advancing her age recklessly by over a year. She was counting on Pauline's notorious inability to do sums, since Sophie had still been ten when Pauline took her in the previous winter.

Pauline touched one of the ringlets Nunzia had produced at the cost of many tears and several small burns on Sophie's scalp. "And you are all dressed up, are you not? You look very fine. What is the occasion? Are you going out?" She frowned. "I do not think you should accept invitations without consulting me, Sophie."

"No, no—I am not—I did not—" Sophie took a deep breath

and started on her prepared speech. "Cousin Pauline, I have spoken with Signora Russo, and she has agreed that I am doing well with my lessons and may attend you now sometimes during the afternoon and evening if you should wish for my company." This was not as much of a lie as Sophie's claim to be thirteen. Sophie had indeed talked with her governess but had given that elderly lady the distinct impression that the idea came from Pauline.

"Well," said Pauline doubtfully. "Well, I must think about it. Thirteen is still a bit young, don't you think, Camillo?"

"My birthday is in three months," said Sophie hastily. Her birthday was in April, true, but she would be turning twelve.

Donna Anna intervened. "This is all nonsense. She is much too young to attend you, Daughter." With a grimace of distaste, she touched Sophie's cheek and held up her reddened fingertip. "Imagine! Rouge, on a girl of her age!"

Sophie's eyes flashed, and she tilted her chin up. At that moment, although she did not know it, her expression was the perfect mirror of Pauline's.

"I will think about it," Pauline repeated, in an entirely different tone of voice. "Sophie, you may accompany me to my sitting room."

That was how Sophie had become a junior lady-in-waiting to the princess.

Several weeks passed, and she had still not met the German prince. Pauline usually summoned her only in the afternoon or for informal events in the palace, although she took special care to include her on outings when Donna Anna was also present. But now at least she had heard more about him. The other attendants treated her like a doll, playing with her hair and arranging her clothing. They also spoke over her head to each other, as if, like a doll, she could not hear. So she learned that the prince never visited now when Camillo was present, that Pauline would meet him sometimes in the gardens of the Borghese villa and return to the palace wet and wind-blown from what was officially a carriage ride. That Camillo was wildly jealous and was trying to arrange to have his rival recalled to Germany.

One evening Sophie had been dismissed after a small dinner party and was getting undressed when she realized that she still had a pair of Pauline's earrings tucked into her petticoat. The princess had decided halfway through dinner that they were too heavy and had beckoned Sophie over to remove them. Normally, Sophie would have waited until morning to return them, but the prince was away from Rome for a few days, and Sophie now knew her way around the palace quite well. There was a back stair to Pauline's suite of rooms, which ran up one side of the palace and opened onto a salon below Sophie's room. Taking a candle, she threw on a shawl and made her way across to the central stair, down two floors, through a series of dark receiving rooms and into the side room that gave access to the stairwell.

Beneath the small door set in the wall, Sophie saw a line of light. It didn't occur to her to think that anything was wrong; Pauline's page often used this stair to run errands for her. Pauline herself even used it when she wanted to return to her rooms to change without entering the central reception hall. So Sophie clicked open the panel—and stopped open-mouthed. There was the page, on his way up to Pauline. And there, with him, was a stranger who could only be the infamous German prince.

He was wearing a half-mask, although Carnival would not start for several weeks. He was thin and blond, and his eyes glittered like blue-tinged frost inside the mask.

"It's only Sophie," said the page, as the stranger stepped back in dismay. "Come on." And he tugged the blond man's sleeve.

Sophie stood speechless, frozen, horrified. This was what she had wanted, was it not? To know Pauline's secrets. To see the mysterious lover for herself.

Paolo turned back, frowning. "What are you doing here, Sophie? Surely the princess didn't send for you?" He jerked his head meaningfully toward the masked man. No, Pauline would not want any other visitors right now.

She still couldn't speak. Mutely, she held out the earrings.

"Oh! Right, she wondered where they were. I'll take them up." And he put them casually in his vest and then led the German on up the stairs.

Sophie had made herself wait until she heard Pauline's low laugh and musical voice echoing down the stairwell. Then she had crept back to her room, got undressed, climbed into bed, and burst into tears.

A few days later, the prince had returned. All seemed peaceful for a day or so, and Sophie found herself glad to think that there would be no visitors on the staircase now. Then, on the Friday after his return, everything had changed.

Sophie and another young woman had been with Pauline in her dressing room. Camillo had stalked in and started shouting before they could even get up from their chairs. Terrified, they fled, but they heard plenty on the way out.

"You slut! You whore!" The normally gentle Camillo was

white with anger. "You are a disgrace to your brother, a disgrace to my house! Have you no shame? No modesty? You are no more fit to be a princess than the girl who sweeps the kitchen! We have not even been in Rome for two months, and you give me horns! Where is my heir, madame? Don't I get a son before you start opening your legs to every man in Rome?"

Camillo had found out, who knows how—from one of the servants, from his mother, from Angiolini, who reportedly had spies in the household. Not from Sophie; she couldn't bear to think about that meeting, and if she had ever imagined herself taking vengeance on both Camillo and the German prince by telling the former about the latter, that notion had died on the dark staircase with the sound of Pauline's laughter.

Pauline shouted back—Sophie was too far away to hear the words now—there was the sound of something breaking, and then Camillo emerged, his face like stone. He walked past the shocked attendants without even looking at them and shut himself in his rooms.

An icy silence settled over the household. Servants spoke in whispers. Sophie prayed for once that Pauline would *not* summon her to help her dress or to go with her to the shops.

A week later, Prince Georg left Rome. The pope had suggested that he was needed back home. And the next morning, Sophie, summoned to Pauline's bedchamber, found Camillo lying half-dressed on a sofa, looking very pleased with himself, while Pauline turned in front of him modeling a sleeveless gown of flowing gold tissue.

"Ah, Sophie!" Pauline whirled over to her. "This is my costume for our ball on the last night of Carnival. You shall have one in white, trimmed with the gold, to match. And here is my mask." She held up a delicate crescent of gilt pasteboard and swan feathers. "Do you like it?"

Sophie nodded. She looked at the prince, lounging on the sofa, and back at Pauline. They were reconciled, that was clear. She should hate him again.

"Now come over here and pick your own mask," Pauline commanded. On a side table lay a pile of fantastic papier-mâché concoctions—animal heads, crowns, birds, flowers, pagan gods, even a stone tower. Sophie looked at this last, fascinated. It had two little windows for the eyes. "Not that one, silly. That is a man's. Here." She led Sophie over to another group of masks, clearly for smaller heads. "Let's try this one." It was a wood nymph, with leaves for hair. Sophie felt the mask settle over her nose and then tighten as Pauline fastened the strings.

"Perfect!" Pauline led her to a mirror. Startled, Sophie saw a stranger—her own body, taller and more slender than she remembered, then a graceful white neck, a childish chin and mouth, and the knowing, distant face of the dryad. The leaves were silk and mingled with her own hair as though Nunzia had worked for hours on the effect.

"What do you think, Camillo?" Pauline appealed to her husband.

"Lovely," he said politely.

But he was not looking at Sophie. His gaze was fastened possessively on his wife.

Sophie had loved Carnival, at least at first. When she wore her mask and domino, she felt truly grown up. Strange men approached her and kissed her gloved hand and begged her to tell them her name. The great palace was open at all hours of the day and night; Sophie could come and go as she pleased so long as Pauline did not require her. The streets and piazzas were full of people. There were musicians, clowns, jugglers, acrobats, tame bears, singers, dancers. It was like one of the fairs her parents had taken her to in the villages near Pontoise, only it was the whole city, and it was not one day but eight.

Pauline seemed to like it as well. Every day she wore a different new gown beneath her domino. Every day she set the swan feathers on her head, looked in the mirror, and announced, "Let us enjoy ourselves today!" Camillo, in a bronze owl mask, escorted her for the first few days, but then he grew preoccupied—Sophie heard him talking to his secretary about a surprise for Pauline at the Borghese ball—and Pauline chose one or another of the young Romans who vied for her attention to escort her to a concert or a dance.

On the fourth day, Sophie had handed Pauline the swan mask as usual. But when she put it on, she did not smile and say "Let us enjoy ourselves today!" Instead, she looked at herself in the mirror for a long time, in silence. Then she turned suddenly to Sophie. "Sophie, this evening we shall watch the horses race down the Corso. I have sent a footman to reserve a place for us at the Palazzo San Marco."

That was when Sophie knew there was going to be trouble.

For the next three days, she had stood next to Pauline on the balcony overlooking Piazza Venezia. Each day, as the horses pounded into the square, a brawny young man in a harlequin mask would wrestle one of the stampeding animals to a walk and hand it over to the waiting grooms. Then he would strut across the piazza and bow elaborately, looking up at Pauline.

She would look down at him and smile. And even naive little Sophie understood that it was not really the horse he was wrestling into submission.

She had hoped that it would end with the last race, although it was a faint hope and grew even fainter when she saw Pauline throw him a glove with a note inside. But nothing had happened that evening or the next night. And tonight had been the last night of Carnival. The night of the Borghese ball.

Sophie had looked anxiously for a harlequin mask among the guests at the villa. Hours had passed, the clocks had struck midnight, and she had started to relax and enjoy herself. Tomorrow she would be little Sophie again; tonight strangers had brought her iced drinks and tiny bouquets of flowers and asked her to dance. One had even kissed her hand. She was pleasantly dizzy from champagne, which she thought much nicer than wine. How lovely it was to pretend to be a grown-up! Perhaps, she had thought, she would have one more candied fig before she went to find the servants who would take her and Donna Anna back to the palace. She had turned to look across the terrace to where the coaches were lined up behind the hedge.

It had been purely by chance, then, that she had seen him. In another few minutes, she would have been gone. She would never have known. But now she did know. Sophie hugged her knees and stared out the window. The sun was rising; she could see reflections of pink in the low clouds. Soon the household would gather itself and go off to mass and come back with ashes on their foreheads.

Pauline.

Camillo.

Ashes.

He had been standing by a dragon-lantern, right where the steps of the terrace went down into the formal garden. The hedge behind him cast a shadow over his left side, so that he seemed to be cut in half vertically—a short, broad-shouldered figure, with the bright parti-colored silks over the upper portion of his face. Instinctively, Sophie had looked around for Camillo. He was in the next room, talking earnestly with an older man who was not wearing a mask.

Where was Pauline? Sophie's heart was pounding and she was sweating. She felt as though she were in a bad dream. The champagne bubbles in her stomach suddenly felt like globs of slime. She had stood watching, helpless, as Pauline walked up to the harlequin man. Pauline was laughing, of course. She had smiled and said something, and then tapped him once on the shoulder, lightly, like a child playing a game of *cache-cache*. And then she had run, laughing again, to the far end of the garden and disappeared into the darkness beyond the lanterns.

The harlequin man had followed her.

Sophie had not gone back to the palace with Donna Anna after all. There was some twisted devil of curiosity in her that wanted to see what would happen. Perhaps Pauline would return in a few minutes. Perhaps the prince would not realize that she was gone. Perhaps she had imagined the whole thing. She had stood in her corner as the party grew wilder and wilder around her, looking out at the terrace steps and waiting for something—she was not sure what.

Several servants had already come up to her and asked if she had seen Pauline, by the time Camillo found her.

"Sophie, do you know where Pauline is?" he had said. His face was pale and strained.

This, she realized with dismay, was that nameless something she had been waiting for. It was horrible. It was terrifying, and painful, and unfair. Why had she ever wanted to join the world of adults? Her hands were shaking; she twisted them into her skirt and willed them to stop.

She had tried to answer calmly. "I am sorry, Your Excellency," she said. "I saw her earlier when you were both receiving guests, but now it is so crowded." What could she say? She was no longer sure whom she was protecting, Pauline or Camillo. She only knew that it was essential to prevent Camillo from finding the harlequin man. "She—she was complaining that her mask was uncomfortable, so that she might have changed it for another, and perhaps if she went outside, she took a domino as well."

"Is she on the terrace?"

Sophie darted a quick, guilty glance toward the fateful lantern at the foot of the stairs. "Yes, I think so. Yes, I saw her there a few moments ago."

The prince looked over toward the terrace. Sophie cursed herself. What if he went out there? What if he asked someone about Pauline, someone who had seen her run by, laughing, half an hour earlier, pursued by a young man in a harlequin mask? She corrected herself hastily: "Or perhaps—perhaps she has gone back to the supper room."

Camillo seemed to will himself back from someplace very far away. He gave Sophie an attempt at a smile. "I will look for her there, then."

She had watched him walk away to rejoin his guests, his

shoulders straight, nodding to this person and that, giving directions to the servants.

She hadn't fooled him. No, she hadn't fooled him at all.

And now she was sitting by her window, in her own personal Lent, remembering his face. That small, not-quite-successful smile. She was thinking about Camillo, and she was trying to hate him, and she knew he did not deserve it. The person who deserved her hatred was Pauline.

So why did she love Pauline? Why did Camillo love Pauline? It was a mystery.

SEVEN

Bagni di Lucca, August 1804

Pauline was sick.

Again.

And they had quarreled.

Again.

Camillo paced back and forth on the balcony adjoining the dining room of their villa. There was a spectacular view: rocky cliffs and crisp green treetops falling away to the river far below, with its ancient stone bridge. Pauline had exclaimed in delight a month ago, when they had first arrived in Bagni di Lucca. It was so lovely! The air was so clear! It was so cool here, so fresh! Thank heavens they were not in Rome, now that it was high summer. She knew she would feel better very soon.

She did feel better—for a day, or a few days, or a week. And then she would feel worse again.

He had convinced himself that this time she really was improving. Just two days ago, she had been dancing at a public assembly with the dazzled mayor of the little spa town, shrieking with laughter as the music got faster and faster, ignoring the raised eyebrows of the more aristocratic guests. This morning she had been doubled over in pain, white and sweating. A servant had carried her to her bath; she could not walk. She had eaten nothing since breakfast the day before.

A polite cough behind him. "Your Excellency?"

It was Pauline's doctor. Camillo turned and waved the older man to a seat.

Peyre sank down onto one of the marble benches with a grunt. "How is she?"

"I gave her some laudanum. The attack will pass. She should feel more herself in a few days."

But, thought Camillo, watching the doctor's face.

"But she must rest." The doctor slapped the polished surface of the bench. "Your Excellency, she must rest! After the last episode, I advised her to remain in bed for a week, as you know."

Instead, she had gotten up thirty-six hours later and danced all night with the mayor, and the Russian count, and the Florentine minister of the exchequer, and everyone and anyone else except Camillo, who stood by the punch bowl, pretending not to watch her.

"Don't look at me," said Camillo with a grimace. "She never listens to me."

"Well, she certainly doesn't listen to me." Peyre sighed. "*Now*, while she is in pain and weak, she will do anything I recommend. And cry, and promise to be good, and have her attendant write down lists of things she must not eat. But the moment she feels better again—" He gestured with his hand as if he were throwing something over the balcony railing.

"She doesn't listen to her mother, either, if that is any consolation."

Peyre nodded gloomily.

"How is the signora? You saw her this morning, didn't you?"

Letizia Bonaparte had arrived in Italy with Pauline's brother Lucien in late spring and had joined Camillo and Peyre in persuading Pauline to leave Rome once the summer weather arrived. She had accompanied Pauline and Camillo to Pisa, then to Florence, and now here to Lucca, where she was taking the waters along with her daughter. Her lodgings were down in the valley, much closer to the baths, and in spite of Pauline's attempts to coax her from her rooms, she was refusing almost all invitations; the heat in Florence had brought on an attack of quartan fever and she was observing a strict regimen of diet and rest.

Peyre gave a dry smile. "Madame Letizia is following my orders and is much improved. Unlike your wife."

Camillo sank down onto the bench and asked for the hundredth time, "What is wrong with her this time? Do you know?"

Peyre shrugged.

"The usual?"

"I believe so."

Pauline had been ill, off and on, ever since her return from the West Indies eighteen months earlier. She had seen doctors in Paris and doctors in Rome, but none of them could do better than the humble and loyal Peyre, who had accompanied her back from the Caribbean. His theory was that Pauline had contracted a tropical disease in Saint-Domingue, which had settled in her intestines. Or perhaps it went back even further, to an attack of fever that had followed the birth of Dermide. Whatever it was, it seemed to come and go as capriciously as Pauline's own whims. When it came, she was miserable. When it went, she forgot at once how ill she had been and sprang out of bed, convinced that *this* time she was truly healthy again.

Until the journey to Rome, Camillo had been blissfully ignorant of his bride's various ailments. While they were courting, they only saw each other once or twice a week, usually at the sort of brilliant occasions for social display that acted like a tonic on Pauline. Then, after the first wedding ceremony, their clandestine "honeymoon" under Napoleon's own nose in Paris had provided an even better tonic: sex, and plenty of it. Until suddenly, once the marriage became public, Pauline had fallen ill again, just in time for the monthlong trek to Italy.

Camillo was no doctor, but over the course of the last seven months he had noticed a pattern to Pauline's illnesses. When she was bored, she was ill. When she was amused or intrigued, she was well.

That, in fact, was the theme of their most recent quarrel.

It had started yesterday, when Pauline did not appear for dinner. A picnic originally planned for the evening had been canceled at the last moment, and Camillo and Pauline were to dine alone for the first time in weeks.

Camillo had spent half an hour with his valet, dressing as formally as if the Queen of Etruria were coming to dine with them. He arrived in the anteroom adjoining the smaller of the two dining rooms and waited.

And waited.

Finally he rang for a servant.

"Please see when Donna Paolina will be ready to dine," he ordered.

The footman returned a few minutes later. "Her Excellency sends her regrets; she is not well. If you will wait one moment, signor, the table is being reset."

So, she was not well? All afternoon she had been feverishly planning her outfit for the picnic, sending the maids running to the kitchen and the garden and the stables to look for charming little items for the rustic "basket" that Pauline planned to carry on her arm.

A moment earlier, he had been starving. Now, he suddenly had no interest in food whatsoever. He brushed past the startled servant, stamped up the stairs to Pauline's room, and burst in without knocking.

She was lying in bed, wearing a nightgown and an old shawl, with no makeup on. There were dark circles under her eyes. She was sipping something that smelled dreadful and clearly tasted worse, since she was making faces with every mouthful. A maid was wringing out a cloth in a basin and looked up, startled, as Camillo banged the door open.

He didn't know what he had expected—to find her in bed with a lover, perhaps?

"I am sorry you are not well," he said stiffly.

She glared at him over the rim of the cup. "I would like to be left alone." She took in his careful toilette. "Oh, I see you are going out. That is just as well. I shall be asleep when you return; please do not disturb me."

"I am not going out." He raised his eyebrows at the hovering maidservant, who took the hint and scurried out.

"How dare you send my servant away?" She sat up in bed, her cheeks flushed.

He pulled a chair up to the bed and sat down. "Doesn't it seem odd to you," he said, ignoring her question, "that yesterday you had no difficulty dancing hour after hour with half the male population of Bagni di Lucca? That a few hours ago you were hopping on one foot with impatience while trying on dresses? And yet suddenly, when you are merely requested to come down for dinner with your husband, you are too weak and ill? You cannot stir yourself to walk down one flight of stairs?"

Her eyes flashed. "Not when I am dining with a prig and a fool."

"Then you admit that you are not really ill?"

"I admit nothing of the sort!"

He changed tacks. "Why did you insist on going to the ball, when Monsieur Peyre had expressly forbidden it after your last attack? When both your mother and I asked you to rest for at least another day?"

Her mouth formed the most perfect, delectable pout. "I felt fine yesterday."

"Yes, because there was a ball. Because you could get dressed and put on jewels and have men admire you."

She raised her eyebrows, every inch the princess. "And what is wrong with that?"

"What is wrong with getting dressed and putting on jewels and being admired by your husband?"

"Oh, please." She set down the cup.

"Don't you think I notice these things? That if you are posing for Canova, for that damned statue, you are happy to take all your clothes off in the middle of March and lie there with nothing on but a scrap of drapery? But when I ask you to come to mass in our family chapel, it is too cold, in a fur coat, and gloves, with a hand-warmer and a rug in the carriage? That if some adventurer dares you to drive his cockleshell of a chariot around the seven hills of Rome, you spring up there like a monkey, but when my mother asks you to host a reception in our own palace, your legs are too weak to stand for half an hour or so to greet our guests? That in Pisa—Pisa, where you proposed to rest and recover your health—you complain of every ailment known to mankind and worry that even in the hills it is too warm, but you leave at once when the queen invites you to Florence—Florence, which is baking in the midsummer sun—and promises parties and banquets and legions of admiring courtiers?"

"You are simply jealous," she snapped.

"I would have no cause for jealousy," he said coldly, "if all they did was look."

"Out!" She erupted from under the covers, waving her arms. "Out! Out!" She was trembling with anger. "You want me to behave like a good Roman matron? Like your mother? I might as well lock myself in a convent! Christ's blood, I would be better off in the convent! I wouldn't have you or your mother or my mother or my uncle or my brother to plague me!" And she burst into tears.

The fights were always the same, and they always ended the same way. Pauline would begin to cry, and Camillo would melt, and apologize, and beg her to stop, and they would end up in bed.

Not this time, he vowed.

He was halfway to the door when he heard her start to cough. And then the coughing turned to hacking, and he was rushing back toward the bed.

"Go away," she tried to say, waving him off.

"You really are ill," he stammered. She was. She was always really ill, and he always thought, until the last minute, that she was shamming. It was as though she could will herself to be sick when she wanted to avoid him or avoid something else unpleasant. He had said as much once to Peyre, and Peyre had replied somberly: "No, it is the other way around. She is ill, but she can will herself to be healthy. For a time."

He didn't believe that. He wouldn't believe that.

Sitting on the edge of the bed, he held her shoulders until the coughing subsided. "Here." He handed her the cup of whatever tonic she had decided would cure her this time.

One sip. A sour grimace. Another sip.

If he let his hand slip down, he could reach her breast. He could see it through the sheer lawn of her nightgown. She would stop coughing as he stroked her, or her stomach would stop hurting, or her headache would go away. That was how it always ended. Sex as peacemaker. Sex as medicine.

What had happened to sex as joy?

"I'll send your maid back in." His tone was distant, formal. He stood up and straightened his neckcloth. He would go eat his cold food, in his cold dining room, alone.

"Thank you." Her tone matched his.

He had rung for the maid and left without looking back.

So here he was, with Peyre, trying once again to solve the insoluble problem: What was wrong with Pauline?

"I asked her last night why she had gone to the ball when you had advised against it," he confessed.

Peyre whistled. "That was brave, but probably unwise."

"She was furious." But Peyre already knew that. The whole household probably knew it; her shouting must have penetrated every corner of the villa.

The doctor rose. "I should look in on her again, I think."

"Yes, thank you, Monsieur Peyre." He hesitated.

"Is there anything else?"

"No, no." Camillo shook his head.

This, too, was a regular feature of their encounters. They had discussed Pauline's diet, her lungs, her circulation, her nerves, her complexion, even her urine. The one question Camillo never asked, and the one question Peyre never answered, was this:

Could Pauline still have children?

Camillo was fairly sure he knew the answer; he simply didn't want to hear it.

He was fairly sure Pauline knew the answer, too. And that she didn't like it any more than he did.

In his darkest, most bitter moments, he brooded over the ironic fate that had locked him in a dynastic alliance—for surely that was all it was, at this point—with a princess who could not bear him a son.

Frascati

Dermide missed his mother, and Sophie was paying the price.

"I want to go outside. I want to send my boat to the dragons."

"It's raining," Sophie said. "You can play with your boat to-morrow, if the weather is good."

"Make it stop raining."

"Don't be silly; I can't do that. No one can."

"Then take me outside!" He stamped his foot.

Sophie folded her arms. "No."

The little boy scowled. "I'll put you in the corner with Carlotta."

He had banished his nurse to the farthest chair in the room after she had dared to suggest a nap. The long-suffering Carlotta rolled her eyes at this threat.

"I won't go in the corner," Sophie said calmly. "I'll leave." She stood up.

"No!" It was a wail. "Sophie, don't go!" He seized her skirt and tugged her back toward the sofa. "I won't make you go in the corner, I won't. But stay with me, please, please stay."

She sighed and sat back down. Dermide was usually so cheerful and affectionate. She didn't know what had gotten into him. He liked Frascati. The Villa Mondragone, perched atop a hill outside of Rome, had an enormous park and gardens perfect for a small boy in the summertime: secret paths, balustrades perfect for climbing, a summerhouse, a pond, a stable with ponies, and—Dermide's favorite—a fountain full of stone dragons. He spent hours constructing little boats from scrap paper or pieces of bark and then shrieked with delight as they were dashed to pieces against the scaly bodies of the monsters. Camillo's brother, who owned the villa, was an indulgent host, and Pauline's brother Lucien was also nearby; he had come to Rome with his mother and had bought the Villa Rufinella, a few miles away. Dermide visited frequently and was especially fond of his cousin Drina, who was exactly his age and game for any sort of adventure. The two of them were a constant trial to Carlotta and Madame Ducluzel.

After some of Dermide's more outrageous "games" with Drina—like tying enormous webs of twine across all the hedges in the formal garden—Madame Ducluzel would walk around telling anyone who would listen how she regretted advising Pauline to leave Dermide behind. And on days like today, even Sophie, who endured far less from Dermide than either of the two older women, would catch herself agreeing.

There had been a long debate about whether Dermide should accompany his mother. Pauline at first had wanted to take him with her. Sophie, well informed by the servants of the latest gossip, had been told on good authority (Camillo's valet) that the prince most emphatically did not want the boy to come along. He and Pauline had just made up after yet another jealous quarrel, and he did not want to play step-papa. The trip to Pisa had, in fact, been partly his suggestion, although Dr. Peyre had enthusiastically seconded the notion. After Camillo warned Pauline that accommodations at Pisa would be small and spartan, she had changed her mind. Then she changed it back. And back again. Ten days before the departure for Pisa, it had finally become clear that she could not postpone the decision any longer, and a delicate dance had ensued, with Camillo steering his bride ever so gently toward leaving her son behind.

Pauline had worried about the heat in Rome and the foul air from the river.

Camillo had countered with a lurid portrait of jouncing carriages, rough roads, and damp beds in strange inns.

Pauline had conceded that Dermide did not like to stay at inns but thought she would miss him too much if he did not accompany her.

Camillo had mentioned that there would be dances and entertainments at Pisa, so that she might not be able to spend much time with her son even if he did come along.

Pauline had hesitated but returned to her concern about Rome's climate.

Camillo had now brought out his trump card: an invitation from Francesco. Dermide could stay at Frascati, in the hills, away from the pestilential air of the city. Pauline's brother Lucien had purchased a villa just below Mondragone and would be nearby with his wife and children to help Madame Ducluzel and Carlotta and the tutor supervise Dermide.

At this, Pauline had yielded. The invitation had been accepted, and Dermide had been packed off to Frascati with an entourage of adoring servants and the promise of pony rides and visits with his cousin Drina.

Since Drina—along with half of Lucien's household—was currently confined to bed with some sort of cold, Sophie supposed that she was the closest thing to a playmate available. Well, really, she did like Dermide. It wasn't his fault it was raining. She gave him a little smile and squeezed his shoulder. "I'll stay. For a bit, anyway."

Dermide leaned against her. But he still didn't look happy. "Sophie?"

"Mmm-hmmm?"

"When is Mama coming back?"

Carlotta rolled her eyes again at this query. It was apparently the question of the day. He had been asking about Pauline every ten minutes.

And that, like his fretfulness, was a little odd. They had been at Frascati for two months. Every so often—about once a week or so—Dermide would ask when Pauline would be there. At first, Sophie had given a long, careful answer. Mama had been feeling ill in Rome, and her doctor had decided that she needed to go to Pisa, to drink some special medicine there. She would be back soon, when the weather grew cooler. But Sophie soon realized that Dermide was not interested in why Pauline had left or even in the precise date of her return. He simply wanted reassurance that sometime, eventually, she would reappear.

Today, however, had been different. Right from the start. A very early start.

Dermide had climbed into Sophie's bed this morning, as he often did when he woke up. He was usually good about snuggling quietly until Sophie herself awoke, but today he had pushed her until she turned over and opened her eyes.

"Sophie!"

"What is it?"

"When is my mama coming back?"

Sophie, still half-asleep, gave the new, much shorter answer, which had worked perfectly well for the past seven weeks: "Soon, when it is cooler."

"I want her now. *Now.*"

She blinked and sat up in bed. "What?"

"I want my mama! I want her today!"

She peered over at the window. It was barely even light out.

"Dermide, go back to sleep," she said crossly.

He burst into tears. "Write to her! Write to her, Sophie! Tell her to come here and fetch me!"

Sophie was taken aback by his desperate insistence. "You wrote to her yourself, remember? Just the other day."

"But I didn't tell her to come back," he sobbed.

Dermide's letters, as dictated by his tutor, consisted of a greeting ("Dearest Maman"), two sentences of reports on his lessons ("I am learning to use my compass. Monsieur says that I am doing very well."), and a closing ("Your affectionate and dutiful son, Dermide").

"You can write to her again, then. Later today."

"No I *can't*." More tears. "Monsieur is sick. And I don't know how to do it myself."

Sophie wiped his face with the edge of the sheet. "I suppose I can help you," she said, not very graciously.

"When?"

"After breakfast. If you let me go back to sleep now."

Dermide obediently lay down next to Sophie, but a minute later he was shaking her again.

"Stop it," grumbled Sophie.

Dermide ignored her. "Since monsieur is sick, can I go and play with Drina today?"

"Drina is sick, too. And Christine. And your uncle. Remember?"

"Why is everyone sick?"

"Dermide! Go away! I want to sleep!"

He had climbed down off the bed and stomped to the door. "You're *mean*" had been his parting shot.

Afterward, Sophie wondered. If she hadn't sent him away that morning, would she have noticed anything? Would she have heard something wrong in his breathing or realized that he was hotter than usual when he lay next to her in bed? But Carlotta had not found anything odd when she bathed and dressed him after he left Sophie's room. Madame Ducluzel, Pauline's housekeeper, who had served as an unofficial substitute for

Pauline for years in Dermide's life, had given him breakfast and read to him. Nothing had seemed amiss to her, either. Luncheon had been served; Dermide had not eaten much, but then he often picked at his food. He had sat with Sophie that afternoon, complaining about the rain, rubbing his eyes, and asking for Pauline.

Carlotta had thought he needed a nap.

In Sophie's view, the explanation was simpler than that. He was peevish, yes, and bored. But his playmates were ill, and it was raining, and he missed his mother. Since Sophie was also peevish and bored and in a continual state of frustrated resentment because Pauline had left her behind with Dermide, her cousin's bad temper seemed perfectly logical to her.

She herself had been snapping at everyone for weeks. When the rare and hastily scrawled letters to Madame Ducluzel arrived, she would hover next to her, nearly dancing with impatience, hoping that this time the letter would say that Pauline and Camillo were coming back to Rome. Instead, the letter from Pisa said they had been invited to Florence. The letter from Florence said they were going to try the baths at Lucca. The letter from Bagni di Lucca said that Pauline hoped Dermide was being a good boy and minding his tutor.

At least, Sophie thought, Pauline had not hoped that Sophie was being a good girl and minding her governess. Her campaign to be promoted to a junior attendant had succeeded at least to this point: Pauline did not mention her at all or give any instructions for her entertainment or care. She had not even thought about where Sophie would go when she left Rome in June, and when Sophie finally gathered up the courage to ask her, she had waved her hand impatiently.

"Wherever you please," she had said.

As angry as Sophie had been about being left behind, she had, at least up until that point, had the consolation of knowing that Dermide and most of Pauline's attendants were being treated the same way. But it had staggered her a bit to realize that Pauline had made no provision for her at all.

Arrangements had been made for everyone else in the household. Two ladies-in-waiting were returning to their families for a visit. Two were remaining in Rome with Donna Anna. One, the lucky favorite, was accompanying Pauline. The servants were divided: a few with Pauline, a few with Dermide, most staying in Rome.

Sophie had been completely overlooked, and at the last moment the decision had been dumped in her lap: Scylla or Charybdis? Remain in Rome through the heat of the summer, in a half-empty palace, trying to maintain her pretense of adulthood? Or revert to a child and go with Dermide to Frascati? Perhaps she had grown tired of playing the young lady; perhaps she had wanted to stay with Carlotta and Dermide, who were the closest thing she had to a family at this point. She had chosen Frascati.

She would regret that choice for the rest of her life.

It was the Feast of the Assumption of the Blessed Virgin, and Pauline had dragged herself out of bed to go to mass in one of the churches in town. She had not spoken to Camillo since their quarrel two days earlier, but the presence of God, a priest, and her mother in combination seemed to bring her to some sense of her duty as a wife and princess, and she actually gave Camillo a wan smile as they left the church.

He handed her politely into the carriage with her mother.

They had come in separate vehicles, ostensibly so that Pauline could stop on the way for Letizia but, in fact, because neither wanted to be within ten feet of the other. Now Pauline edged into the middle of the coach and cocked her head to one side, indicating the seat opposite hers. She was ready to forgive him, it seemed.

He looked at her dark eyes, with their unspoken question, and pretended not to notice. He would not—would not—be Pauline's toy any longer. It was a marriage of state. He repeated that phrase to himself like a schoolboy reciting his lessons. A marriage of state.

She patted the seat across from her impatiently.

He bowed coldly and closed the door of the carriage.

A marriage of state. He should find himself a mistress. That was what noblemen did. Their wives were for land and money and political power and legitimate children. Their mistresses were for affection and pleasure and companionship. One of Pauline's ladies-in-waiting had already made it quite clear that she would be happy to console him for Pauline's neglect. She was blond and plump and friendly, the kind of woman he had always found appealing. In fact, she resembled his Venetian singer, without the intimidating reputation for prowess in the bedroom.

When he tried to picture the woman, he could not even remember her face. Or her Christian name. He could ask Pauline, of course. "Excuse me, but what is the name of your lady-in-waiting who has been trying to seduce me? The blonde?" She would probably be happy to tell him. If she was speaking to him, after his rejection of her overture in the carriage.

Everything was closed for the feast day, which made it difficult to find excuses to delay his return to the house. He took a brief walk around the town, which essentially consisted of two streets and a bridge across the river. He paid a call on an elderly friend of his mother's, who was also here taking the waters. Eventually hunger prevailed, and he sent for his carriage. As it lumbered up the steep zigzags of the road through the gorge, he stared out the window.

Dinner was a solitary meal, eaten in silence. After the plates had been cleared, he sat at the table with a bottle of the local red, a jejune table wine that his butler in Rome would not have served even to the servants. Its coarse sourness suited his mood perfectly.

He was on his fourth glass when the footman knocked and stepped into the room.

"Yes?"

"Her Excellency sends to ask if you would come to bid her good-night."

A long swallow. "Tell Her Excellency I am asleep."

The servant, a local youth, clearly did not know what to do.

Camillo set down his glass. "Tell—my—wife—I—am—asleep," he repeated, staring at the footman.

He gulped. "Yes, Your Excellency."

"And tell the other servants I am not to be disturbed."

"Yes, signor."

"And ask the *maggiordomo* to bring me another bottle of this wine."

"At once, Your Excellency."

As Camillo was halfway through the second bottle, the footman reappeared, looking extremely nervous. His wig was askew, and he adjusted it as he stepped into the room.

"I beg your pardon, signor—"

"I thought I told you I was not to be disturbed," Camillo growled.

"Yes, Your Honor—I mean, Your Excellency." The young man was stammering. "It is very urgent, or I would not have—"

Camillo was already on his feet. "What is it? Is Donna Paolina worse? Where is Signor Peyre? You fool, why didn't you tell me at once?"

The footman simply gaped, then stepped aside.

Behind him, covered with dust and sweat, was a courier. Camillo recognized him; it was Giacommo, one of his brother's senior grooms. The man staggered forward and held out a sealed note.

Camillo took it, then frowned.

"This is addressed to Donna Paolina," he said.

"Don Francesco told me that you should open it first," said Giacommo. He looked haggard.

"My God," whispered Camillo as he read. "My God." He looked up at the groom. "When did you leave with this?"

"Yesterday evening. I rode straight through the night." Giacommo swallowed. "Should I take it to Donna Paolina?"

Camillo shook his head. "I will tell her. Go get something to eat, a change of clothes. I will send someone else back to Frascati; you must be exhausted."

"Thank you, signor."

The footman was still standing, paralyzed, holding the door.

"Fetch Signor Peyre," Camillo told him. "At once."

He paced back and forth impatiently until the doctor hurried in. "Have you seen my wife this evening?" he demanded.

Peyre nodded.

"How is she?"

The doctor pursed his lips. "I've seen her worse. I've seen her better. She is very weak just now; I purged her. She insisted on it."

Camillo handed the note to Peyre. "Do you believe I should show her this?"

Peyre turned pale as he read. "When did this arrive?"

"Just now. My brother's groom rode straight through."

"It's a three-day trip from here in a fast carriage," Peyre muttered. "A rough trip, over bad roads. And she will want to start back the moment she sees it."

The two men looked at each other.

"Tomorrow?"

The doctor nodded. "Tomorrow evening, so that it will be too late to leave until the next day." He looked at Camillo. "Do you want me to be there?"

Camillo didn't answer for a moment. "No," he said heavily. "No, I'll do it myself. She will need you afterward."

Both men knew it would take Pauline a long time to forgive the unlucky messenger who brought her the news that her son was dead.

EIGHT

Frascati

W here is he?"

Pauline, white-faced and haggard, jumped out of the carriage without even waiting for the footman to lower the steps. She looked around at the frightened circle of people standing in front of the entrance to the Villa Mondragone: her brother Lucien, Camillo's brother Francesco, Madame Ducluzel, Carlotta, Sophie. Dermide's tutor was still confined to bed. So were Lucien's wife and both daughters. Lucien and Madame Ducluzel were barely recovered. The sickness had swept through the two households like a summer storm. Sophie wished she were ill, too. She wished she were anywhere else but here.

It was mid-afternoon, on a blazing August day. The yellow stone of the massive building radiated heat without offering any shade. Off to the northwest, through a smudge of haze, lay the Tiber valley and Rome.

No one stepped forward. No one said anything. What was there to say?

"Lucien!" Pauline had spotted her brother. She ran to him and seized his shoulders, shaking him. "Where is he? Where is Dermide?"

He couldn't speak. Tears were running down his face. Everyone except Pauline was crying, in fact, even Don Francesco.

Her face was so pale; her eyes were so dark. Sophie thought she looked like a ghost. Lucien put his arms around her, but he left a little space, as though she were not really there. As though she had died and not Dermide.

"I am so sorry," he whispered.

"I want to see him. Please, Lucien, I must see him. I must say good-bye." She was begging, her voice cracked and broken. When he did not answer, she broke free and turned to the others, staring hollow-eyed at each one in turn, seeing in their faces the news she had already received from the courier: she would not be able to see the body. It had been wound and sealed in the coffin almost at once. In this heat, with the fever still spreading, even Pauline's frantic messages could not prevail.

"We put your hair in the coffin, Paolina," Lucien said, his voice hoarse. "That, at least, we could do."

"Yes," she said. "Yes, I sent you my hair. I did do that."

The courier had ridden all night and all day. There had been a letter wrapped around the locks of hair, but the writing was so jagged and smeared that no one could read it.

Lucien stepped over to her and put his arm gingerly around her shoulder. "We put it all in."

"There was a lot of it this time." With a savage little smile, she pulled off her bonnet and tossed it onto the paving stones.

Lucien stepped back; Madame Ducluzel gasped. Sophie, horrified, put her hand over her mouth to cover her own instinctive cry.

Pauline had hacked her hair off nearly to her scalp. Little dark tufts were sticking out at odd angles. Her hair was shorter than a boy's, shorter than a priest's. Without her bonnet, she looked even more pale and drawn.

"She did the same thing when her husband died," Carlotta whispered to Sophie, her eyes huge. "Only this time it is even worse. She looks like a patient from an insane asylum!"

It was a mistake to speak. Pauline whirled at the sound and pointed at Carlotta. "You! Were you with him? When it happened?"

The nursemaid stood paralyzed with fear.

"What about you? Was it you who watched him die?" Pauline turned to Madame Ducluzel. "I trusted you! I trusted all of you!" she screamed suddenly.

"*Le bon Dieu—*" the housekeeper started to say, her voice shaking.

"God has nothing to do with this," said Pauline fiercely. "God would not take my little boy away and not even let me see his body! God is not that cruel!" *But you are,* said her burning eyes and set face. "Who was it? Who was at his side, in my place?"

"There is no one to blame," Lucien said, his tone suddenly stern. "We all took turns nursing him. He had the best of care. Don Francesco"—he gestured toward Camillo's younger brother—"brought two doctors from Rome. Many others fell ill with the same fever—nearly a dozen of us. I was in bed for four days. Alexandrine is still sick; so are Lotte and Drina."

"They're not dead," said Pauline bitterly. "Only my son is dead."

Don't ask again, prayed Sophie. Don't ask who was with him when he died. And, like an answer to her petition, she heard the sound of horses' hooves on gravel. Another, much larger coach emerged from the end of a long avenue of live oaks and drew up alongside Pauline's.

Whoever was in this coach was not eager to get out. The shades remained down over the windows; the doors remained closed. There was no movement, none of the normal gentle rocking that indicated passengers getting ready to alight. When the footman jumped down and unfolded the steps, everyone waited in fascinated silence to see what would happen when he pulled open the door.

Nothing. No one appeared.

It was so bright in the sun in the middle of the open stone space that it was impossible to see inside the carriage. Was there anyone there?

The footman stepped up to the black hole, reached out a hand, and assisted an elderly woman down the steps. Pauline's mother. Sophie relaxed. She had been unconsciously holding herself taut, ready for something terrible.

Madame Mère hobbled stiffly over to her son and embraced him, kissing him on both cheeks and the mouth. "A sad business," she said, looking around at all the spectators to the family drama. "Although I must say that I raised eight of my thirteen, mostly on my own, as a widow of modest means, and lost none once they had passed the age of two. But here is Pauline, who cannot manage to rear her six-year-old even with the help of a tutor, a governess, a nursemaid, and dozens of other servants.

Joseph and Lucien have each already lost one out of their three and have only one son out of six babies. Napoleon has no children at all; Elisa's son died at five months, and Louis's son—if it *is* his son—is even more sickly than Dermide. Hortense is increasing again, so I suppose we will see if one of my children besides Caroline can manage to produce a healthy boy."

She looked at Pauline and pointed back to the larger carriage. "There is your husband. Do your duty and behave as a proper wife, and perhaps God will grant you another son."

Camillo was just emerging from the interior of the coach, unfolding his tall form somewhat awkwardly in the narrow opening.

Sophie tensed again.

But Pauline said nothing as Camillo came forward. She looked tired now and wilted, as though some force that had been sustaining her had suddenly disappeared. Moving even more slowly than her mother, she took Lucien's arm and walked with tiny, shuffling steps toward the house where her son had died.

Pauline sent for Sophie that evening.

She was in the chapel, one of the few rooms in the great stone house that Sophie had never entered. She had expected it to be grim and dark, but even at night, lit only by lamps and candles, it was charming and ornate. The ceiling curved up overhead in elaborate white-and-gold panels, each framing a picture of what Sophie supposed must be saints or angels. Most of the images vanished upward into darkness, but a trick of reflection lit the central boss of the vault, decorated with the figure of a dove surrounded by golden rays. Sophie stared up at the dove until a touch on her arm reminded her why she was there. It was Camillo, and he put a finger to his lips and led her forward to a small niche off on one side, where Pauline was kneeling in front of a bank of guttering candles.

"Here is Sophie," he said gently.

Pauline crossed herself and rose. She looked at Sophie, and Sophie's heart sank. Pauline had discovered who had been with Dermide on that last, horrible night. Who had watched him die.

"Not here," said Camillo. He led them back into the main wing, up a flight of stairs, into a small sitting room. Pauline lowered herself into an armchair. She did not invite Sophie to sit, although Sophie's knees were trembling so hard that she thought she might fall over.

"You were with my son."

Pauline looked sad now, not fierce and terrible as she had out in the sun in the courtyard. But Sophie was still afraid.

"Yes," she said, so softly that even she could barely hear it.

"You will tell me about it."

Carlotta had dragged Sophie into a deserted anteroom earlier, after the scene in the courtyard. "Don't tell her," she warned. "She'll ask, but don't tell her." Five minutes later, it was Madame Ducluzel, with the same warning. Then Lucien Bonaparte. Then the page, Paolo. So she had had plenty of time to think about it. To think about what she would say.

It all went out of her head at the sound of Pauline's low, commanding voice.

"What—what do you want to know?"

"How did he get sick?"

Sophie looked at Camillo. Tell her, his nod said. "Everyone was sick," she said, twisting her hands in her skirt. "I think Lotte had it first, and she wasn't very ill, but then she never got better, either. And then some of the servants, and then Monsieur Lucien . . ." She faltered.

"And Dermide?"

"He didn't seem ill at first, but then later we realized he must have been sick already that morning. He was impatient with everything and didn't want to eat. That evening he had the flux, and so then we knew and put him to bed. But he still wasn't very bad. It looked like what had happened to Lotte—he was in bed for two days, but he was bored and restless and kept asking to get up. Only he still had a bit of fever." There was a huge lump in her throat; she could barely speak. "The doctors said he was doing well but that he shouldn't get out of bed. And he was asking for you."

"He was?" Pauline brightened.

Camillo was looking daggers at Sophie, but she continued.

"Yes, starting the first morning he got sick. He wanted you to come back. He wrote to tell you so. I helped him."

Tears were pooling in Pauline's eyes; she brushed them away impatiently. "Go on."

"Well, that was the first day. Before we knew he was sick. But then after that, when he asked for you, Carlotta would come get me, and I would help him write another letter."

"Do you have them?" Pauline said eagerly. "Do you have the letters?"

Sophie nodded. "The first one was sent. But the rest are in my copybook. He was going to make fair copies when he was allowed out of bed."

"So, that last night, you were helping him write a letter."

"Well, we started the letter. But then he got bored and wanted to play a game. So I went to get some cards. Carlotta stayed with him," she added hastily. "And then I came back, and we were going to play, and I touched his hand, and he was so hot! Much hotter than the first two days." Her knees were shaking again.

"Where was my brother? Where was Madame Ducluzel? Where was the tutor?"

"They were all sick." Sophie closed her eyes. Everyone had been sick, except Sophie and Carlotta and some of the other servants—strangers, people Dermide barely knew. "We sent for the doctor again. He was very puzzled. He thought the fever would go back down, that it was just the time of day. That Dermide would be better in the morning."

"And then what happened?"

Sophie took a deep breath. "He was angry that we had called the doctor; he wanted to play cards. So I took out the cards, but when I was laying them out on the bed, he fell asleep. And he was sleeping, and Carlotta went to get some water or some towels or something—I don't remember what—and then he gave a little sigh. And it looked like he had just woken up for a minute and then gone back to sleep, but he hadn't. And then Carlotta came back—"

Sophie covered her face with her hands and sank down onto her knees. *Please believe me*, she prayed silently. *Please believe me, and think of him falling asleep, with the cards sliding off the coverlet.* Every night since Dermide's death she had had the same nightmare, of the little body convulsing and twitching, over and over, the eyes rolling back in his head, the thread of drool running out of the side of his mouth. She would sit bolt-upright in bed, gasping for air and trying to tell herself that it was only a nightmare.

Except it had been real.

She felt a hand underneath her elbow. It was Camillo. He had pulled a chair forward, and now he lifted her into it. She leaned against him for a moment, oddly grateful.

"So." Pauline's voice had a vicious edge. "I give you a home. I treat you like my own daughter. When you are ill, I nurse you around the clock. I bring you back from the dead. And this is how you repay me. My son is dying and you are fetching cards and playing games."

Sophie shrank down in the chair. *I should have stayed in Rome,* she thought, numb with despair. *I should never have come to Frascati.*

"Well?" demanded Pauline. "Have you nothing to say for yourself? Look at me!"

Sophie raised her eyes. Pauline's face was a mask of anger, rigid and hollow. "Go now," Camillo said in her ear. "She doesn't mean it. She is mad with grief. Go. I'll talk to her."

With a choked sob, Sophie fled. She could hear Pauline screaming after her.

"Don't think I'll forget!"

Camillo wished he could run away as well. He had not been alone with Pauline for four days, ever since the moment when he had made her lie down, warned her that he had bad news, and given her the letter from Frascati. She had been rational only long enough to confirm the news—no, it was not a mistake; yes, he had spoken to the courier himself. Then she had curled into a ball at the foot of her bed and started to wail—a thin, high-pitched sound like nothing he had ever heard before. She didn't respond when he called her name, when he touched her, when he shook her. He had summoned Peyre and left her to whatever comfort medicine could provide.

"Let me know if she would like to speak with me," he had told Pauline's page. "At any time of the day or night. If I am asleep, wake me."

There had been no summons. Pauline wanted no one and nothing. She had refused to see her mother. Her servants were forbidden to enter her room except when sent for and were instructed not to speak at all in her presence. She had left at dawn the following morning, riding alone in one of the smaller coaches, without even her maid or her page. Ahead of her, a courier galloped on a fresh horse, carrying a letter wrapped around the newly cut dark curls. It had been left to Camillo to make arrangements to pack, dismiss servants, fetch Madame Mère, send servants ahead to engage rooms for the night. Pauline had not even stayed at the same inns as Camillo and her mother.

There was a long silence after Sophie left. Pauline sat stiffly upright in her chair, staring grimly at the place where Sophie had been sitting.

"It is not Sophie's fault," Camillo said finally. "She is still a child herself, you know."

The response was a glance of utter contempt.

"It is *no one's* fault," he went on. "Do you hear me? Not the doctors, not my brother or your brother, not Madame Ducluzel or Carlotta. There was nothing anyone could have done."

"How do you know?" She stood up, clasping and unclasping her hands. "How do you know that? Don't you think that if I had been here, I would have noticed something earlier? Or nursed him more carefully?"

There was no safe answer to that question, so Camillo said nothing.

"I must be cursed," she muttered. "My husband is sick, I

cannot save him. My son is sick, I cannot save him. The only one I manage to save is that little witch Napoleon planted in my household to spy on me and tell tales to Joseph and my mother."

That little witch adores you, Camillo thought bitterly. He remembered Sophie looking away, embarrassed, when he had asked her where Pauline was on the last night of Carnival. *She lies to protect you from your own husband and she hates me cordially on your behalf. You treat her like dirt, and she only loves you more.*

"I must go away," said Pauline, more to herself than to Camillo. "I must go back to France. I hate it here; everything is dreadful here." She was breathing quickly, small, shallow breaths. "Yes, I have to go home. Dermide will be buried beside his father; I will take him to Montgobert."

She began pacing in circles around the armchair where she had been sitting. "I must send to Rome for the berlin," she said. "The carriages here are not large enough to hold the coffin. And I will need outriders. And footmen; more footmen. We only have two with us now. A courier can be sent tomorrow morning to tell my brother I am returning to France. If I leave the day after tomorrow, I can be there by the second week in September." It was as though Camillo did not exist; she didn't look at him or acknowledge him in any way. She walked around him as if he were a second armchair.

Only after the second circuit did Camillo notice that she was trembling—her hands, her arms, her head.

"Pauline!" He stepped in front of her.

"No," she muttered, drawing the word out. She was shaking so hard that her voice vibrated: *no-uh-o-uh-o-uh-o-uh-o.* "Don't tell Napoleon. What if he says I cannot leave Italy? Just get in the carriage and start north."

He grabbed her by the shoulders.

"Let me go!" she screamed, clawing at his chest.

"You're ill, you must sit down." She quivered between his hands like a wounded animal.

She laughed. The sound set his teeth on edge. "I am not ill. I went to the baths, I drank the waters, I purged, I bled, but I was not ill." Tears were pooling at the corners of her eyes, and she blinked them away. He could feel her trying to hold herself together. "I left him. I left him, Camillo. I took the doctor." She looked up at him for the first time. "Do you understand? He was the one who was sick, and I had our doctor with me. Because I am a selfish, lazy mother, who can only think about herself."

Now she was crying in earnest.

"You are not lazy and selfish," he said mechanically. Then, with more conviction: "Doctor Peyre could not have done anything more than the doctors from Rome did. He told you so. I heard him."

She sagged against him all at once, sending him staggering back one step. "Why didn't I take him with me?" she wailed. "Frascati is too close to Rome; I should have known that. He has always been subject to summer fevers."

"Don't do this," he whispered. "It isn't your fault. Don't think that, don't ever think that." He picked her up and carried her over to a sofa, where she lay sobbing, facedown, pounding the silk upholstery with her fist.

"Shhh." He stroked her cropped hair, making soothing noises like the ones he made to his mare when she was nervous. "We will go back to France. Whatever you want. I will make all the arrangements." He knew he shouldn't say it, but he did anyway. "I love you."

She turned over then and looked at him, her tear-drenched eyes so full of pain that he felt his heart squeeze with pity. "You can't love me. I killed my son."

"Pauline, no." He didn't know what to do or what to say. All he could think of was to sit by her and hold her hand. He took off her sandals, covered her feet with a shawl, tried to wipe her face with his handkerchief. Nothing seemed to comfort her. Eventually he slid down alongside her; she was still sobbing but turned into his arms with a sigh almost of relief and hid her head on his chest. When she would start to speak, he simply shushed her, like a child, gathering her closer and murmuring her name until she subsided.

They lay entwined for a long time. The candles burned down; the lamps began to sputter. Camillo felt sad and happy all at once. It was a little calm space in the storm of Pauline; he knew it would not last. For Pauline, grief was anger. He drifted off to sleep, breathing in her scent and feeling the ragged edges of her soft hair under his chin.

He woke at dawn, suddenly cold. His arms were empty. Pauline was standing next to the sofa, brushing the creases out of her skirt, her movements savage and careless. When she saw him looking at her, she gave him a mirthless, terrible smile.

In a flash of understanding, he saw what was coming.

"I want to thank you, prince husband, for consoling me." Her voice dripped with sarcasm. He could picture it eating into his skin like acid. "In my grief, you see, I became a bit confused. I blamed myself for driving off to take the waters without Dermide. But after you went to sleep, I remembered something. I remembered that it was *your* idea to go to Pisa. *Your* idea to leave my son at Frascati. I wanted to take him with us. But 'the lodgings were too cramped, the inns were too dirty, the carriage ride would make him sick.'" This last was delivered in a scornful imitation of his patrician Roman accent.

She pointed her finger at his chest. "Your brother could keep him here, in the hills, where he would be safe from the contagion in Rome. Safe! Yes, and my brother and his family would be nearby. You told me that, too. It was one of his cousins who infected him!"

He looked up at her, not bothering to defend himself. It would be no use, not when she was in this mood. And if she was set on blaming one of them for her son's tragic illness, he would rather she blamed him than herself.

Still in her stocking feet, she scooped up her sandals and headed for the door. Wrenching it open, she turned. "You killed my son," she said flatly.

He said nothing, just looked at her. Her eyes were red; her clothing crumpled and tear-stained; her cropped hair was jagged and ugly. He remembered the day he had decided to marry her, when he saw her exhausted and filthy by Sophie's sickbed. Why did he think she was beautiful no matter what she wore, no matter how ill she was, no matter how spiteful or cold her expression?

"You killed him," she repeated. "And I will never forgive you. Ever."

The door slammed behind her.

PART II

The Yellow Rose

Warmth, Jealousy,
Promise of a New Beginning

Paris
Frimaire 13, Year 13
[December 4, 1804]

Dearest Jerome:

You have been away so long, and by the time your letters
reach me from America they are months old. But I will
be one of the first to send you this news: our brother was
at last crowned emperor two days ago, and the balls and
parties continue as I write this; no one is sleeping, there
is noise and activity everywhere, and food and drink of
every possible description. The prince joined me here
some weeks ago and it is some comfort to have him with
me, but I still mourn for my son and must find some
quiet time to be alone occasionally and suffer constantly
from headaches. In any case Camillo will be gone in a
few weeks; Napoleon has given him a commission in the
Grenadiers, and he will be sent to Prussia, or perhaps it
is Russia? I don't see why all the men in our family have
to be in the military. Certainly I wish he had never made
you a naval officer; you are so far away all the time.
Please come home soon, dearest brother, you were still a
boy when you left and I long to see you and embrace you.

Your Pauline

Plombières-les-Bains
25th September 1806

Dear Napoleon:

*I must ask what it is that keeps Camillo so constantly with
his regiment. I see other officers in Paris and even here in
the spa towns in the mountains; why is my husband home
so seldom, for such short periods? Surely now that I am
an imperial princess and a duchess I might expect to enjoy
some of the privileges of rank? Also, I request that you
authorize some additions to my household staff, notably, the
appointment of a Monsieur de Forbin as a chamberlain. I
met him here while taking the waters; he is of good family
and will be a great help to me when I return to Paris and
must play my part and help you at court.*

Your affectionate sister,
Pauline

Gréoux-les-Bains
30th June 1807

To the Comte Auguste de Forbin, Hôtel de Charost, Paris

*Auguste, my dearest love, what delays you? I command you
as your beloved, not your employer, to make haste to join
me here at Gréoux. Surely as my chamberlain you need no*

excuse to be with me. I am not well, and it is very hot here in the south at the moment, but I know I will be better the moment you arrive. I have been very good and am drinking the waters every day.

You ask about my husband—Camillo has been promoted to general and writes me very affectionately. There was great excitement here a few days ago when we received dispatches from the army; it seems Camillo led a ferocious charge against the Russians and was personally commended by my brother. So he is well, and I do not think he will be in France at all this summer but if he does come we must bear it and be discreet. Caro, come quickly to

your beloved, P.

Nice
13th March 1808

Dear Napoleon,

I wish you would not order me about as you do your soldiers. Camillo will simply have to take up his new post as governor in Turin without me. I am not at all well and cannot possibly travel over the mountains right now; the climate of Turin is also very bad and my doctors advise me to remain here in Nice.

Your dutiful sister,
Pauline

ment of six million francs to Pauline's personal fortune. Her staff
had trebled in size: she now had an almoner (a cardinal, no less),
two chaplains, a *dame d'honneur*, twelve ladies-in-waiting (not including Sophie), six chamberlains, and four equerries. And those
were only the official attendants; she also had a physician, a music
master, readers, an ever-revolving bevy of pages, and an army of
servants. Her clothing and jewels were worth a king's ransom (or,
indeed, an emperor's ransom, as future events would suggest),
and she now traveled in such state that one coach was designated
largely to carry her tub, held ready for her daily ritual of bathing
in milk.

Still, it stood to reason that the unhappiness of an imperial
princess should be greater than that of a mere princess.

Part of her discontent was, in fact, the direct result of Napoleon's
coronation. Four years ago, she had been the only princess in the
family. Now all her sisters were imperial princesses, and Elisa
was also Duchess of Lucca (which, unlike Guastalla, was a large
and wealthy province), while Caroline was a Grand Duchess of
Cleves and Berg. Her sister-in-law Julie, a queen, outranked her
(Joseph was King of Naples and Sicily); so did Catherina, Jerome's wife, since Jerome had been named King of Westphalia;
and Hortense, wife of Louis, the new King of Holland. Only one
of her sisters-in-law remained in Pauline's good graces: Lucien's
wife, Alexandrine. True to his revolutionary ideals, Lucien had
refused to accept any titles or offices from Napoleon and had denounced his older brother's assumption of imperial power.

Worse than the proliferation of royal titles in the family was
the loss of privacy. Four years ago, her love affairs had, for the
most part, been a game—a vicious one, to be sure—between

herself and Camillo. Estrangement, jealousy, reconciliation, passion, estrangement. It was a dance they both knew well. The players were extras, visitors to Rome or Paris or whatever spa Pauline believed would cure her that year. They came; they fascinated or were fascinated (briefly); they left.

Now the affairs had become matters of state. And the players were members of her own household. Napoleon's re-creation of court life in the miniature monarchies fashioned for his siblings meant that Pauline was constantly surrounded by attractive, ambitious young men. She had already had a liaison with one of her chamberlains and, more recently, had seduced her music master, a shy young Italian. But her courtiers and ladies-in-waiting were loyal to the emperor, not to her. She was a public figure, and sooner or later, her brother would receive reports that his sister was creating more scandal.

That was why Her Imperial Highness Pauline was having difficulty persuading Napoleon to allow her to leave Camillo and go back to France. She could plead illness all she liked; he did not trust her, and so far he had refused every one of her increasingly abject letters begging him to let her leave Turin and go to France.

"I am ill, and would like to take the waters in Aix-en-Savoie," she wrote.

"You may go to one of the hot springs in your husband's province," he wrote back.

"I am *very* ill, and my doctors recommend Aix," she tried next.

"It is likely just a spring cold; your duty is to your husband and the people of the region" was the reply.

She turned to Camillo's secretary, Monsieur de Villemarest. One afternoon, she realized that she had eaten something that disagreed with her; she made certain to have the secretary shown to her apartments during a violent episode of vomiting.

He wrote the letter.

Napoleon told Villemarest to make sure that Pauline got the best of medical care. But she belonged with Camillo, in Turin.

Pauline did not want to be in Turin, hemmed in by clouds and mountains. Hemmed in by the rigid, narrow-minded matrons of Piedmont and the even more rigid rules Napoleon had laid down for her behavior. The rules specified everything from the number of forks at dinner down to the time and place of the weekly public receptions he commanded his new governor-general to host for the people of northern Italy. The rules said that Pauline was to be a dutiful and discreet spouse. The rules required her to receive the wives of the local nobility in her private apartments at least once per week. The rules stated that Pauline was to appear at every public event at Camillo's side.

Above all, Pauline did not want to be with Camillo. Because Napoleon's coronation had not only transformed Pauline's siblings into kings and queens and Pauline's own life into a constant battle with her own attendants. It had also transformed Camillo. And Pauline had to be honest: the whole thing was her fault. She was the one—at least indirectly—who had sent Camillo off to war.

Napoleon had always liked Camillo. Unlike the French hostesses who thought Camillo an idiot, he spoke to him in Italian and therefore actually received replies to his questions. And the first time the First Consul had seen his would-be brother-in-law on a horse, he had whistled in astonishment. His later comment to Lucien, who transmitted it verbatim to Pauline, was "My

God, that fucker has the best seat I've ever seen!" (Pauline had to admit that the sight of Camillo on horseback was often all it took to prompt her to move from the "jealousy" stage of their marital game to the "reconciliation" stage, to be followed as soon as possible by "passion.")

In the benign afterglow of the coronation, it had not been hard to persuade Napoleon to find an excuse to keep Camillo in France. And, therefore, an excuse for Pauline to remain in France.

At the time, she had not been thinking very clearly. It had been barely five months since she had returned to Paris with Dermide's body; she would still wake nearly every night in the small hours of the morning, terrified, convinced that something dreadful had happened, and then realize, as sleep dissolved, that something dreadful *had* happened: her son was gone forever. Because Dermide was so young, she had not been required to observe a formal mourning period; this meant that she had been immediately swept up into the maelstrom of preparations for the coronation. By the time the grand event was over, she had been exhausted, disoriented, and could only think of one thing: she wanted to stay in France. Italy was a dangerous place, where boys were playing in fountains one minute and dead the next. France was safe; she had been happy here; she must find some means of postponing her return to Rome. Her brother was now emperor; he could help her. He could create some position for Camillo in the new regime.

She had forgotten that Napoleon was an emperor second and a soldier first.

The emperor had granted Camillo French citizenship. The soldier had made Camillo an officer in the Horse Grenadiers.

Camillo had been delighted, and, at first, Pauline had been delighted as well. Her husband had looked very dashing in his bearskin hat and gold-braided uniform. Mounted on his black charger, he had looked even better. On the day he rode the horse to the Hôtel de Charost for the first time, she couldn't even wait to get back into the house. They made love in the stables, with the gelding kicking and stamping in the next stall. Afterward, Pauline had sewn the epaulette back onto Camillo's jacket herself. It still had four tiny little dents where she had bitten into it.

Pauline should have known better. She had, after all, been married to one of Napoleon's senior officers before. Yet somehow she had deluded herself, had pictured Camillo going off to war for a few weeks, perhaps a month—just time enough for a charming flirtation while he was gone—and then returning on his sleek, muscled black horse to whisk her off to the stables again. After a month or two, he would sally forth on another mission; again, a few weeks later, he would return. Pauline would stay in Paris and he would circle around her, at a distance, like a kite on a string.

Unfortunately, both Camillo and Napoleon believed that officers in cavalry regiments belonged with their troops. So Camillo went off to Boulogne and disappeared into the gaping mouth of Napoleon's war machine. He was promoted to colonel, then general.

The man who came back in 1808 to assume his governorship was very different from the man who had left Paris for Boulogne in 1805. This Camillo was proud instead of shy. This Camillo could not be goaded into fits of jealousy or tearful and passionate reunions. He had seen battle; he had led cavalry charges; he had held his own in the most elite fighting unit in Europe. No one could accuse the prince now of being a fop or a coward. No, this Camillo had proved that he was a soldier, a fighter.

He just wasn't interested in fighting for Pauline.

Pauline had tried everything she could think of. When he arrived in Nice, where she had been spending the winter, she had expected they would resume their usual magnetic oscillation between attraction and repulsion. Since she was, at that time, feeling exceptionally healthy and contented, she had decided to forgo the normal first stage (a violent quarrel) and proceed straight to the romantic reunion. That evening, she gave Camillo her most meaningful smile as they retired from the salon after dinner and set about making herself ready for him in her bedroom. She remembered that he did not like bright light or complete nudity and considerately quenched the lamps and retained a wispy film of drapery over her torso. When all was ready, she disposed herself charmingly on her pillows and waited.

Two hours later, she roused herself from the light sleep she had fallen into, put on a wrapper, and rang for a maid. "Please inform His Excellency that I am waiting for him," she said.

The maid reappeared after a few moments to tell her that Camillo had retired for the night. Quite some time ago.

Very well, she thought. *We will try jealousy. It had always worked before.* She got up early the next morning, determined to provoke Camillo into acknowledging her hold over him.

Pauline's latest lover, Felix, had made himself very scarce from the moment it was announced that the prince was coming to Nice to collect his wife and take her to his new capital of Turin. She found him packing his trunk in the small room he was now sharing with one of Camillo's aides, engrossed in sorting through a pile of sheet music.

Yesterday she would have been delighted to hear that he was leaving. Now she needed him. "Felix!" Her tone was horrified. "You are not leaving; you cannot leave!"

He whirled around, startled.

"But—your husband," he stammered.

She tossed her head. "Don't be ridiculous."

He was turning bright red. Really, thought Pauline, he was so young!

"I was told—the secretary—he showed me the list of appointments to your husband's household. I am not on it."

This was more like it. "Well, you are now," she said. "Wait here."

She found Camillo conferring with two of his aides on the terrace. There was a breeze off the sea, and the wind ruffled Camillo's hair. He stood straighter now, she noticed, and his profile looked almost stern. The contrast with the timid, blushing Felix was very appealing.

"I must speak to my husband," she informed the aides imperiously.

Camillo raised his eyebrows. "One moment, madame." He pointedly continued his conversation for another few moments, then excused the young men.

"You have dismissed my music master," she said accusingly.

He frowned. "Who is that?"

"Felix," she said, deliberately using his Christian name. Then, ostentatiously correcting herself. "Signor Blangini."

"I have dismissed no one."

"He told me you did! Villemarest showed him the list of appointments, and he was not on it!"

"Ah." His frown cleared. "That list is not mine. It was drawn up by your brother."

"Well, I do not see why I cannot have my music master with me! If I must go to Turin, I should have some few pleasures still left to me!"

"Certainly," he said, his tone indifferent. "I will tell Villemarest that he is part of your personal staff."

Pauline stamped back to her room, forgetting that she had left Felix waiting for word from her. Obviously, Camillo did not understand that Felix was his rival. Perhaps he had not heard the gossip yet, or perhaps, having met Felix, he had judged him too young and timid for the gossip to be true. And, in fact, she conceded to herself, it had taken quite a lot of persuasion to get Felix into her bed. He was not a very bold Romeo.

The villa she had borrowed for her stay in Nice had a lovely garden lined with orange trees, which had just finished blooming. Pauline set the stage again. This time the cast was larger than it had been for the aborted drama in the bedroom. She was the principal, of course. There was a wrought-iron bench beneath the trees at the far end of the garden; Pauline had two of her pages carry out cushions, a tray of wine and refreshments, and some music. She and Felix would sing duets.

Next came the question of the messenger. Someone had to bring Camillo out at the right moment. Not her new ladies-in-waiting; she did not trust them, and they were strangers to Camillo. Not Madame Ducluzel; she would never forgive Pauline for involving her. The pages would not be able to make sure Camillo arrived on cue.

"Sophie," she muttered. "And it will be good for her, too."

Sophie was now in an awkward phase: tall and gangly, her breasts just starting to round out, half-girl, half-woman. She showed no interest at all in the pages, who were good-looking boys only a little younger than she was, or in the equerries, equally good-looking young men a little older than she was. She drifted around looking soulful and pure and tripping over her own feet. Pauline was, for once, thankful that Sophie was not Catholic. She was at that age when many girls (although never Pauline) decide they want to enter a convent.

And so, the play commenced. Pauline summoned Felix; they arranged themselves beneath the sweet-scented trees. The sky was crystal-blue, the Mediterranean Sea below a deep turquoise. They sang the first duet. Partway through the second, Pauline put her hand over the music and smiled at Felix.

"It is so lovely out here, don't you think?" She tossed the sheets aside and reclined invitingly on the cushions.

With a nervous glance back toward the house, Felix snatched the music up. "For Christ's sake, Pauline, your husband is fifty feet away!"

"A hundred. He cannot see us, you know that." They had used this spot before. It was completely invisible from the house, tucked into a corner of the garden.

He still looked terrified.

"Just a kiss. Just one kiss. It's the music, it's the spring breeze, it's the sea and the sky! We are meant to be happy—can't you feel it?"

It wasn't one kiss, of course. She knew he wouldn't be brave enough to go much beyond kissing, so she kept it light, teasing him with her tongue, slipping her dress off one shoulder and inviting him to fondle her breast. That would be enough.

Steps on the gravel path. Sophie's voice, a little breathless.

"She said she needed to show you something at once, something about some ships that shouldn't be in the harbor—"

Felix choked and scrambled to his feet, knocking over the carafe of wine in the process. Pauline let her dress slip a bit farther down, then looked up, as if surprised.

Camillo completely ignored Felix. "A very charming scene," he said. He glanced down the hill to the water. "I take it the only ships that are in the wrong harbor are here in the garden?"

"What do you expect, if you neglect me?" Pauline shot back.

Felix was attempting to stammer excuses. Camillo gave him a cold stare. "Escort Signorina Leclerc back to the house, please," he said. He turned to Sophie and made a formal bow. "My apologies, Sophie."

The girl gave Pauline an anguished look, then turned and ran, followed by Blangini, calling after her and stumbling on the loose gravel as he went.

"Well," said Camillo when they were alone. He sounded tired and disgusted, not jealous.

"Well," said Pauline, in sarcastic imitation.

"You needn't have gone to so much trouble," he informed her. "I already knew."

She sat up, indignant. "Then why did you give me permission to take him to Turin?"

"Do as you please. Bring him and anyone else you fancy with you; I don't care." He started to walk away.

"Camillo!"

Was it her imagination, or did he stiffen slightly? He did turn back. Grudgingly.

"You were *gone*. I saw you twice in three years! Don't tell me you were faithful to me the whole time you were with the army!"

"No," he admitted. "But I was at least discreet. There are not five people in the world who could tell you the names of my mistresses. Whereas, even out on the borders of Russia, I knew the name of every one of your lovers. And so did most of Napoleon's army." He folded his arms and leaned against the garden wall. "Do you know what was waiting for me when I staggered off the field at Friedland?"

Friedland. Pauline thought she remembered that name. A battle, somewhere. Somewhere far to the east, near the Baltic.

"Thirty thousand dead," he said. "Most of them the Tsar's, but still. And I got back to my tent, covered with blood, and found a little packet."

"Letters?" she whispered. Who would have written to him? His mother? One of her ladies-in-waiting? No, they only reported to Napoleon.

"Not letters. Cartoons. My wife, in the newspapers."

She had seen those cartoons. She had laughed at them. Apparently, Camillo had not found them amusing.

"I didn't believe the one that showed you in bed with your brother," he said. "For one thing, I credit him with too much good sense to entangle himself with you. But the rest? They seemed all too plausible. Especially after I had been informed by several eyewitnesses that you had at one point actually been so lost to decency that you had packed up and gone to live in the house of one of your male servants to make it easier for him to service you."

"He was my chamberlain, not my servant," she objected hotly.

"When you are a princess," he said calmly, "your chamberlain *is* your servant."

"It was a perfectly nice house," she muttered. "His family is older than ours."

"Than *yours*," he corrected.

"So what do you want?" she demanded. "Do you want me to take a vow of celibacy? You certainly don't seem interested in performing your marital duties."

He sighed. "I don't want anything from you. Go your own way, and I shall go mine. It's no use my asking you to behave with some modicum of propriety; you won't listen. Since you are clearly barren, I at least don't need to worry about a cuckoo in the Borghese nest. But I refuse to waste my time any longer trying to mend this farce of a marriage."

He was halfway down the path before she recovered her wits. "Camillo!" she screamed. "You don't mean it! I know you don't!"

This time he had not turned around. Pauline had been left alone under the orange trees, with wine soaking into her skirt.

Seduction had failed; jealousy had failed; next she had tried sympathy. She still remembered how tender Camillo had been to her in Lucca, how frightened. Of course, she had really been quite ill then. But she could reproduce those same symptoms, especially since travel always made her stomach unsettled.

The following week, they had set out for Turin. As the parade of carriages crawled over the mountains into Italy, Pauline drooped hour by hour. She refused to eat. She fainted conveniently into an equerry's arms when he helped her from the carriage. She stayed up all night in the inns and kept her servants running for obscure remedies.

Her husband never came near her. Whenever she sent him a

message detailing a new symptom, he sent back his best wishes for her recovery, followed by a visit from the doctor. Vastapani had been appointed by Napoleon to replace Peyre, who had resigned in disgust during one of Pauline's more flamboyant affairs. Vastapani would take her pulse, check under her eyelids, examine her urine, and shake his head.

"I don't understand it," he would say. "Everything seems quite normal. Perhaps another dose of calomel will set you right."

There was no point in swallowing calomel or extract of rhubarb if Camillo was not paying attention; eventually, she had dismissed Vastapani and "recovered" in time to make a grand entrance to Turin in an open carriage at Camillo's side.

For the past six weeks, she had tried one last ploy: she had tried being good. She was charming to the Piedmontese burghers; she danced the local dances; she ate the disgusting, bland, creamy local dishes; she smiled by Camillo's side and did nothing, absolutely nothing, that her own mother would not have done.

It was choking her. She was drowning in her own tediousness.

Very well, then. It was time to leave. Napoleon thought she was not really ill? He forbade her to return to France? She would show him, and Camillo, and all of them.

TEN

"So." Pauline handed Sophie a glass of sweet wine. "How old are you now, Sophie?"

For four years, Sophie had been bouncing back and forth between the schoolroom and Pauline's little court. First, there was her brief stint in Rome as a pretend fourteen-year-old. Then, the summer at Frascati with its dreadful conclusion. After Dermide's death, she had been happy to remain in the world of lessons and early bedtimes. She was convinced that Pauline blamed her for her son's illness, that Pauline would never want to see her again. But when she had arrived in Paris, several weeks behind Pauline, Pauline seemed to have buried her anger with Dermide's coffin. She greeted Sophie warmly, housed her in rooms next to her own, and insisted that Sophie be included in the coronation ceremony. Sophie found herself once more a junior lady-in-waiting, being fitted for dresses that were so heavy and stiff she could barely move in them. The promotion lasted until the prince went off to the front. Then, once again, Sophie was banished to the top floor of the *hôtel* and a governess arrived to resume her lessons. She had a sort of duenna, too, a superior maidservant who was the sister of one of the prince's men. Her name was Bettina, and she reported every single scandalous tale about Pauline to Sophie with great relish. "You're back in the schoolroom because *she* wants to put someone in her bedroom," Bettina told her. "Just wait and see."

Bettina had been right, of course.

When that lover disappeared (he had joined the army and gone off to fight in Austria; Sophie was never sure if he had volunteered or been forcibly conscripted by an angry Napoleon), Sophie was once again Pauline's favorite companion. Lessons had been curtailed, then suspended. The governess had left. Pauline had taken Sophie with her to Nice; she had given her jewelry and teased her about her lack of interest in men. One day, Sophie was dismissed again, this time to a small room at the back of the villa, which she shared with Bettina. "She's at it again" was Bettina's dark prediction. A week later, Felix Blangini had arrived and been installed in Sophie's old suite, right next to Pauline.

Now they were in Turin, and Pauline wanted Sophie back.

"You be careful," Bettina had said gruffly this morning when Sophie opened the note from Pauline. "She'll be all sweet to you now, and then cold as ice tomorrow."

Sophie knew that.

She had never had a proper letter from Pauline before, though. It was addressed to her dearest cousin Sophie, and it informed her that she would be expected to meet with Pauline every afternoon at two from now on. Sophie had assumed that there was to be some sort of public reception every day, and she had struggled into her court dress and had her maid curl her hair. But when she had gone across the hall to Pauline's chambers, there had been no one else there. Just Sophie and Pauline and the heavy furniture and Chinese vases. Every room in the palace had at least three vases, and Sophie was sure she would break one sooner or later.

Pauline had looked at Sophie's outfit and burst out laughing.

"Sit down, you goose. It's just to be the two of us. Don't wear anything like that tomorrow; it makes me itch just to look at you! Here, have some wine." She led Sophie over to an embrasure by the window; two chairs had been pulled up next to a table. The window looked out onto the Piazzetta Reale, which at the moment was gray and wet.

"Dreary, isn't it?" Pauline made a face, then turned her back to the view and poured two glasses from the decanter on the table. It was heavy, sweet wine, dark gold in color.

"So, how old are you now, Sophie?"

She took a cautious sip from the crystal goblet Pauline handed her. It seemed very strong to her. But Pauline was drinking hers. "Fifteen." She gave her true age. Fifteen, to Sophie, was magnificently old, and she had only arrived at that estate ten days earlier.

"Is that all?" Pauline poured herself another glass. "Well, that explains a lot. I must have been confused; I thought you were older." She tilted her head to one side and studied Sophie. "Good eyes, good skin. A bit bony, but you'll fill out. Don't let your maid curl your hair like that again; it makes your face too long." She leaned across and patted Sophie's knee. "I have been neglecting you," she said. "But now I mean to make it up to you. A girl your age needs a mother, someone to tell her about men and marriage and the way the world works. You'll come and visit me at this time every day—unless there is some state ceremony, of course—and I'll answer all your questions." She sat back and beamed at Sophie.

Sophie was holding her glass suspended between the table and her mouth, gaping.

"Drink up," Pauline encouraged her. "I wasn't shy at your age, but I know you, Sophie. You're a prude, like Camillo. You won't tell me anything until you've had a glass or two."

Mechanically, Sophie took several more swallows from her glass.

"Let's start with the young men attached to the court," Pauline said briskly. "Who do you fancy?" She saw Sophie's face and clapped her hands. "So, there is someone! I thought you were looking a bit less ethereal since we arrived in Turin."

Sophie silently cursed her too-expressive face. "No, no one," she lied.

Pauline laughed. "I'll have it out of you, never fear. How can I help you if I don't know who it is?" She frowned suddenly. "It isn't d'Aniano, is it? He has the pox already, even though he's only sixteen."

"No," said Sophie, feeling her face start to burn.

"Well," said Pauline. "That's a blessing. But as long as we are on the subject, I'll tell you how you can check to see if your lover is infected. It's usually a little sore about this big—" She held up her fingers in a small oval. "It looks a bit like a button, and it feels hard when you touch it. If you spot something like that, send him off to get dosed with mercury salts before you sleep with him."

Wine, or curiosity, or both, got the better of Sophie. "Where—where is the sore?"

"On his cock, of course. Where did you think?"

"Oh." It wasn't possible for her face to get any hotter.

"Have another glass of wine," Pauline said. "Are you still a virgin? I assume so, but one never knows."

It took three days and six glasses of wine for Pauline to worm the name out of her. Sophie had resolved that she would be boiled in oil, stretched on a rack, and crucified before she confessed. But Pauline was like an unstoppable force of nature. She bombarded Sophie with names. Was it a Frenchman? Villemarest? Mont-Breton? Or an Italian? De Sordevalo, perhaps? She interspersed her queries with comments about their physique, their erotic history, if any, and their marital prospects. For the first time, Sophie discovered that she herself was a desirable bride: Napoleon had set aside a dowry of fifty thousand francs for her.

Sophie held out until the inquisition took a disturbing turn. In the middle of some unflattering comments about the potency of one of the equerries, Pauline suddenly stopped in mid-sentence. "How could I have been so stupid?" she exclaimed. "I am forgetting what I was like at fifteen! I am asking about all the young bachelors, but of course it is a married man! They are always the most attractive to girls."

"No," protested Sophie. For some reason, it was very important to her that Pauline be disabused of the notion that Sophie would fall in love with a man who was married to someone else.

"No?" Pauline looked at her searchingly. "He isn't married?"

Up until now, Sophie had not answered any of Pauline's questions, just ducked her head and sipped her wine. But now she did answer: one word, "No." And like a dam with a small crack in it, that one answer quickly led to more. All Pauline needed was a "no," and she was on to the next possibility. Was he French? No. Italian, then. One of the pages? No. Equerries? No. A soldier? One of the officers in the militia? No. A member of the household? No. Of the Piedmontese nobility? No.

"Mother of God," gasped Pauline, after this last response. Her eyes lit with amusement. "I know who it is. It's that young hothead, that idiot from Milan who wants to throw the French out of Italy! What is his name? Visconti? I've seen him with you, in fact! But he was scowling; not very lover-like."

Sophie said nothing, at least out loud. Inside her head, the words unrolled like a furled banner opening: Gian Andrea Visconti. Gian Andrea Visconti. Gian Andrea Visconti.

"Hmmmm." Pauline was thinking, one finger perched on her lower lip. "He would do nicely as your first lover," she decided. "Although he might need some training. But of course you cannot marry him."

Gian Andrea was descended from an ancient and powerful northern family, and he carried himself like a prince of the blood. Tall, slender, and hawk-faced, with a swatch of dark hair that continually fell into his eyes, he seemed to Sophie like the hero of some chivalric romance. The nineteen-year-old had come to Turin with a letter of introduction from his great-uncle, who owned half of Milan, but it soon became clear that he had no intention of playing courtier.

No, Gian Andrea was a patriot, and he had come to persuade Camillo that he was betraying his own country by governing on Napoleon's behalf.

Had he been older or from a less powerful family, he would likely have been arrested right away. The militia had strict orders to suppress anything that looked like a nationalist uprising. But Camillo and his court treated Gian Andrea like a misguided schoolboy, listening politely to his earnest speeches and inviting him to go hunting, or boating, or drive out to a picnic in the foothills. No one took him seriously, especially because, after he had been there for a few days, it was obvious to everyone that he had fallen head-over-heels in love.

Not with Sophie, of course. With Pauline.

Sophie's life that fateful May in Turin therefore consisted of intervals of exquisite torture set into vast gray fogs where she ate, spoke, and slept without paying any attention to what was around her. When she was with Gian Andrea—or with Pauline, talking about Gian Andrea—the world was so real, so brightly colored and sharp-edged that it hurt. When she was somewhere else, the pain was gone, but so was she.

She had seen right away that her hero had fallen victim to Pauline and had resigned herself to watching him from afar at public events. But within a few days of his arrival, he himself had sought her out.

They were at Stupinigi, at the old royal hunting lodge. Pauline had demanded a change from the damp air of the town, and Camillo had moved the court to the hills for the day for a "bucolic fete." Sophie had been playing idly on a very out-of-tune pianoforte in the music room when Gian Andrea had knocked on the open door.

Her fingers produced a mangled chord, and she snatched them back from the keys.

"May I come in?"

She nodded.

"Don't let me interrupt you," he said politely.

"I'm finished," she said quickly. "I don't have my music here, and in any case, the instrument is dreadfully flat."

"May I escort you somewhere, then?"

She couldn't believe this was really happening. *Where*, she asked herself frantically. *Where could I say I was going?*

He seemed to guess at her difficulty. "Perhaps to the bridge, in the park? It is a lovely view."

As if in a dream, she rose and took his arm.

"You probably don't remember me," he was saying. "We were introduced the evening I arrived. But I heard from the princess that you were a freethinker, and I wanted to ask you about it. I am very intrigued by the movement."

You are intrigued by Pauline, thought Sophie cynically, *and you have discovered that I am her ward.*

It was not a total lie. He actually was interested in free thought. He had read Collins and Diderot, and believed that free thought was essential to the nationalist cause he championed. But after one or two meetings, Sophie was not surprised when his questions veered away from philosophy and settled on Pauline. Or, more precisely, on Camillo.

Every day he had a new and ugly story about the prince, which he shared with Sophie. "You're the only one who takes me seriously," he would say. Sometimes he would smile at her, and her heart would turn over. Once he put his arm around her, but he spoiled it by ruffling her hair. "Sweet Sophia." He laughed. "What would I do without you? You're like my priest; I confess everything to you."

Yesterday he had suddenly asked about Dermide.

"The prince didn't really kill Donna Paolina's son, did he?"

"Of course not!" Sophie gave Gian Andrea her fiercest glare. "How could you even think such a thing!?"

They were walking in the gallery that connected the larger palace in the royal square to the smaller one, where the Borgheses held court. He trailed his finger across one of the marble console tables and said nothing.

She knew how he could think Camillo guilty of murder. Hadn't she herself pictured Camillo as a poisoner, four years ago? Gian Andrea was bewitched, as Sophie had been. Pauline could tell no lies. Camillo was an unfeeling monster who oppressed his beautiful wife. And Gian Andrea, of course, was ready to be Pauline's knight errant and save her.

They stood in silence for a moment, looking at the silver-plated clock on the table. It was an eagle. Camillo's new subjects had decided that the palace needed Napoleonic eagles, and they had showered him and Pauline with clock-eagles, candlestick-eagles, chairs with eagle legs, china services decorated with eagles, cushions embroidered with eagles, even a box of sugar candies fashioned to look like eaglets hatching from their eggs. Soon the palace would have an eagle to go with every Chinese vase.

"Well, what did happen?"

"What? When?"

"When the princess's son died."

"Oh." Sophie did not want to think about Dermide. "He died of a fever," she said reluctantly.

Gian Andrea gave her one of his I-am-too-worldly-for-you looks. "Some fevers are natural; some are not."

"Stop it!" Sophie stamped her foot. "Everyone in the house was ill! Dermide was always a bit sickly; it hit him harder than the others, that is all. The prince wasn't anywhere near Frascati. He was in Lucca with the princess."

"All right, I believe you," he said, alarmed at her expression.

The tears that had threatened at the mention of Dermide retreated, and Sophie started to relax again.

"But he wouldn't let her bury the boy in the Borghese chapel," he said, persisting. "That I do know. He made her take the body all the way back to France."

Sophie gave him an incredulous stare. "Who told you that?"

He looked uncomfortable.

"Pauline," she said, nearly spitting out the words, "*insisted* that Dermide be buried next to his father in Picardy. She traveled back to France with his coffin. Even though it was August, and the fever was everywhere. She fought with the prince, and her doctor, and Napoleon, and she only got her way because they were afraid she would do something dreadful if they said no."

He looked skeptical.

"Listen to me," she said, her voice intense. "You don't have to believe anything else I say, if you only believe this. You think my cousin is Italian. She grew up on Corsica, so she speaks Italian better than French. She looks Italian; she is married to an Italian prince. But she isn't Italian. She is French. No one *ever* has to compel her to go back to France from Italy. France is home. That is where she wants to be. She writes Napoleon every week asking for permission to return."

"I happen to know why she wants to go back to France," he said stiffly. "She told me herself."

"Oh?"

"To get away from her husband." Leaning over, he said in a low voice. "He mistreats her."

Sophie couldn't listen to any more. "The prince is worth ten of her!" she snapped, exasperated. Then she hurried away, appalled at what she had just said. *He'll never speak to me again*, she thought, and as her footsteps echoed on the marble floors of the gallery, the silence behind her echoed louder still.

When she met Pauline that afternoon, her red eyes gave her away.

"He's been unkind to you!" declared Pauline theatrically. "The villain!" She spoiled it by laughing. But only for a moment; then she became sympathetic. "He thinks you are too young, doesn't he?"

Sophie nodded. "Once he said I was like his little sister," she said glumly. "Another time he compared me to a priest."

"Well, that won't do. We must think of a way to get his attention before you leave."

Leave? They were leaving? When? Where were they going? Were they coming back? She nearly choked on her wine. Terrified, she dabbed at her mouth with her handkerchief until she thought she could command her voice. "Are we leaving soon?"

"Sometime soon, yes. I am waiting to get permission from my brother."

"And—and I am going with you?"

"Yes, of course." Pauline didn't appear very concerned about it, but Sophie's whole world was crumbling.

"Will the court—" She was floundering. "Will the prince—that is, will the people here at court be coming?"

"You mean will your young admirer come with us," Pauline said matter-of-factly. "No, I imagine not. This will be a private trip, just you and me and a few of the servants. That is why we need to do something soon. Something to pique his interest in you." She must have seen how upset Sophie was, because she added, with one of her pats on Sophie's knee, "Don't worry—it won't be for several weeks yet. More likely a month."

A month. A month had seemed an eternity when Sophie was waiting in Paris for Pauline to return from one of her spur-of-the-moment visits to a spa, or from her stay last year at the home of her lover. Now "we leave in a month" sounded to Sophie like "we leave tomorrow." Her stomach clenched; she thought for a minute she might pass out.

"Let me think," muttered Pauline. "The banquet, perhaps. That would be a good time."

There were often several banquets a week at the palace, but Sophie knew which one Pauline meant. Camillo had decided to celebrate the feast day of Saint Philip, Apostle of Rome, with a mass in the Chapel of the Holy Shroud in the morning and a large banquet at the palace in the evening. Not only was this Camillo's name-day (his second name, Filippo, was his name in the church), but an earlier Camillo Borghese, Pope Paul V, had been the first to recognize the saint, beatifying him less than twenty years after his death. Sophie had already heard plenty from Gian Andrea about the planned celebration.

"I don't think he will go," Sophie said nervously. Gian Andrea had first denounced the whole institution of name-days as superstitious nonsense. Then, warming to his theme, he pointed out that this particular ceremony, with its links to Pope Paul V, was obviously meant to remind Camillo's subjects of his family's power and papal connections. "It's nothing but politics," he had concluded in disgust. "Politics and religion. Bah."

"He'll go if I speak to him," Pauline said.

Sophie must have shown something in her face; Pauline laughed. "No, no; he's far too young for me. And so serious! He never smiles. He's all yours." She took back Sophie's glass of wine. "No more wine for you today; we need to try on dresses. Three days isn't long enough to have something made up; we'll have to alter one of mine."

Sophie started to object; she had plenty of dresses already. Then she thought about her dresses, and Pauline's dresses, and held her tongue. Hers were muslin, in pale colors, trimmed with ribbon, with square bodices. They were dresses for a girl. Pauline's were silk, decorated with jewels or gold embroidery, cut low in the front. They shimmered when she walked and cupped her breasts invitingly. Now that Sophie actually had breasts (tiny, but breasts nevertheless), Pauline's dresses had started to look appealing rather than shocking.

Pauline rang for her maid. "Bring me the blue silk," she ordered, "the one with the chiffon overskirt. And the yellow sarcenet. Although—" She looked at Sophie. "I don't think you will look well in yellow, but it is a very pale yellow. We shall see."

Within a few minutes, Sophie was standing on a stool while two maids and a seamstress pinned fabric around her. She felt a bit light-headed and dizzy; it was a good thing Pauline had taken away her wine.

"Too short, of course." Madame Ducluzel had been summoned to assist in the proceedings and was eyeing the blue dress approvingly. "But we can put on a border; the color is perfect."

Sophie, looking in the mirror over the heads of the maids, did not approve, but no one seemed to be interested in her opinion. She remembered this dress on Pauline; she had worn it in Nice, less than a month ago. On Pauline, the deep neckline and high waist had hugged the princess's curved figure. On Sophie, the dress hung like a sack; her thin shoulders stuck out of the tiny cap sleeves and the bodice flapped, half-empty, over her under-endowed chest. And, of course, the hem didn't even reach her ankle bones. On Pauline, the rich blue color had set off her white skin and dark hair. On Sophie, the color simply made her pale hair and eyebrows look even paler. She sighed.

"Bend over," said the seamstress, her mouth full of pins. She was doing something to Sophie's chemise, and her fingers tickled Sophie's rib cage. Obligingly, Sophie inclined forward.

"More."

She bowed at the waist, almost losing her balance.

As her breasts shifted forward, the seamstress caught them in a fold of fabric, twisted, and pinned. Sophie suddenly felt as though she couldn't breathe; there was a band around her chest that gripped it like iron.

Up, gestured the woman.

Sophie straightened, looked automatically in the mirror, and gasped. The loose neckline was loose no longer. It clung like a second skin, and thrusting up to fill the scallop-shaped bodice were two lovely, creamy globes, straining at the fabric as though they were twice their real size. Slightly cross-eyed, she peered down. She had *cleavage*.

Meanwhile, the seamstress was twitching at the fabric of the sleeves, adding a ribbon of chiffon to match the skirt. Sophie's shoulder bones disappeared. Finally, a border of fringed silk was tacked onto the hem.

"That is more like it," said Pauline, satisfied. She pointed at one of the maids. "You. You will do the signorina's hair. No curls. Put it up à la Grecque, and twine this in it." She handed the girl a box.

Sophie craned her neck to see what was in the box. It was a rope of sapphires.

"Here, I'll show you," Pauline said. Hopping up onto the seamstress's chair, she lifted Sophie's hair into a rough twist and draped the jeweled strand across her head.

Instead of pale hair, Sophie suddenly had gold hair. Gold hair with sparkling blue highlights. At that moment, she would have lain down and let Pauline walk on her. Except that it would ruin her dress.

At Pauline's insistence, Sophie attended mass with the rest of the court on the morning of the banquet. "He has to see you in the morning, looking like the Sophie he ignores," Pauline told her. "Then, at the banquet—the transformation!" She snapped her fingers. "He will be *bouleversé*." Pauline had been speaking French to Sophie lately. It made Sophie nervous; it reminded her of the mysterious voyage looming in her future.

As a budding freethinker, Gian Andrea should not have been

at mass, either. But Pauline insisted he would be, and there he was, in the row right behind the prince and princess. He managed to position himself so that he took communion next to Pauline, too, and when he touched his lips to the goblet, he looked not at the bishop but at his neighbor, bending sideways to place his mouth exactly where Pauline had placed hers. Sophie, conspicuously isolated on her seat while everyone else lined up at the altar, noted this bit of byplay and flinched inwardly. It was exactly the sort of thing Pauline had been teaching her in her "lessons."

Sophie, Pauline decreed, had to learn how to flirt. In the three days since the dress-fitting, the princess had spent hours each afternoon coaching her. Sophie was exhausted from listening and watching and trying to do everything Pauline suggested. The results had not been promising.

"Now, young Visconti sees you in your new dress, and he is *épris*." Pauline had imitated a smitten look. "He comes up and kisses your hand and tells you how lovely you look. What do you do?"

"Say thank-you?" Sophie guessed.

That option obviously had not occurred to Pauline. "I suppose you could," she conceded. "But that is not the important part. I'll be you. Come here and kiss my hand."

Feeling utterly ridiculous, Sophie stepped awkwardly toward Pauline, raised her hand, and kissed it.

"Now, watch," instructed Pauline. As Sophie lowered Pauline's hand and started to let go, Pauline held on and stepped forward, so that Sophie was now much closer to her—a hand's breadth away instead of the length of her arm. And she lowered her eyes, peeping up at Sophie from underneath her dark lashes.

Sophie's eyes followed hers automatically. Then, realizing

that she was staring straight down Pauline's dress, she hastily stepped back.

"That's what you want." Pauline jerked her chin down toward her décolletage. "You want to bring him right up to you and then lower your eyes so that he looks down, too. You look modest and charming, and he gets an eyeful of your titties. Plus the smell. You have to get him close enough to smell you."

That had been bad enough, but then there was the discussion (more like a lecture, because Sophie had been too shocked to say much) about virginity. With some regret, Pauline had decided that Napoleon might be upset if Sophie slept with Gian Andrea. "He would blame it on me, for one thing," she said. "But really, there is quite a bit that you can do without actually letting him inside." And she had proceeded to describe those options with great relish.

Sophie had gulped down three glasses of the sweet wine in a frantic attempt to numb her brain but had still understood far more than she wanted to. Now, alone on her bench in the red-and-black marble vault of the chapel, she watched Gian Andrea take communion and tried to shut out the images of his mouth doing something else. Something unspeakably embarrassing and revolting. She fervently hoped that her father was right that there was no God, because if He existed, He would probably strike her with lightning for thinking about things like that in the chapel that housed Christ's burial shroud.

Mass was long, and Sophie's knees were bruised by the end. She had also worked herself into a state of utter panic. The thought of the banquet terrified her. To be on display, in public, in that dress suddenly seemed like a nightmare instead of a fairy tale. And what if Pauline was right? What if Gian Andrea did take her aside afterward and kiss her? Put his tongue in her mouth? Put his hand down her dress? Was that what she, Sophie, wanted? Or was it what Pauline wanted? Her head was pounding; her stomach felt like she had swallowed a dead toad. She couldn't go; she wouldn't go; she was sick. As the rest of the court filed out, Sophie huddled in her corner, unable to move. The silver lamps around the altar in front of her wavered and dimmed; black spots danced in front of her eyes.

"Are you all right?"

It was Gian Andrea. He squatted down and peered at Sophie's face.

"Just a little dizzy," she said, sitting up and blinking.

"You didn't fast, did you?" He took her arm and helped her up. "You don't need to fast if you are not taking communion, you know."

Sophie tried to remember when she had last eaten. Her appetite had been poor lately. Sometimes, after the glasses of sweet wine in the afternoon, she couldn't eat supper at all.

"I don't go to mass very often any longer," he was saying. He still had her arm. "But Donna Paolina asked me to go, as a favor, and of course, since she is my hostess, I thought it would be rude to refuse."

Bettina, who had been seated in back with the servants, bore down on them and almost snatched Sophie away. Gian Andrea didn't seem to mind. "She's looking a bit piqued," he told Bettina, as though Sophie were not there. "She should rest if she is coming to the banquet later."

Sophie roused herself at the word "banquet." "Are you coming?" she said, trying to sound casual. "To the banquet, I mean?" Her terror did an abrupt about-face: What if she and

Pauline had gone to all this trouble and he did not appear? She suddenly wanted, more than anything, to have Gian Andrea see her in the blue dress. Yes, and kiss her. And maybe even other things.

"Of course I am coming." He smiled down at her, his dark eyes crinkling slightly at the corners. "I am escorting you. Didn't your cousin tell you?" He strode away, nodding slightly to Bettina.

Sophie gazed after him until he disappeared.

"Holy Saint John protect us," muttered Bettina under her breath, looking from the star-struck Sophie to the receding figure of Gian Andrea. "Now what is that *puttana* up to?"

ELEVEN

Gian Andrea did not follow Pauline's script. When he met Sophie as she arrived at the bottom of the scissor staircase in the main palace ("There is something very appealing for men about watching a woman descend to their level," Pauline had said), he stepped back, not forward.

"Sophie?" he said, incredulous.

She didn't follow the script, either. She laughed and whirled around in front of him. The motion lifted the chiffon overskirt in little waves around the blue silk and sent the fringe fluttering at her ankles.

He did take her hands then, but not to bow over them. He held her still and surveyed her, from head to toe and back again. "You look—"

"Different?"

It had taken three hours to get ready; she had a headache from tilting her neck to have her hair put up; her bodice was so tight she could feel every stitch of the seam. And she was gloriously, deliciously happy, because when she had looked in the mirror, she had seen a complete stranger. Willowy, not thin. Blond, not straw-haired. This Sophie had dark eyelashes and delicately curved brown eyebrows, setting off her blue-gray eyes. This Sophie smiled.

Even Bettina had been impressed. "Look at you!" she had gasped, before she had remembered that this was all vanity of vanities and repeated her warnings about young men and wine and dancing.

There was to be dancing. First the banquet, then dancing, then a late supper and fireworks. In this dress, Sophie *knew* she could dance. Not like those other times, when she tripped, or stopped at the wrong part of the music, or went up the line when she should have gone down.

"Shall we?" He was offering her his arm.

She tucked her gloved hand into the crook of his elbow but held him back when he started toward the state dining room. "We're to wait. The prince and princess will be here in a minute, and we are to follow them."

"Ah, yes, that's right. The princess mentioned that to me." He looked expectantly up at the landing. Sophie just stood there, drinking in the delicious feeling of his arm enfolding hers. Every once in a while she would steal a glance at his fierce profile and then turn away, or lift her hand slightly and then settle it again, so that she could enjoy the contrast: not looking, looking. Not touching, touching.

It was not a minute, or even two, but it was less than a quarter-hour. A sudden hush fell over the group assembled at the foot

of the stairs, and Camillo and Pauline appeared at either side of
the gallery on the floor above. They bowed to each other across
the intervening space, then began to descend, crossing in front of
each other twice as the separate stairways met and parted again.
Both were dressed in white; as they drew closer, Sophie could
see that Camillo's jacket and waistcoat were embroidered with
gold and silver thread. Pauline's gown, however, was completely
unadorned. It fastened at one shoulder with a small gold brooch
and swept down to her feet from the cinch beneath her breasts.
She wore a small gold necklace at her throat, and her hair was
caught up with a simple band of pearls. When she reached the
bottom, at exactly the same moment as Camillo, they turned in
unison and joined each other in the middle of the lofty receiving
hall, as though they were performing the steps of a dance.

"Magnificent!" breathed Gian Andrea. He hadn't taken his
eyes off Pauline during the two minutes it took to execute the
stately, carefully timed descent. And really, thought Sophie, you
could hardly blame him. It *was* magnificent. She was magnificent. Every single person in the room, male and female, was staring at Pauline. That was just the way it was.

Dinner was magnificent, as well. There were sixty guests in the
state dining room, and at times it seemed to Sophie that there
were sixty different courses. The palace kitchen had endeavored
to please both local palates and the imperial couple, and so pi-
geons in cream sauce jostled against vol-au-vents; truffled veal sat
next to courgettes carved into elaborate shapes and piped with
cream; the traditional Piedmontese *bonet* was served for dessert
in plain glass custard bowls while an intricate centerpiece of spun
sugar and pastry in the shape of the dome of the royal chapel was

carefully cut and handed round after tantalizing diners all during the meal.

Sophie barely ate. Nervous, exhilarated, and half-strangled by her gown, she preferred to sit and look around and sip her wine. It was lighter and easier to drink than the dark gold liquor Pauline served; she had several glasses before the second course was even removed. Gian Andrea, too, seemed nervous. He would look at Sophie, smile absently, then pick at his food. She noticed that he hardly drank any wine. Toward the end of the meal, he beckoned over a page, whispered something to him, and sent him off to the head of the table.

Sophie, her heart sinking, watched the page head for Pauline. What was it? A note? An agreement to meet later? The page slipped behind the royal couple, leaned forward—and said something to Camillo.

The prince looked up, surprised. The page turned, indicated Gian Andrea, and said something else.

Gian Andrea had gone completely still next to her. His hand was gripping his untouched wineglass; he seemed afraid to move.

Camillo looked straight at him and nodded. And smiled.

That was what Sophie remembered afterward: Camillo's smile. Friendly, a little curious, a little drowsy; the smile of a man who has just fed sixty people a delicious dinner in his palace.

"Now we shall see," Gian Andrea said to her in a low voice, his eyes glittering.

"What is it?" Sophie looked at Camillo, at Gian Andrea, back at Camillo.

"I asked if I could offer a toast, after the mayor. On behalf of the people of Milan." He leaned back in his chair. "My ancestors were Dukes of Milan, you know. Three hundred years before the Borgheses swindled their way into the papacy."

"You're not going to say anything like that, are you?" Sophie asked, alarmed at his expression.

"No." He pulled a thin, leather-bound octavo volume out of his jacket. "Just some historical stuff, about his name."

"Oh." Sophie didn't think anyone could make much trouble talking about Philip of Neri. From what she could gather from Bettina's comments after mass that morning, he had spent his life tending the poor and sick, in classic saintly fashion.

The footmen began clearing away the plates; the prince and princess rose and led the way to the ballroom. More guests were to join the diners here; many had already arrived and were milling about between the marble columns. The orchestra was in place, tuning their instruments.

"When do you suppose the dancing will begin?" Sophie said, looking down the expanse of the polished floor. She had her hand tucked into his arm again; he seemed very stiff, his shoulder unyielding and tense.

"First there will be the toasts," he said. "See?" A small army of footmen in green and gold had entered, carrying trays of champagne. Sophie took a glass and let the bubbles break under her chin. She loved champagne, but she didn't think she could swallow anything else without bursting a seam. Gian Andrea waved the servant away. "Come on," he said, pushing through the crowd. "We have to be up front, with the prince."

The mayor was already speaking. Sophie couldn't hear very well; people were still talking, and new arrivals, crowding in, were calling the footmen over to obtain their share of the champagne.

As they grew closer, she could see him, though, a short, stout figure with a sash across his chest, gesturing expansively and bowing repeatedly toward Camillo and Pauline. His voice faded in and out, like music heard through a window:

". . . signal honor of Your Excellencies' hospitality . . . this happy occasion . . . His Imperial Majesty . . . many blessings . . ."

He was just finishing as they pushed their way through to the open space around Camillo and Pauline, and was cheered loudly, if for no other reason than because everyone finally felt free to drink the champagne they had been holding. Camillo's short speech of thanks was completely drowned in the applause and the clink of glasses.

The musicians picked up their instruments; the concertmaster looked at Camillo expectantly. The prince shook his head. No, wait, his gesture said. He motioned Gian Andrea forward.

Holding Sophie like a shield, Gian Andrea stepped out into the empty circle facing the prince.

"Citizens of Turin," he began. His voice was clear and pitched to carry. Some people stopped talking and turned, curious to see what was happening, but most did not. "Citizens of Italy!" he tried again, louder.

Sophie had been to many, many banquets by now. She had heard many toasts. They did not begin with the word "citizens"— at least, not since her childhood, during the Terror. They began with "Your Excellency, Your Imperial Highness, and distinguished guests." Or "Your Holiness, Your Eminence, and distinguished guests." Or "Your Majesty, Lord Mayor, and distinguished guests." She tried to move away from Gian Andrea, but he was holding her arm clenched to his side in an unbreakable grip.

That second, louder "citizens" had done it. Into the hush that followed, Gian Andrea spoke. "Fellow guests," he said, "as a small and inadequate acknowledgment of the hospitality I have received these past few weeks from the prince, I have asked him for permission to honor his name-day with this toast. Indeed, as a Visconti, as a son of Milan, I consider it my right and my duty to celebrate the history of the great families of our nation."

There were some approving murmurs and a gracious smile from Pauline.

"This morning," he went on, "in the chapel adjoining this ballroom, we honored Saint Philip, and remembered his generosity and concern for those who were weak and suffering."

More nods. Footmen were circulating unobtrusively, topping up glasses for the unexpected second toast.

"I ask you now to remember and honor someone else, someone whose name the prince also bears: the great Roman hero Camillus." He pulled out the book and flourished it like a sword. "Here," he said, holding it up, "in the pages of Livy, we find his story. How he led the people of Rome to victory after victory, conquering all the neighboring towns."

There were a few murmurs at this, some surprised, most impatient. Sophie was trying to remember if she knew anything about Camillus. Was it Camillus who held the bridge? No, that was Horatius.

"And his greatest achievement, of course, was after the invasion of the Gauls."

Suddenly there was complete silence.

"The Romans, besieged and starving, had given up. They had surrendered. They were actually weighing out the gold, the ransom for their cowardly lives, into their barbarian conqueror's hands," Gian Andrea went on. His voice echoed down the line of columns. "But at the very last moment Camillus appeared with his army and ordered the Romans to take back the ransom and prepare for battle. *He* would not allow the Romans to pay tribute to Gaulish brigands."

A woman laughed, nervously, and was instantly shushed.

"He told them this: 'Ransom your country with swords, not gold.'" He glared around the room, then repeated slowly, "Swords, not gold. Then he and his men defeated the invaders and drove them back out of Roman territory." Now he let Sophie go, but only so that he could take her glass—he had none—and raise it, holding it up next to the book. "I give you Camillus," he shouted, "a true Roman hero. May all the Gallic invaders of Italy meet a like fate!"

There was complete pandemonium. Men roared in anger; women screamed; some of the soldiers present dashed for the door; others headed purposefully for Gian Andrea. Camillo, standing next to Sophie, looked tired. "Young fool," he muttered. He stepped forward and raised his hand.

The crowd began hushing each other; the soldiers paused.

"Thank you, Cousin, for that reminder of Rome's noble past," he said. "But now I think we have been waiting too long for the promised ball. Princess?" He held out his hand to Pauline; the musicians struck up a local country dance. The soldiers, moving again toward Gian Andrea, suddenly found a line of dancers forming.

"Cousin?" said Sophie, seizing on the smallest of the many things she did not understand at the moment. "You're not his cousin, are you?" Somehow, she didn't know how, she had ended up with both the book and the glass of champagne. Gian Andrea had spilled most of it when he gestured at the end of his speech.

"He's trying to protect me," Gian Andrea said scornfully. "Let them arrest me! I am ready for them."

One of Pauline's pages came running up. "She says you are to dance," he whispered, breathless. "Right now. She is saving a place for you."

And so, Sophie danced in her blue dress with Gian Andrea at the head of the long line of couples, right behind Pauline and Camillo. She dipped and twirled and stepped forward and back, moved in rhythm across the shining floor with her skirt brushing against the columns behind her. It was nothing like she had imagined it would be. She felt nothing now when he touched her arm or laid his hand briefly on her waist to steady her during a spin. He was not going to kiss her. She knew that now. He was going through the motions of the dance, but he was paying no attention to Sophie at all. He was drunk on his own bravado.

And Pauline, moving down the line next to Sophie, was watching Gian Andrea with a very familiar look on her face. It was the look a cat gives a canary. There was nothing Pauline liked better than a rebel.

Sophie left the dance early, pleading a headache. She did have a headache; she had had one all day. That had not mattered before that stupid toast, before Gian Andrea dragged her out into the middle of the ballroom and spouted treason while holding her hand. She would gladly have danced with a headache, and eaten ices, and walked in the royal gardens. But she had no desire to stay in the ballroom and watch Pauline circling Gian Andrea.

Bettina had already heard what had happened. The local servants had been terrified, convinced the militia would haul everyone in the palace off to jail. "Ungrateful, uncouth, boorish scum of a Visconti," she fumed as she peeled off Sophie's dress. Bettina was very jealous of the Borghese family honor. "Imagine telling the prince he wanted to give a toast, and then pulling a stunt like that! He should be horsewhipped."

She slid the sapphire chain out of Sophie's hair. "In the old days, he would have been called out. Right then and there. Pistols or swords."

Bettina wasn't much over thirty, so Sophie wasn't sure how much she knew about "the old days." But she was quite certain Gian Andrea would have been delighted to fight, with swords or guns or fists, on the slightest provocation. Earlier this evening, before Gian Andrea's speech, the thought of a duel would have provoked a lovely, tragic daydream about weeping over his wounded body. Now she just felt sick and anxious. After Bettina left, she curled up in her nightgown on a seat by the window and waited for the fireworks. Her suite had a view of the gardens, and a small balcony, as well. She wondered drearily when Pauline would move her out—the rooms were right across from Pauline's—and install Gian Andrea in her place.

Sophie was dozing when the first firecracker went off, and she woke with a start. One part of her wanted to close the balcony doors and go back to sleep, but she knew the noise would be too loud. She might as well see the display. Throwing on a shawl, she stepped outside and looked down into the garden.

The fireworks were at the far end, by the trees, and at first they were so bright against the dark sky that she saw nothing else. She could hear guests below her, talking and laughing, with an occasional burst of applause for an especially dazzling pinwheel or rocket. Gradually, as her eyes adjusted, she could make out the shapes of people right below her: just shapes, with occasional glimpses of white gloves or white dresses, or flashes of jewelry, when the rockets fired. All the lanterns had been quenched to highlight the display, so the only light was from the crescent moon overhead and the flash and trailing dust of the firecrackers. After a little longer, she could see the apparatus for the fireworks—wagons, dark silhouettes against the trees, visible for one moment as each rocket was fired. Every once in a while the artificers would wheel out something on a frame and light it: the little colored sparklers would flare up all at once on their board and make a shape or a word. There was an eagle, of course, and a dragon, for the Borghese house, and then, a bit later, a very elaborate one, lit in sections, row by row, which spelled out in fiery gold letters: HIS EXCELLENCY THE GOVERNOR-GENERAL SALUTES THE PEOPLE OF TURIN. That one burned for so long in one place that Sophie could see the men working with the rockets quite clearly, running back and forth and signaling to each other when it was time to light the next row of letters.

Afterward, it was dark for a minute or two; something had gone wrong with the next rocket. The guests began to murmur; some started to drift back inside. Sophie stood, her hand on the rail. She knew the fireworks were not finished; Pauline had told her they would end with a fire-fountain accompanied by music. She had seen the servants setting out the chairs for the orchestra halfway between the palace and the trees. Right below her, in the light spilling out from the palace, there were four men with trumpets, looking at each other uncertainly.

She looked back toward the artificers. They were running back and forth with lanterns, pulling more rockets from one of the wagons. It was only by accident that one lantern swung wide, into the trees, and showed her the soldiers standing there, hands on their weapons, with an officer gesturing to them. *Not yet*, said his gesture. *Wait.*

They could be part of the ceremonies, she told herself. Perhaps they were to fire a salute. She tried to squint, to pierce the darkness again. The artificers had set up a new series of rockets and were lighting them; she could see the fuses. The guests who had gone inside were hurrying back out; the musicians headed purposefully toward their assigned places.

The soldiers had not moved. They were not going to fire a salute; how could she have been so stupid? They were not in dress uniforms; they were not lined up in formation. They were half-crouching, waiting. Waiting for the fireworks to be over, for the guests to go home. She was pulling on her slippers, tearing off her nightgown. She grabbed the first dress she found in her wardrobe and threw it over her head.

Where was he? Was he out in the garden, with the other guests? No. He was with Pauline, she was sure of it. And Pauline was wearing white. She would have seen her. She scanned the garden again, to make sure. The music had started, and the rockets were arching over the flowerbeds. The ladies in white stood out like little candles below the shooting stars overhead.

Too fat, too tall, the dress had sleeves, the dress was flounced. No, no, no, and no.

She ran across the hall. The doors to Pauline's suite of rooms were closed; there was no light showing beneath them. Footsteps—on the stairs. Was it the soldiers already? She gasped and then heard the reassuring sound of a flint striking. A servant was relighting one of the sconces. Cautiously, she tried the door handle. It was not locked.

Once she stepped inside and closed the door, the noise of the music and fireworks suddenly dimmed, as though she had sunk underwater. The sitting room was dark; the curtains had been drawn. Sophie stood still, afraid she would break something if she blundered into a chair or table.

"I heard a noise." It was Gian Andrea's voice. Sophie stopped breathing.

"The fireworks." Pauline, of course. The voices were coming from Pauline's bedroom. Now that Sophie was looking, she could see a tiny, tiny thread of light under the door.

"No, like a door opening."

"They're all out watching the show. And if you are worried about Camillo, I assure you he would never abandon his guests." There was a sound of something rustling; clothing, perhaps, or bedsheets. "Come over here."

Sophie felt her way toward the inner door. Chair, chair, small table, carpet, side table. She slid her hand along the back of the table. This one. It was red-and-gold, if she remembered correctly. And not too big to lift. She picked up the vase and hurled it against the door. It broke with a huge crash, then fell, with a little tinkling sound as the smaller pieces hit the bigger ones.

"My God, what was that?" Gian Andrea.

The door flew open, and Pauline stood facing her, holding a candelabrum. In the room behind her, Gian Andrea was lurching out of a chair. They both still had their clothes on, and the bed was smooth and undisturbed. Only later did Sophie realize how different things would have been if she had seen something else when that bedroom door opened.

"Sophie!" He started to stammer something—excuses, explanations, apologies. Pauline silenced him with a gesture. She was looking straight at Sophie and there was no apology in her glance at all.

"Soldiers," choked Sophie. "Militia. All around the garden. I think they are waiting for the guests to leave."

"Do you see well in the dark?"

"Yes."

They both ignored Gian Andrea completely.

"Go to the window—carefully—and pull the curtain aside and tell me if there are more soldiers out in the piazza."

There were.

"Back in the bedroom," Pauline said to Gian Andrea.

"They can arrest me," he said, eyes flashing. "I won't hide behind your skirts."

"They can arrest you somewhere else," Pauline said coldly. "Not in my husband's house, after he lied in front of half of Turin to protect you. Get in there and shut the door, and wait until we tell you to come out."

When the door had closed again, she lit a lamp and surveyed the broken vase.

"Now we ring for a maid," Pauline said.

"What?"

"We ring for a maid. And send for Carlo and Nicola." These were two of the older pages. "If you are stopped on the way out, you are a guest. You broke the vase accidentally. You are taking the pieces with you when you leave, to repair it."

"But—" Sophie looked at the red-and-gold fragments. No one would ever be able to repair that vase.

"Go get dressed." Pauline shoved her toward the outer doors. "In something you might have worn to the banquet. Not the blue dress—it is too conspicuous."

"I don't understand," muttered Sophie as she went back across the hall. She put on one of her girlish white dresses with the square necklines, found a pair of white-and-gold slippers, and scurried back across to Pauline's suite.

The maid had arrived and was sweeping up the larger pieces of china into a napkin. One of Pauline's pages ran in, listened to something she said, and ran back out.

"Fix her hair," Pauline told the maid, pointing at Sophie. She was arranging the napkin and the vase fragments in a small basket.

Once more Sophie twisted her neck and held still while her hair was pinned up. This time there were no sapphires, just a gold chain around her neck. More pages ran in and out, carrying bundles of clothing. One bundle was a cloak, for Sophie. Another, taller page, disappeared with his bundle into the bedroom.

Pauline lifted her head suddenly. "Do you hear that?" Sophie listened. Below Pauline's window, the sound of horses' hooves and carriage wheels echoed up from the piazza. "The carriages are lining up to take the guests home. You'll have to lead them down the back way," she told the older page.

Gian Andrea emerged from Pauline's bedroom. He was dressed as a footman, in green-and-gold livery with a powdered wig and old-fashioned buckle shoes. They must have been a bit small because he walked as though his feet hurt. The jacket was a bit tight across the shoulders, too.

Pauline handed him the basket with the broken vase. "My sedan chair will be waiting at the far side of the piazza," she told Sophie.

Gian Andrea was frowning at the basket. "What is this?"

"Your disguise," said Pauline impatiently.

Then Sophie understood.

Ladies do not carry boxes, or parcels, or baskets full of broken china. Footmen carry them. A footman escorting a lady in evening dress out of the palace would look very suspicious. A footman *carrying something* and walking behind a lady would look perfectly normal.

It wasn't very difficult.

The page took them down the servants' stair to the ground floor. When they stepped out into the entrance hall, they merged with the flow of departing guests. The page escorted Sophie; the Gian-Andrea-footman walked dutifully behind. Sophie hoped he was not limping.

Down the steps, out into the piazza. Sophie looked straight ahead, focusing on the sedan chair. She could see it, beyond the line of carriages. She could also see the soldiers, standing in two lines, scrutinizing the guests as they moved toward the waiting carriages.

No one stopped them. No one even looked at them.

When they reached the sedan chair, the page glanced around

to make sure that they were unobserved. Then Gian Andrea swung inside, the door banged shut, and the bearers picked it up.

"Wait!" His voice was muffled by the closed screens on the windows. After a bit of a struggle, he pulled one partway open.

"What about this?" He held out the basket.

"Keep it." She gave a sour little smile. "A souvenir."

"Good-bye, Sophie," he said softly. "Thank you."

She nodded.

I'll never see him again, she thought, as the sedan chair swayed into the line of vehicles leaving the piazza. *And now I'll have to remember him in that stupid wig.*

TWELVE

It had grown cool, and since this was Turin, it was already damp. A chilly breeze off the mountains was lifting stray leaves and flower petals in the piazza, the last remnants of bouquets and garlands discarded by guests as they left the banquet. Nevertheless, the young captain of the militia was sweating. He kept taking his handkerchief out and dabbing at the back of his neck under the high collar of his dress uniform.

Camillo kept his voice low and even. "I assure you that the Visconti boy has left. There is no need to search the palace, and I will take it as a personal affront if you do so." The argument had been going on for more than ten minutes. The captain insisted that his colonel only wished to speak with Gian Andrea ("a formality"); there was no reason for Prince Borghese to protect the young man. Camillo insisted that Visconti was no longer in the palace.

"My men did not see him leave."

The prince raised his eyebrows. "Do you doubt my word?" He drew Pauline, who was standing at his side under the arched entranceway, a bit closer. "Do you doubt the word of my wife, the emperor's sister?"

"Of course not, Your Excellency. But—"

Pauline interposed. Giving the officer her most sympathetic smile, she said softly, "I am sure this is very difficult for you, Captain."

What was difficult, thought Camillo sourly, was that the governor-general of a province of the French empire had no control over the troops of the imperial garrison. Those troops reported directly to Napoleon, and they had standing orders to arrest Italian nationalist agitators. He was lucky they hadn't just closed down the ball and seized Visconti right after the toast. But as the captain had explained, they had deferred to Camillo's obvious hint that he wished to avoid a scene. It had never occurred to the officers of the militia that Camillo would continue to obstruct them once the guests had departed.

"You must see that it would be most improper for your troops to enter the palace without my husband's permission," Pauline continued.

"If, as you both claim, the boy has left," said the captain stiffly, "then I fail to see why you will not grant that permission."

"Because," said Camillo patiently, "I have reliable information that Visconti is gone. And after spending the entire day, at considerable expense, wooing the people of Turin, I do not propose to ruin the effect by leaving my subjects with the image of soldiers looking under beds as their final impression of this event."

"How do you *know* that he has left?" the younger man persisted. "Your Excellencies, if I may say so, had many guests here this evening. No one could expect you to have kept track of every one of them."

He was offering them an out, Camillo saw. He was damned if he would take it, though. He drew the line at letting Napoleon's troops into his own home.

"I saw him leave," said Pauline firmly.

The captain looked at Camillo, startled, then dropped his eyes. It wasn't hard to guess what he was thinking; everyone had seen the boy dancing with Pauline after Sophie had left. Everyone had seen the two of them disappear from the ballroom within a few minutes of each other, right before the fireworks.

She reached across and touched the young officer's sleeve. "Captain, I know you will have to write up a report."

That was true. Napoleon's empire sometimes seemed to Camillo to run in triplicate and to require more clerks than soldiers.

"I would appreciate it," she said in a low voice, "if you could omit the details I am about to give you. But I believe that your mind will not be at ease until you are certain that we are not concealing the young man."

"No, Your Highness; that is, yes, Your Highness."

Would Pauline really be willing to tell the captain about her latest infidelity right in front of her husband? Camillo had to force himself to stand there with his arm around her waist when every instinct screamed "step away, step away."

"Well, the truth is, my little cousin, Signorina Leclerc, has formed a *tendre* for Visconti. And she was very upset after his rude and foolish speech, as we all were. You must have seen her; she was with him when he gave the toast. The girl in blue."

Where was this going? Camillo suppressed a sigh. But the officer was nodding.

"She left after the first dance."

Another nod.

"I asked him to dance. I was worried that he would make another speech." She gave the captain another wry little smile, a "really, what is all the fuss about a silly toast?" smile. "But, in fact, he wasn't thinking about politics. He was very concerned because Sophie—my cousin—had left. Evidently the relationship was not as one-sided as I had thought."

Camillo didn't believe that for one minute. He had seen Gian Andrea mooning over Pauline since the day he had arrived in Turin.

But the captain must have been a romantic. He was nodding again.

"I suggested that he go and apologize to her right away, persuade her to come back downstairs to the ball. But, of course, it was necessary for me to accompany him to her room."

"What happened?" The captain was hooked. She was reeling him in.

"She threw a vase at his head," Pauline said dryly. "One of those Chinese things, red-and-gold. And he left. I saw him go myself, down the back stair. One of my pages showed him out; I can send for him if you don't believe me."

It was the detail of the vase that did it. The captain sighed. "I don't understand why my men did not see him leave. He is quite conspicuous, with that nose and his height."

"Perhaps your men were watching the fireworks instead of the gates," Camillo suggested.

"Perhaps." The captain saluted. "My apologies, Your Excellency, for troubling you." He bowed to Pauline. "Your Highness."

Then he was gone.

Camillo waited until the captain had collected his men and marched off. He still had his arm around Pauline's waist, and without looking at her, he said in a detached voice, "Was any of that true?"

"Most of it." Pauline laughed. "She did throw the vase. Mother of God! I didn't think she had it in her."

"You mean—it really was Sophie?"

"What did you think?"

"That you slept with him, of course," he said brutally. "And then sent him off down whatever secret stairway you have discovered in this palace to bring your lovers in and out."

"He did go down the back stairs," she conceded. "But no, Camillo. I didn't sleep with him. I've been trying to be good." She looked down. "You haven't noticed."

He had noticed. He just hadn't believed it was real.

"I noticed that you have bombarded your brother with requests to leave me and go back to France."

"Because you're ignoring me!" She stepped away from him. There were footmen waiting to open the doors, two feet away, and she didn't care. Her voice was shaking. "You just pretend I don't exist, except when we are out in public together. I'm not a nun! I'm a woman and I'm your wife, and if you won't treat me as your wife, I don't see why I should have to stay here in Turin and be a puppet princess! I can go to some little town and live my own life and you can be rid of me." She burst into tears.

They ended up in bed, of course. He had practically dragged her up the stairs, her dance slippers skidding on the marble floors.

"Out," he said breathlessly to the maid, who was sweeping the sitting room. Eyes round with curiosity, she left, although not without a backward glance.

Pauline was giggling. She was so beautiful, he thought. Her eyes still had tears in them, and she was giggling and pretending to resist as he tugged her toward the bed. Her teeth were beautiful, and her eyelashes were beautiful, and her arms were beautiful.

"How does that thing unfasten?" he said, looking at her white, one-shoulder dress. It looked like it was glued to her body.

She giggled again. "Watch." She pulled open the gold pin at her shoulder.

The dress slithered to the floor. Just like that. As usual, she wasn't wearing anything underneath it.

"You," she said, her eyes narrowing, "have far too many buttons on your clothing."

It was true: his jacket had buttons; his embroidered waistcoat had buttons, his shirt cuffs, his trousers. He was ripping all of them open as fast as he could.

She danced around him, completely naked, mocking him for being so slow. "Ouch!" She hopped on one foot over to the bed and sat down. Picking up her right foot, she pulled it up by the lamp so that she could see it, giving Camillo an excellent view of her crotch. "Never mind, it isn't bleeding." She patted the bed next to her.

He got out of his tight-fitting pants by peeling them off inside-out, then dove onto the mattress. She had changed him, he realized. He didn't mind being naked. He didn't want her to turn down the lamp. He looked back on his younger, more prudish self and wondered where that Camillo had gone. Good riddance, he decided, surveying his wife.

There was an indented line on the skin of her left shoulder from the seams of the dress. He traced it down to her breast, touched the nipple, ran his finger back up.

"Oh," she sighed, collapsing sideways to lie next to him. "You have the most wonderful hands." She pulled his other hand from underneath his head and brought it to her mouth, sucking on one finger after another.

Each finger brought him new, cascading shivers of delight.

Then she hooked one of her legs over his hip and wriggled a bit lower on the bed.

He looked down. She was right there, wide open; he was poised for entry. One little shift—

She put her other hand on his hip and tugged.

He had meant to take it slow; he had been thinking, all the way up the stairs, of her hands and her mouth and all the things she had taught him. But that little tug drove everything else out of his head. He slid into her in one firm push and felt her heel settle into place in the center of his lower back.

She felt so good. It wasn't just that her face was a classic oval, or her hair like silk, or her body perfectly proportioned. She *felt* different from other women: tantalizing and pliable and moist. She fitted him like that dress had fitted her.

"Don't move," he gasped.

She wriggled, perverse as always.

He pinned her down with his free arm. "Stop." It came out as a growl. Then he inched back and forth, just a little. A little more.

She took a shuddering breath.

With tiny, tiny incremental thrusts, he brought them both to the point where they were gasping and clutching at each other. Then he stopped. He lay there, holding her still when she wanted to begin again.

How many months had it been? He wanted to savor this. But he felt her impatience and yielded. There would be tomorrow, after all. And the day after. Or even later tonight, although it was almost dawn. He shifted his grip, rolled her up on top of him, and thrust up into her, suddenly fast and powerful where he had been slow and delicate.

She came at once, arching her chest above him, and he pulled her hips closer as he pumped frantically into his own release. The lamplight and candles at the edge of his vision suddenly exploded into sparkling little pinwheels. He had made his own personal fireworks display.

As usual, Pauline jumped out of bed within a few minutes. She was always restless after sex. He lay half-dozing, hearing her humming a local folk song. She didn't know the tune beyond the first few bars, so she would start the song, then stop, then start over.

"Damn!" She was hopping again, holding one toe. He could see something on the floor; she must have stepped on it. *Poor Pauline*, he thought sleepily, drifting off again. She was very fond of her feet and would sometimes display them to shocked visitors by peeling off her shoes and stockings in public. Now she had bruised her toes twice in twenty minutes.

Behind his closed eyes, the obstacle on the floor suddenly took on a very distinctive size and shape.

He opened his eyes. It wasn't his imagination. There, on the floor, just visible in the lamplight, was a small octavo volume. Leather-bound. He knew what it was. It was a text of Livy.

My God, he thought. A moment before, he had been sweating; now he suddenly felt very cold. *What a fool you are, Camillo*, he told himself savagely.

He sat up, pushed his legs over the side of the bed, and nudged the book closer with one foot. Then he bent over and picked it up. Pauline was still humming, dabbing her face and breasts with water over by the washstand. He opened the book. Any faint hope he had entertained that some other book, identical in appearance, had found its way into the bedroom of a woman who never read books, died at once. It was Livy, and on the fly-leaf was an inscription in Latin: "To my dear Gian Andrea, from his most affectionate godfather, Pietro Verri."

He thought again about Pauline's story to the captain. About the maid, cleaning the sitting room at two in the morning. About the first, still unexplained, injury to her foot. The lamp was right next to him; he picked it up and walked methodically around the room, shining the light onto the floor. There, in the corner by the door to the sitting room, was a tiny triangular piece of red-and-gold china.

"What are you doing? I can't see if you take the lamp that far away."

He held up the lamp in one hand, the book in the other.

Her mouth opened, but nothing came out. She looked stunned.

"I don't know why I should be so surprised," he said. His face felt stiff and old; the words sounded like someone else talking.

"Camillo, don't." She dropped the washcloth. "It isn't what you think."

"Oh? What is it, then?" He set the lamp down on the floor, bent over, and scooped up the little piece of china. "Is this the vase Sophie broke? Did she find you here with the boy she thought she loved? That part was true, wasn't it?"

"Who cares about Sophie!"

"Who, indeed. Obviously not you." He stalked over to the heap of clothing he had abandoned—was it only half an hour ago? It felt like a year. In silence, he turned his breeches right-side out, pulled them on, and stuffed his arms into his jacket. His shoes and stockings and shirt and vest he simply picked up in one untidy lump.

She ran to the door and stood there, blocking his way. "I didn't sleep with him!"

"I don't care," he said wearily. He pushed her aside and headed for the outer doors. Another piece of china skittered across the floor as he kicked it out of his way.

"Camillo!" she screamed. "You have to believe me! Nothing happened! All he wanted to do was talk politics!"

He turned at the door, even though he didn't want to. Something made him look back at his wife, standing naked in the doorway of the bedroom, fists clenched, with the lamp on the floor sending a beam of light streaming out between her legs.

"Go to France," he said. "Get away from me. The farther the better."

THIRTEEN

The day after the banquet, Sophie went to the most neglected, unused, unlikely room in the palace she could find and sat there all afternoon. She didn't think Pauline would expect her for their daily conversation, but she wasn't taking any chances. Once she was sure it was dinnertime, she made her way back to her room, reconciled to going to bed early and hungry so long as she didn't have to see Pauline.

"I'm sick," she told Bettina, and climbed into bed wearing her chemise and stockings. "Don't let anyone in. Especially Donna Paolina." She wasn't sure how much Bettina knew about what had happened last night, but she could always count on her to think the worst of Pauline. She decided to be sick tomorrow, too. And the day after that. She burrowed down under the coverlet and brooded in the stuffy darkness, staring into nothingness and scraping her thumbnail back and forth over the sheets. A bit later, she heard Bettina talking to someone at the door to the outer room—it sounded like the prince. Whoever it was, they went away.

Footsteps. It was Bettina.

"Do you want anything to eat? Some soup? Some custard?"

"No."

"Do you want your nightgown?"

"No."

Eventually, she fell asleep.

The next day she had breakfast in bed, lunch in bed, and dinner in bed. Between meals she napped or tried to read, and snapped at Bettina whenever she asked Sophie any questions. That night she kept finding crumbs in the sheets. She tossed and turned until the small hours of the morning, unable to sleep. When she finally did manage to sleep, Bettina woke her two hours later so that the doctor could examine her.

She snapped at him, too.

After her second day in bed, she realized that she had succeeded in completely inverting her schedule. She was asleep during the day and awake all night. Perhaps she could just become an owl and flit through the castle when everyone else was asleep. Then she could spend at least some time out of bed.

On the third day, she woke from a very deep post-luncheon nap to find Pauline shaking her.

She closed her eyes as hard as she could. "Go away," she said, trying to sound ill and wan.

"Stop pretending to be sick, Sophie. It's childish."

"I'm not pretending."

"Doctor Vastapani says there is nothing wrong with you."

Sophie sat up. "When he says that about *you*, you always tell me he is an idiot!"

"He *is* an idiot." Pauline sighed. "I miss my dear Doctor Peyre."

Sophie was tempted to remind her that Peyre had quit in disgust when Pauline had moved into the house of her chamberlain-lover last summer, but instead she subsided back down onto the pillows and closed her eyes again.

"I know what you need," said Pauline briskly. "You need something to take your mind off yourself."

Sophie ignored her.

"Get up." She pulled the covers away from Sophie and tossed them on the floor. "We're going to visit some people who are really sick."

That made Sophie open her eyes. "What?"

"You heard me. We're going to the Hospital of San Maurizio."

Bettina had told Sophie repeatedly that it was the duty of those who had been blessed with wealth and good family to console the sick and poor and dying who were in their charge. As Bettina was fond of pointing out, Donna Anna had set an excellent example for her daughter-in-law; the Dowager Princess Borghese went every Tuesday morning to the Hospital of San Giovanni in Rome and dispensed jellies, tonics, and moral advice to the patients. Camillo had assumed that his new princess would accompany his mother on these visits.

Pauline had absolutely refused to go near the place. She had a horror of hospitals; she was convinced they were cesspits of infection and that the patients were all criminals and prostitutes. She complained to Camillo of her own delicate state of health and hinted that seeing all the invalids would remind her of the tragic illness and death of her first husband. Camillo had backed down, and Pauline had sent a gift of money to the monks instead.

For the first time, Sophie looked carefully at Pauline. She was dressed soberly in a dark cambric gown. She wore no rouge, and her hair was pulled back with a simple band. And she looked as though she hadn't slept in three days. At least Sophie had had her daytime naps. The last time Sophie had seen Pauline looking so haggard was after Dermide's death.

"Is something wrong?" Sophie sat up again. "Has someone died?" A horrible thought occurred to her. She clutched Pauline's arm. "Did they arrest Gian Andrea? Did they shoot him?"

"Oh, for God's sake," said Pauline, disgusted. "Don't be such a nitwit. No one has been shot. Now get up and get dressed."

They really did go to the hospital. Sophie kept glancing over at Pauline, trying to figure out why she looked so stern and severe and why she was suddenly interested in tending paupers and cripples. The brothers who ran the hospital were overjoyed to receive a royal visit and insisted on showing every ward to Pauline and her attendants (in the end, four other ladies-in-waiting had been dragged along as well). Sophie found the sight of room after room of sick, dirty people disgusting, and the smell even more disgusting, but she said nothing and tried to hang back at the rear of their party as they moved through the wards. Pauline, on the other hand, was full of curiosity. What was wrong with this man? Why did this woman have yellow spots on her face? She stopped and spoke with several patients and even helped one woman sit up and hold her baby. At the end of the visit she had tears in her eyes, and in the carriage on the way back she gave an agitated speech to her ladies-in-waiting about the poor state of the hospitals in Paris. She would write to her brother and commend the model of the Italian institutions.

Hanging back, once they had returned to the palace, didn't work. Pauline thanked all the other ladies-in-waiting and dismissed them. But Sophie found herself once more in Pauline's room, sitting in the chair by the window with a glass of syrupy wine. It was even sweeter and more yellow than she remembered it.

She kept her eyes obstinately focused on the wine, wondering what Pauline would say. Would she tell Sophie more court gossip? Sophie was three days behind now in Pauline's running catalogue of who was sleeping with whom. Would she make fun of the men who admired her? She had described one languishing Piedmont landowner as a basset hound because he had mournful eyes and large ears that drooped slightly. A young Frenchman had made the mistake of writing her a poem; she had read it to Sophie, interspersed with merciless comments on the author's bad posture and unwashed hair. One thing Sophie was certain of: Pauline would not apologize. Apologies were for ordinary mortals.

"Are you angry with me?" Pauline said finally.

Sophie didn't answer.

Pauline sighed and let her go.

Within a few days, the afternoon meetings had resumed their normal pattern. It was hard to resist Pauline when she was exerting herself to be charming. Sophie started out determined not to talk; then decided she would talk but not smile; then decided that it was difficult not to smile when Pauline was smiling at you and teasing you to eat little crumbs of galette from her hand like the bird on her shoulder. The bird was a gift from the mayor and looked like him: round and small and bright-eyed. It was while they were feeding the bird two days later that Pauline had finally brought up Gian Andrea.

"You mustn't be too disappointed in him, Sophie," she said. The bird cocked its head to the side and nibbled Pauline's ear. "He is really still very young."

I'm not disappointed in him, thought Sophie. *I'm disappointed in you.*

"They get these obsessions at his age," Pauline continued, lifting the bird down to her lap. "Hunting, or war, or boxing. Something *manly*. Something that proves they are no longer boys. Sometimes it is even women. But it isn't any particular woman—it's just women in general. With him, it is politics. He thinks he is going to singlehandedly save Italy from my brother."

She offered the bird another bite of galette. "Nothing else is real to him. You could put him in a room with Helen of Troy, and he wouldn't have the slightest idea of what to say to her."

Perhaps this was Pauline's roundabout way of reassuring Sophie that the scene in her bedroom had, in fact, been completely innocent. That would *almost* qualify as an apology. Perhaps Pauline really was sorry.

"I mean," Pauline continued, "I stood right in front of the lamp—right in front of it! He should have been able to see everything; that dress is practically transparent if you put a source of light behind it. And do you know what he did? He took out his book and started to read to me in Latin!"

Then again, perhaps not.

* * *

The prince had left for Florence right after the banquet; Sophie was not sure why. He returned five days later to get ready for a state visit. Pauline's brother Joseph was traveling from Naples to his new kingdom of Spain and would stop in Turin on his way. There was to be another banquet, although without dancing and fireworks, and a ceremonial escort to the border, with the prince leading his personal guard.

On the first day after Camillo's return, he came to find Sophie in the garden.

"I gather that you were ill," he said awkwardly. "I hope you are recovered."

"Yes, thank you." In fact, her headaches had come back, and she actually felt worse now than she had when she was in bed for three days. But she was certainly not going to admit to Camillo that she had not really been sick.

He looked a bit ill himself, she thought. And Pauline still had hollows under her eyes. She knew what that meant: they had had another fight.

"Cousin Pauline has been feeling poorly as well," she said tentatively. Pauline had taken to her bed a few hours before the prince was due to return. Yes, they must have had a fight. And now Pauline was pretending to be sick. Sophie had learned to feign illness from a master of the art.

At the mention of Pauline, his face closed. "Yes, so I hear," he said. He looked so grim that for one moment Sophie was almost afraid of him. She shrank back slightly on the bench where she was sitting. She revised "fight" to "Fight." Or perhaps outright war.

He composed himself once more. "May I escort you inside?" he said politely.

She supposed she should go in. She had been out in the garden for quite some time, and even though she was sitting in the shade, the damp heat combined with her headache was starting to make her feel a little queasy.

When she wobbled a bit as she stood up, the prince grabbed her elbow. "Are you certain you are not ill?" he said.

"I'm fine," Sophie said.

Then she threw up all over the bench.

This time Sophie really was sick. And so was Pauline. Vastapani no longer announced that everything looked normal when he examined them, and he hadn't mentioned calomel once. Pauline was doubled over with cramps; Sophie could barely keep down a glass of water. Both were covered with sweat and shivering.

"I need to go to Aix-en-Savoie," Pauline told the doctor. She didn't have to force herself to cry, either; the tears came easily now. He was worried; she could see it even under his usual courteous professionalism. "Please ask my husband to let me go." Camillo had not come to see her at all; Vastapani was serving as her go-between.

He returned with the usual answer: "The prince believes that he has no authority to give you leave to travel outside of the province. He has written your brother urging him to grant your request."

"Napoleon?" She coughed. It was a horrible, rasping cough. It even scared her. "He thinks I am shamming. I've written him three times already since we arrived here. He insists that Val d'Aosta is just as good as Aix."

"I have included a statement of my own in His Excellency's letter, noting that the sulfur springs of Aix are specifically indicated in your case and that of your cousin."

Two weeks. It would take at least a week for the letter to reach Napoleon, and a week for the response to come back. She thought morbidly that she might not survive two weeks of her current symptoms. If she could only see Camillo in person, she could persuade him to ignore Napoleon's earlier orders.

She wrote him a note and begged him to visit her.

He did not answer.

She wrote him another note. Napoleon would surely give his permission when he heard Vastapani's report; could he not have pity on her and spare her the two weeks of misery waiting for the emperor's official approval?

This time she received a reply. "His Excellency Prince Borghese regrets that he has no authority outside his own province and must refer this matter to your brother." He hadn't even signed it; Villemarest had written it for him.

Luckily, Pauline had more than one brother.

Joseph arrived the following afternoon and was shown up to Pauline's room immediately. He was still in his traveling clothes and brought in the distinct smell of horse and dust as he hurried to her bedside. She had actually forgotten that he was coming and was so relieved to see him that she burst into tears.

"What is this I hear, that you are sick again?" He would have kissed her, but she pulled away.

"Don't come too close. Vastapani says that Sophie and I contracted something at the hospital. It would be dreadful if you became ill as well."

He pulled up a chair and sat down, studying her. "You really do look terrible," he said bluntly. "When they told me you were confined to bed, I thought it was one of your little pets. But I've never seen you like this." He tilted his head sideways. "Your skin is almost green."

"Stop it," she said crossly, wiping her eyes. "I know I'm feeling awful; you don't need to make it worse by making me feel ugly, too."

"You're never ugly," he said. But his smile was perfunctory. He really was worried, she could tell.

She took in his dusty clothing. "Did you come straight to my room?"

He nodded.

"So—" She hesitated. "You haven't seen Camillo."

"He met me at Moncalieri and escorted me here."

"Oh." *How did he look?* she wanted to ask. *What did he say about me?*

Joseph cleared his throat. "I take it things are not going well between the two of you."

The tears started again. "Please, Joseph, you have to help me! The doctors think I should go to Aix, but Camillo thinks I am faking. I'm not faking, surely you can see that?"

"No, no," he reassured her. "No one thinks you are pretending this time. This isn't like a headache or a fainting spell. Sophie is almost as sick as you are, with very similar symptoms. And Vastapani says there is blood in your mucus when you retch."

"There is?" She had a moment of panic. She hadn't wanted to be quite this ill, just sick enough to convince Camillo to let her go back to France.

He patted her arm. "Don't worry about it; it sometimes happens with these inflammations."

"Joseph, I'll die if I stay here!" She really was frightened now.

"Camillo says he can't let me leave the province without Napoleon's permission. They wrote to him yesterday, but even if he believes the doctor this time, it will be weeks and weeks!"

He frowned. "What do you mean, you can't leave the province?"

"It's just Napoleon being stupid and petty!" she said, getting indignant all over again. "He keeps writing me back and telling me I may go anywhere in Camillo's departments, but that I need *his* permission to cross into France proper."

"Well," said Joseph, bristling. "He may be an emperor, but he isn't the head of the family. I am. As far as I am concerned, you can leave as soon as you are well enough to travel. And I will tell the prince as much right now. I'm about to be King of Spain; I should have some authority to do something for my sister."

Pauline was too sick to make the arrangements. Madame Ducluzel did it for her, and, as a result, her entourage was larger than she would have liked. There was the housekeeper herself, Sophie's attendant, three ladies-in-waiting, three pages, two equerries, and various grooms and maidservants. The largest coach had been refitted so that Sophie and Pauline could travel lying down; behind that vehicle came carriages for the attendants and servants, one for Pauline's bathtub and one for her sedan chair.

At Camillo's insistence, Vastapani also accompanied her. She would have been happy to take this as an expression of concern. Camillo's note had made it clear, however, that he still had not forgiven her. At least this note was in his own handwriting. "I have instructed the court physician to attend your party at least as far as Aix-en-Savoie," he wrote, "and to remain until he is satisfied that Sophie has recovered. I feel confident that he will discharge this office responsibly and thus relieve me of any anxiety I might have felt on her behalf."

Who cares about Sophie? Who, indeed?

After that, she decided not to humiliate herself by asking him to come to say good-bye before she left, although she hoped he would come of his own accord. She was his wife, after all, and she was ill, and she was leaving.

He didn't come to say good-bye. He didn't even make a formal appearance in the courtyard as the coaches were loaded up and the equerries sent ahead to clear the route through the city. Pauline was carried to her carriage by one of her menservants, and as he handed her in, she saw Sophie, red-eyed and damp with sweat, already reclining on the other seat. She was clutching a small posy of herbs and lifting them to her face occasionally.

"What is that?" Pauline asked, as she arranged herself on her side of the carriage.

"I don't know." Sophie handed it across. "I feel less queasy when I smell it. The prince told me his grandmother used to make one for him when he was ill as a child."

So, he had made a point of saying good-bye to Sophie. That wasn't surprising, after the note he had written.

Pauline closed her eyes and inhaled. Lavender and mint. It was soothing.

It was also a message. Lavender, in the language of flowers, was loyalty. And mint was wisdom or grief.

There wasn't much difference between wisdom and grief, Pauline decided.

As they jolted over the passes from Turin to Susa, through Exilles, to Cesana, Sophie simply lay there in misery and hoped she would die. Or at least faint—a long faint, several hours' worth. Her little posy of herbs was all very well when they were not moving, but the slightest bump set her stomach churning, and the road was nothing but bumps. It was clear that Pauline was equally uncomfortable, and normally that would have meant short, easy days of travel and long rests every few hours. But Pauline was obsessed with reaching France.

"How far now?" she asked at every halt. Sometimes she would even get out and hobble over to the crossroads to look at Napoleon's new kilometer markers for herself. But she could never remember how far a kilometer actually was, and one of the equerries had to convert the number into leagues for her.

Since she and Sophie were lying down across both seats, Pauline's maid had to sit on the floor. Sophie was constantly afraid that she was going to throw up on the poor woman's lap and was very relieved when Pauline, who seemed to be improving with every new report of the shrinking distance to the border, decided on the morning of the second day that she and Sophie could ride unattended.

"Good," she said as they lurched forward. "Now I can give you some of this." She handed Sophie several small white almond-shaped fruits. Or were they peeled nuts?

Sophie looked at them doubtfully. "What is it?"

"Garlic," said Pauline, putting one of the cloves into her mouth. "Doctor Peyre told me it was very good as an antidote. I ate some yesterday morning and again last night, and I already feel better."

Sophie dutifully chewed and swallowed. The cloves were sweet, but afterward her throat felt like it was full of burning fog. She burped loudly.

"They do give you wind," Pauline said, eating another one. "Both kinds. And, of course, very foul breath. But there's no one here in the carriage with us now, so what does it matter?"

In her five years with Pauline, Sophie had been subject to a number of Pauline's "remedies," sometimes even when she herself was not at all unwell. In certain moods, Pauline would insist that everyone in the household be dosed with whatever cure she had heard of most recently. Most of them simply tasted bad, but at one point Pauline had decided that everyone needed to be protected against smallpox, which, to Sophie's horror, turned out to mean having holes punched in her skin with a needle coated with scabs from the skin of a sick cow. Chewing garlic seemed mild by comparison.

On the third day, they started at dawn to have ample time to cross the pass at Montgenèvre. Pauline was obviously much recovered; as soon as the carriage was underway, she actually sat up, for the first time since they had left Turin.

"Poor Sophie!" She gave Sophie a sympathetic smile. "Are you feeling any better? I am."

Sophie thought about it. Perhaps she was feeling better. Her stomach did not ache so much, and the clammy sweating had stopped. At the moment, her main preoccupation was sleep; Bettina had practically had to drag her out of bed. "Yes, I think so," she mumbled.

"Here." Pauline offered her more of the garlic.

"Later," said Sophie, her eyes closed.

"No, I think you need more." Pauline pushed the cloves into her hand. "I'm worried about you."

It seemed easier to just eat the garlic, so she did. Then she dozed off, starting up occasionally at an especially violent jounce and then falling back to sleep.

When she woke fully, the carriage had stopped. Pauline's seat was empty. The door was open, and she could see rocks and a snow-covered peak looming up beside the vehicle. Sun sparkled on the snow—it was midday—and so bright that it hurt her eyes.

"Sit up!" It was Pauline, filling the doorway. "Sophie, we're in France! We're over the top of the pass! I am so happy! Sit up, and I'll feed you some real French bread." She climbed in, eyes sparkling, her cheeks red from the wind, hair tousled. It was hard to believe she had been too ill to walk a few days earlier.

"This is better than garlic, isn't it?" she said, tearing off a piece from the inside of a coarse-crusted roll. She held it over Sophie's head, like someone training a dog. "Come on, Sophie, sit up," she said, coaxing her.

Sophie struggled up onto her elbow and accepted a tiny bit of the bread. It tasted just like the bread she had eaten last night at the inn in Cesana. Bread dipped in boiled wine. Her diet was very limited at the moment.

A footman came and closed the door, and the coach started moving again.

"Now we go down," said Pauline, her mouth full of bread. "And we'll stop in Briançon, and then tomorrow we'll be in Aix. You'll feel much better by then, I promise you. I didn't mean for you to be quite so sick. Or myself, either. I was actually afraid for a little bit that I had taken too much and would die."

A day earlier, Sophie would have accepted her confusion as part of the general haze of illness and lack of sleep. She was more awake now.

"Taken too much what?"

"Arsenic."

Sophie frowned. "Arsenic is a medicine?"

"No, no." Pauline settled back on the cushions and tucked her feet up underneath her. "I dosed us with arsenic to make us sick. I knew it would work because several years ago in the West Indies I had just these symptoms and Doctor Peyre thought I had an inflammation of the bowels. But what had really happened was that I got a little too brown in the sun, and a Frenchwoman who had lived there for many years told me to eat a little arsenic and I would grow pale again."

Sophie was not sure she was hearing correctly.

"When Doctor Peyre found out, he was furious," Pauline went on. She didn't seem to notice Sophie's horrified expression. "He made me eat twenty cloves of garlic a day. Can you imagine?"

"You gave me poison," Sophie said, her voice hoarse. It didn't come out right. It was meant to be an accusation. It came out as more of a resigned acknowledgment.

"But now you're already getting better, and we are in France." It was clear that Pauline thought this was a completely normal course of events.

Sophie cleared her throat and tried again. "You gave me poison!" she shouted.

"Well," Pauline pointed out, still in her "I am being reasonable" tone of voice, "I gave it to myself, too. I started with a little bit every day, so it wouldn't take me too hard when I had to actually make myself sick."

"Then why did you have to give it to me?" wailed Sophie.

"So that we would both be sick," said Pauline impatiently. "So they would think it was some disease. Napoleon kept writing back and telling me that I wasn't really ill."

"I could have *died*."

Indignant, Pauline shot back, "I was *much* sicker than you were!"

"Well, you deserved to be!" Sophie yelled. "You deserve to be sick *all* the time. You are the most selfish, horrid person I have ever known. You told me when I had the fever that no one would ever choose to be sick, but you chose to make yourself sick, and to make it look better, you made me sick, too!" She sat up and banged on the ceiling of the carriage, signaling the driver to stop.

"What are you doing?" Pauline seemed to realize for the first time that Sophie was truly furious. "Sophie, stop! You're making a fuss about nothing!"

Sophie gave her a withering look. "Do you know what Gian Andrea asked me once? He asked me if the prince had poisoned Dermide. Imagine that! Accusing someone of poisoning in 1808! I thought he had read too many stories about the Borgias. I'm never drinking a glass of wine you give me again."

The carriage slowed down, and Sophie jerked open the door.

"Where are you going?" Pauline looked a bit stunned.

"I'm going to ride with Bettina. She hates you, and so do I." Sophie climbed down from the carriage as soon as it stopped, then staggered. She hadn't walked without someone helping her for several days. Gritting her teeth, she set out to cover the fifty yards between Pauline's carriage, in the lead, and the servants' vehicle, which followed the ladies-in-waiting and Pauline's bathtub. The coachmen and footmen all stared at her as she wavered past them, and by the time she reached her destination, Bettina had already jumped out and was coming to help her.

"What is it?" she said, as she hoisted Sophie in. This carriage was much smaller and was already carrying Madame Ducluzel and three other maids, but they moved aside at once to make space.

I should tell her, thought Sophie. *I should tell all of them. Their princess has poisoned me to trick her brother. I should write Napoleon and tell him to take me away from* her *and let me go back to my father.* She was suddenly homesick for Pontoise and her old house, with its shabby rooms and shabbier furniture.

"What is it?" asked Bettina again, concerned. "Did the princess decide she wanted the carriage to herself?"

"Yes," said Sophie. She closed her eyes. "She said I stank of garlic."

They reached Briançon at six in the evening, and Sophie went at once to her room at the inn, shut the door, and put a chair against it. She remembered her three days in bed after the banquet and thought of Pauline, coaxing her back into a good humor, feeding cake crumbs to the bird and teasing her. Not this time, she vowed.

There was a sharp rap on the door. It was Pauline, of course.

"Go away!"

"Sophie, stop this."

"I'm writing to the emperor," she said loudly. "I'm going to ask him to send me back to my father."

There was a sudden silence on the other side of the door. Then Sophie heard a slithering sound, then a bump. When Pauline spoke again, her voice came from down by the floor.

"Sophie, please."

"No."

"Sophie, you're all I have left." She could hear a little catch in Pauline's voice. "My son is gone, and Camillo doesn't love me anymore. You're my family." There was a creak from the bottom of the door; Pauline was leaning against it. "I would never hurt you, you know that."

"Oh, Pauline," whispered Sophie to herself. She started to laugh silently. "You accused me of killing your son. You used me to deceive and humiliate your husband. You tried to seduce Gian Andrea after I told you I loved him. You poisoned me. And you don't think you would ever hurt me?"

That was the moment Sophie grew up.

She sat down by the door and listened to Pauline sob for a few minutes. Then she pulled away the chair, opened the door, and let her in.

Camillo was reading a letter from his court physician. Pauline and her cousin were both recovering, he wrote. The princess was in good spirits and was planning to travel to Paris later in the summer for the emperor's birthday. Should Vastapani remain with her or return to Turin?

He laid it down on his writing table. It was the fourth report he had received. He hadn't answered any of the others, and he suspected he wouldn't answer this one, either. For the moment, he shoved it into one of the drawers, then lined up his inkwell and pen stand in a neat row on the now-empty surface of the desk. Villemarest handled almost all of his other correspondence; he would give this to his secretary, too.

There was a tap at the door. It was his majordomo.

"Excuse me, Your Excellency, but the wagon from Signor Canova has arrived and is being unloaded. Have you made a decision yet?"

In which of the innumerable rooms opening off the endless, echoing corridors of the palace would he like Pauline's statue? Which was arriving, ironically, just in time to replace the real thing?

"Have it brought into the entrance hall," he said finally. "I will decide later where to put it."

He waited for an hour, pretending that he was not going to go and see it. Then he gave up and went downstairs.

The servants had set it off to the side, to be out of the way of guests entering or leaving. It was partly in shadow, and the long beams of light from the late afternoon sun picked out segments of the marble and lit them in rectangles that continued up the wall behind it. There she was, naked, just as when he had last seen her on the night of the banquet. But smiling now, self-assured, alluring. Her slightly raised brows seemed to promise the answer to some amusing question.

"Where shall I put you?" he asked her. "Shall I scandalize the matrons of Turin and leave you here? Or hide you somewhere where I don't have to see you unless I want to?" He contemplated her charms for a few moments, then patted her shoulder. "I'll be back in a few minutes," he said. "I just remembered some business I must attend to."

He found Villemarest in the outer room of his official suite. His secretary's desk, unlike his private one upstairs, was covered with piles of paper.

"Maxime," he said. "I need you to draw up a letter to my bankers here and in Rome."

The secretary reached for a tablet and paused expectantly.

"From His Excellency, etc., etc., with compliments, etc., etc. As from—well, let's backdate it a little. As from the first of July, the year of Our Lord 1808, no drafts from the Princess Pauline Borghese on the accounts designated below—just append the usual list of the family accounts—are to be honored, nor any drafts from agents acting on her behalf. All inquiries to be directed to etc., etc.—that's you, Maxime. Given by my hand this day, etc., etc. Bring it to me when it is ready to be signed and sealed."

"Yes, sir." Villemarest kept his face completely devoid of expression. "This will only take a few minutes. Where will you be?"

"In the entrance hall."

He would go tell Pauline that he had just cut off all her money and watch her smile in response.

PART III

The White Rose

Innocence, Unity, Death

Paris
17th March 1810

From Her Imperial Highness Pauline, Princess of
France, Duchess of Guastalla, Princess Borghese, to His
Excellency General Prince Camillo Borghese, Governor-
General of the Departments-beyond-the-Alps, greetings.

My brother informs me that you will be present for
his wedding to Marie-Louise of Austria next month.
Please be advised that all conversation between us will
be in public only and I do not wish to see you apart from
those state occasions requiring our presence together. My
brother also tells me you will be staying in my house;
you may have the first and second floors for your household and I will use the ground, third, and fourth floors.
[written by her secretary, du Pré de Saint-Maur]

Gréoux-les-Bains
8th July 1813

Dear Camillo:

I am quite ill; the heat is dreadful, and my new doctor is
very strict so that even the baths are becoming a trouble

and plague to me. I think of you often. Why do you not answer my letters? I will write you regardless.

Your affectionate wife, Pauline

Casa dei Mulini, Portoferraio, Elba
22nd November 1814

Dear Camillo,

I am settled now here on Elba and hoping for word from you. Lucien tells me that you have asked for a number of paintings from your family's villa that are now in the Hôtel de Charost in Paris; I have sold it to the Duke of Wellington, as Napoleon is in great need of funds at the moment, and if you will send my agent in Paris a list of the items, he will forward it to the duke and look into the matter. I suppose it is a good thing that you never did send my beautiful statue by Canova to Paris even though I asked you for it several times after I went back to France. Did you know that when it was shipped from Turin to Rome my brother intercepted it here on Elba briefly? But it was in a sealed crate, and he did not want to risk unpacking it, so he never saw it. In the end it went to Rome, and I came here.

My brother is bearing up well in his new little kingdom, and the British Commissioner, Sir Neil Campbell, is attentive and shows me every courtesy. I am determined to keep

Napoleon occupied and am quite frantically busy arranging plays and musicals and dinners; you would not recognize me as your lazy Pauline.

I hope you are well and that you think of me sometimes even if you do not answer my letters.

Your wife, Pauline

Casa dei Mulini, Portoferraio, Elba
16th January 1815

Dear Camillo,

Still no word from you and I know you are right to be angry with me, but I hope you are reading my letters, at least. Do you remember Sophie? She is with me here on Elba, of course, and she is to be married! He is a young British officer named Speare (which means "spear," but when I teased Sophie about it she flew at me like an offended bird and nearly scratched me; I think she is nervous about her wedding night). He is very handsome and charming and is a great favorite with everyone although he speaks hardly any French and no Italian whatsoever. I shall miss her, but they have rented part of a house just down the hill from our little palace, and Campbell has graciously promised me, in private, that he will make sure the young man stays posted here on Elba as long as possible.

Napoleon is quite well and lively and I am his hostess. None of my brothers or sisters have come to Elba, although they all promised to do so, and I suppose I must stay strong and hope that I do not fall ill, since everyone relies on me here.

If you do not wish to write to me perhaps you will at least send your greetings to Sophie. She is now Mrs. Charles Speare, at the Casa Jana, Portoferraio, Elba.

Your wife, Pauline

Compignano
8th March 1815

Camillo, you must help me. They arrested me the night after I arrived here in Italy from Elba. I am in my sister Elisa's villa in the hills above Viareggio, and there is half of an Austrian garrison camped outside guarding me. I beg you to send someone to intercede for me with the Austrian commander; he will not listen to anything I say and seems to believe that a French army is hiding in my baggage. I have no news of Napoleon; how could anyone think I had something to do with his departure from Elba? It would be laughable if I were not prostrate with anxiety and weariness. No one is with me except a few servants who scream every time they see a soldier.

Pauline

Bagni di Lucca
6th June 1815

Dear Camillo, I thank you if it was your influence which finally prevailed upon the Austrians so that I have been allowed to come here to a place of health and safety. I think of you often and how carefully you nursed me when I was sick here in Lucca that dreadful summer that I lost Dermide. I must ask if you have any news of Sophie. Her husband left Elba with the other British troops after Napoleon returned to France, and she was making arrangements to follow after him when I left two months ago, but I have heard nothing since. I know that you sent her a generous gift for her wedding; perhaps she has sent you word of her whereabouts? If you do not wish to write me directly, please send any information you have to my secretary in Rome; he will forward it to me.

Pauline

Bagni di Lucca
28th June 1815

Dear Camillo, I have heard the terrible news of Waterloo. My poor brother! I am trying to find out where he will go; if it is to America, then I shall join him. Lucien tells me that Sophie's husband was killed on the battlefield. Perhaps you

have not had time to answer my previous letter, but as you
can see, it is now very urgent that I find her.

Pauline

Rome
3rd October 1815

Camillo, everything is dreadful; the British will not let me
go to St. Helena with Napoleon although I begged them and
wrote every one of my London friends. So I must stay here
in Rome, and now you say you wish to divorce me. Well,
you should at least have the courtesy to tell me so to my face
and answer my letters. I have tried to be a good wife to you
and I do not understand why you refuse to meet with me
and will not try to reconcile with me when I am your wife
in the sight of God.

Bagni di Lucca
18th July 1816

Dearest, dearest Sophie,

I am so happy to hear from you! I have been searching
for you since I left Elba and am very sorry to hear of your
illness and of the way you were treated by your husband's

family. Of course you must come to me at once in Italy.
Camillo tried to divorce me, but the pope has ordered him to
recognize me as his wife and I am to take possession of the
palace in Rome again as soon as the weather grows cooler.
He is in Florence with his little blond duchess and does not
care to have anything to do with me, but at least my rights
have been restored. For the summer I am in Lucca, where
I have bought a small villa. You will like it here very much,
and if you are still feeling unwell, you may drink the waters
with me.

I am sending you a draft on my bank so that you can
come as quickly as possible; everything express, the best inns
and couriers. I cannot wait to embrace you.

Your loving cousin Pauline

Bagni di Lucca
23rd July 1821

Dear Jerome:

Our brother is dead. My life is over. I will never forgive the
British; they did nothing even when I begged them to let
me go there and told them what terrible reports we had of
Napoleon's health and now they have finally relented and
issued me a passport, but it is too late.

Pauline

Rome
12th September 1824

Dear Camillo:

*I am very ill, and I wish to come and see you. I must make
my peace with you before I die. Please, I beg you, grant me
this last favor.*

Your wife, Pauline

FOURTEEN

Florence, October 1824

W ho?" Camillo looked from the note in his hand
back to his servant, back again to the note.
"Here in Florence? Right now?"

"Yes, Your Excellency."

"They're not giving up, are they?" he said. This wasn't addressed to his servant, or even to the other occupant of the
room, but she lifted her head from her needlework anyway.

"What is it, *caro?*"

Not everyone could have a widowed duchess for a mistress. A duchess from one of the most eminent families in
Italy. And beautiful, to boot. He smiled as he looked at her.
Livia Lante della Rovere was still lovely, fair-haired and blue-
eyed, grave and gentle. Her fine-boned face had worn well
as she entered middle age, although in his eyes she would

always be his young cousin. Of course, he himself was nearing fifty; there was some gray in his hair and his waistline was gradually expanding. Youth was a relative quality at this point.

"Another message from my wife," he said.

She made a face. "How many letters is that this month? Three from her, one from the cardinal, one from the pope?"

"This isn't a letter." He held up the folded paper in his hand. "It's a message, sent over with a footman from the Hotel d'Inghilterra. She's in Florence."

"Pauline is in Florence!" She looked horrified.

"No, no, one of her relatives. A young cousin. Not so young now, I suppose. A strange girl. I never knew what to make of her." He sighed. "Vivi, I think I must see her."

"Nonsense."

"No, really. We went through some difficult times together. I've always felt that I owed her something."

She took another stitch in her embroidery. "If she's connected to that woman, I advise you to have nothing to do with her."

The servant coughed. "I beg your pardon, Excellency, but I must have given you the wrong impression. The note was not delivered by a servant. A footman escorted her, but the lady herself is downstairs. Shall I tell her you are not at home?"

"Sophie?" He sprang up. "Sophie is downstairs?" Halfway to the door, he was stopped by an outraged "Camillo!" from Livia.

"Show her up," he told the servant, retreating to the sofa. "And bring some refreshment."

When he resumed his seat, the duchess ostentatiously put away her needlework and came over to sit next to him.

"Are you guarding me?" he said, amused.

"If need be."

"We have nothing to fear from Sophie," he assured her, squeezing her hand.

There was a light tap at the door, and a woman came in, nodding gracefully to the footman as he held it open.

She curtsied. "Your Excellency, thank you for seeing me."

Surely this wasn't Sophie? Tall, yes, fair-haired, yes, same gray eyes—but not a girl. A woman, fashionably but quietly dressed, with a neat figure and small lines at the corners of her eyes, which spoke of strain. Then she gave him a familiar, twisted little smile, and he was on his feet, rushing over to her.

"No, no, not Your Excellency! It is still Cousin Camillo, surely. Or just Camillo." He kissed her on both cheeks and held on to her a moment longer than necessary.

Her shoulders trembled slightly in his grip; she was nervous. He almost looked down to see if she was twisting her hands in her skirt. But that was silly; she was a grown woman now.

"Vivi," he said, turning toward the sofa, "may I present Signora—Speare? Is that right? Did I pronounce it correctly? English names have all those letters one does not say. And this is my cousin Livia, the Duchess della Rovere."

The duchess gave a cold nod in acknowledgment.

"I almost didn't recognize you," he said, leading Sophie over to a chair. "How long has it been?"

"Since Napoleon's wedding to Marie-Louise." She thought for a minute. "Fifteen years? Sixteen? Fifteen, I suppose."

"You look very well." He assisted her into the chair. "I have had news of you, of course. I heard about your wedding, on Elba. And then you lost your husband at Waterloo. That must have been very difficult."

"It wasn't much of a marriage." She gave him another one of

her not-quite smiles. "We had about six weeks together, and then Napoleon escaped and off went all the British soldiers to chase him."

A maidservant came in with a tray of little cakes and glasses of sweet vermouth.

"Thank you," said Sophie, accepting some of each. "Pauline said I only married Charles to spite her, because he was English. I hate to admit it, but I think she was right." She took a small bite of cake, then set it back down on her plate.

Pauline. She had said the name. Livia stiffened.

"How is Pauline?" Casual, as though he had not read the letters, in some cases three or four times.

"She's dying." The curt statement was like a blow.

"So it's true," he whispered. He hadn't believed the letters. It was simply impossible to picture Pauline dying.

"But surely she has been ill off and on for many years?" Livia interjected defensively.

"Yes. This is different." Sophie's expression was stark. "That is why I came in person. I knew you wouldn't believe the letters. How many times has she claimed to be dying before? Dozens. Scores. I don't know. This is real. She has cancer. Some sort of growth, on her liver. The doctors are quite certain; they all agree. Oh, some give her two months, some six, some as much as eight. But no more than that." She leaned forward, her voice urgent. "Camillo, you can help her. She needs you."

He shifted uncomfortably. "I am sorry to hear that she is so ill. But we have been legally separated for almost ten years. She has a generous allowance and the use of several of my properties. I am not sure that I am in a position to increase the amount—"

She cut him off. "I don't mean financially. She has ample

funds. I know she was a bit extravagant at times, but she has changed."

"A bit!" He snorted. "Five hundred thousand francs for one necklace? More than a bit, I would say."

"She has changed," Sophie repeated. "Since Napoleon's defeat, she is quite frugal, at least by her standards. It doesn't matter. It isn't about money. It's—" She looked at the duchess and stopped.

"If you will excuse me." Livia rose and gave him an icy glare. "I shall leave you to reminisce in private." She swept out of the room.

"Oh, dear," said Sophie. "I'm sorry. I suppose I was expecting to find you alone, even though I know she has been with you for many years. She seems very nice," she added politely, in spite of abundant evidence to the contrary.

"I'm the one who should apologize." He sighed. "She's afraid of anything connected with Pauline." Then, with a little laugh, "She's somehow convinced you're going to persuade me to take my wife back."

She gave him a level stare, very like the Sophie of old. "I am," she said.

"You can't be serious." Livia's glare was even colder than the one she had favored him with during Sophie's visit. "I'm to move out. Of my home. With you." Her gesture took all of it in: the high-ceilinged room, the bed where they slept together, the paintings he had bought her, the furniture covered with embroidered fabric he had watched her make, the windows looking out on the Via Ghibellina, where they would often walk in the evenings, wandering through the crooked streets around the Duomo and the old prison. "And *she* is to move in. And be waited on. And be your wife again."

"I am still her husband," he reminded her.

"Camillo! She betrayed you! Not once, not twice, but a hundred times."

An exaggeration, he thought, but not an outrageous one. He estimated the actual number at something like thirty.

"The last time you saw her, when you traveled to Paris for Napoleon's wedding, she charged you rent for staying in her house."

True. Of course, that was in retaliation for his letter telling her she could no longer draw funds from any Borghese accounts.

"And refused to see you except in public."

True. He hadn't wanted to see her, either. They had barely looked at each other, even when they had to stand together behind Napoleon when Marie-Louise arrived in Paris. Luckily, he had only been required to stay in Paris for two weeks. Even an emperor cannot afford to prolong his wedding festivities when he is at war with most of Europe.

"And made you live on one floor of the house, while she lived on the other, and forbade you to leave your floor."

True.

"And said she had no room for your servants, so that they had to stay at an inn."

Vivi had a good memory. He had forgotten that one.

"Then you came back to Turin; she stayed in France, and she ignored you completely for five years, until Napoleon was exiled. *Then* suddenly she wanted to live in the palace in Rome and be a Borghese again." She folded her arms. "I'll never understand why the pope wouldn't let you divorce her."

At the time, he had been furious. But papal princes, for obvious reasons, were held to rather strict standards in marriage. And Pauline had powerful allies in Rome, even after Napoleon's defeat. He had ceded Rome to Pauline and retired to the Borghese palace in Florence with Livia. And really, he thought, he had had a very nice ten years here. Florence was small and lovely, the pope and his family and Pauline were safely distant in Rome, and Livia was a gentle and dignified companion.

She wasn't gentle and dignified right now, of course.

"Vivi, please don't make this any more difficult than it is already," he said sadly.

Her eyes filled with tears. "Why? I don't understand. Why do you have to bring her here? Why can't she leave us alone?" She had been pacing around the room; now she collapsed onto a chaise and buried her face in her hands.

"She needs me," he said, unconsciously echoing Sophie's phrase. He sat down next to Livia and put his arm around her. "Vivi, she doesn't have anyone except Sophie. Her family is in no position to help her. Napoleon is dead—and Sophie tells me that the news of his death nearly killed Pauline all by itself; she was frantically writing the British to try to get permission to visit him on St. Helena and they didn't let her know he had died until months afterward. Her mother has become a recluse; her older sister died five years ago. Her brother Lucien lost his post at the university and can barely support his own family. The others are scattered across the globe."

"She has servants, doesn't she?"

"Would you want to die surrounded by people you were paying?" He squeezed her shoulder. "I don't want this any more than you do, but it's my duty. She's my wife."

"She didn't take *her* duties to her husband very seriously."

There was no point trying to defend Pauline to Livia. It was like trying to explain the ocean to someone who dwelt inland. Look at that lake. Now imagine it is bigger. A hundred times, a thousand times bigger. Miles deep. The waves are much taller; they can be forty feet high. All the fish are different. All the plants are different. The water is salty, not fresh. And there are tides . . . At some point, you realize that you cannot explain the ocean to someone who has only seen lakes.

Livia was a lady: virtuous, modest, and conservative. True, she had been living in sin with Camillo for nearly fifteen years, first in Turin, then here in Florence. But in every other way, she was the epitome of a respectable noblewoman. She went to church. She raised her daughters. She entertained graciously in Camillo's small palace but preferred to be quiet, just the two of them. She was a lake. Pauline was the ocean.

It had occurred to him many, many times that he had married the woman who should have been his mistress and was keeping the woman who should have been his wife.

"Do you really think I should abandon my obligations because she abandoned hers?" he asked her. "And remember, I was not always faithful to her, either. Even before she ran away from Turin. I was away on campaign for over two years, and Napoleon's officers were not monks."

"Yes. No." She leaned her head against him. "It won't be for long, will it?" She laughed wildly. "What a horrible thing to say. Never mind, Camillo. I'll try to be good."

He kissed the top of her head.

"Camillo?" A long pause. "Do you think she is still beautiful?"

"I don't know. Sophie made it clear that she is extremely ill."

But he couldn't picture Pauline ugly any more than he could picture her dead.

Sophie had not been fond of the Palazzo Borghese when she first went to Rome, and nothing had happened to improve her opinion of it subsequently. Most of the rooms were closed off now, and there was a desperate attempt to keep Pauline's suite and the two large reception rooms cheerful, warm, and dry, but it was a losing battle. The first thing that hit Sophie when she returned from Florence and walked into the palazzo was the smell of mildew.

"I *hate* this place," she muttered as she followed the footman who was carrying her bags up to her apartment. "It's dark. It's wet. It feels like a crypt. I don't know why she stays here. She has four other houses, including one right here in Rome. We could be at the villa right now, and her friends would come and visit. No one ever wants to come here."

But that was why Pauline had moved back to the palazzo, of course. At the Villa Paolina, she had always held open house; everyone was welcome. That was the point of the villa: to be informal, to have no rules, to entertain dukes alongside piano teachers. With Pauline as the center of everything. When you decided that you were ugly and dying, you didn't want to be the center any longer. You wanted to hide. The majordomo had informed her just now that Pauline hadn't admitted anyone during the entire time Sophie had been gone.

"She wouldn't even read her mail," he told her, worried. "She said no visitors and no letters, unless they were from Florence."

I'm from Florence, thought Sophie. *I'm a walking, talking letter from Florence*. An express letter: two grueling, long days in the carriage each way. She wanted a bath. She wanted to lie down on a real bed and read a book that wasn't shaking up and down while she held it. And it was so hard to pretend for Pauline when she was tired.

She settled for brushing her hair and splashing some water on her face. As she walked into Pauline's apartments, she could hear Pauline's voice, querulous and high-pitched. "Is that Sophie? Is she back? I heard a carriage. I heard the door."

"Yes, it's me," she said, following the voice to the bedroom. Four o'clock on a sunny, crisp October day and Pauline was in bed. That was how it was now. Sophie braced herself and managed a smile as she bent over and kissed her cousin. "How are you?"

"What did he say?" Pauline demanded. She gripped Sophie's hand, hard. "Will he see me?"

"May I at least sit down first?" said Sophie lightly, trying to reclaim her hand.

"Sophie!"

"Yes! He said yes."

"How is he? Did you see *her*? Tell me everything!" She finally let go and sank back onto the pillows.

"The prince is well. He is making arrangements to move you to Florence. He asks that your doctor send him a letter describing what you will need."

Pauline looked at her. After a minute, she said cautiously, "Moving me to Florence? Not just a visit?"

Sophie nodded.

"Where in Florence?" Pauline whispered.

"With him. In the palace. The duchess and her daughters will move out."

Pauline looked away; Sophie knew that she was crying.

"His hair has gone partly gray," Sophie said quickly. "But he is still very handsome. He goes riding nearly every day, and he said to tell you that he will take you for drives. The hills around Florence are very beautiful at this time of year." She groped for something else to say, but the other topics that occurred to her—Camillo's pretty duchess, the latest grim report from the doctor, the lack of news from Pauline's far-flung brothers and sisters—were all disasters. She settled for a small cough instead.

Pauline swiped at her eyes and turned back to Sophie. She made a face. "Drives in the hills. I don't want drives! I want to make amends for my sins. What do you think, Sophie? Will he forgive me?"

"I did," Sophie said, smiling a little ruefully.

Pauline sighed. "Yes, you did. Many times. And now I am dragging you off to Florence, away from your friends here in Rome." She looked at Sophie anxiously. "You will come, won't you, Sophie?"

Sophie gave her an incredulous look. "How could you even *think* I wouldn't come?"

"Well." Pauline picked at the edge of the bedspread. "Camillo and I have not always gotten along very well. And sometimes other people get caught in the middle."

"He's changed. You've changed. Isn't that the whole point of this?"

Pauline was silent for a minute. "Do you think this is crazy? For me to go to Camillo, after so many years? I could just stay here, you know. It would be so much easier. Or we could go to Pisa, like last winter. Just the two of us."

"It's all arranged," Sophie said quietly. "It's what you wanted."

FIFTEEN

On a cold, rainy day in November, the Prince and Princess Borghese were reunited.

Since Livia was no longer there to remind him of his dignity, Camillo did run downstairs this time. He even went outside, in spite of the rain, and opened the carriage door himself. He had been pacing for hours, ever since he had received word that Sophie and Pauline would arrive today. Every few minutes he would go to the window overlooking the narrow street and peer down. He was trying to prepare himself, to nerve himself—but for what?

Sophie emerged first, then a maid. He peered into the darkened interior. Someone was half-sitting, half-reclining, swathed in shawls and blankets. One shawl covered the lower part of her face. All he could see was a bit of forehead and two enormous dark eyes. Pauline.

He climbed in. "Do you need help getting out? Shall I send for a footman?"

She pulled down the shawl that covered her mouth. "Aren't you even going to say hello?"

Something held coiled inside him relaxed when he saw her face and heard her tart question. Yes, it was still Pauline. The illness hadn't eaten her yet.

He made a little half-bow, the best he could do sitting in the carriage. "Welcome to Florence."

Her hand stole out and touched his wrist. "Thank you for having me." It was said in a gentle voice that he had almost never heard from her. Thank God she had snapped at him first. Then, briskly, "Yes, I am afraid someone will need to carry me. Not you, Camillo. Though you look better than I had expected."

"So do you," he said, before he could stop himself. He didn't know what he had been picturing, but her face, at least, had not changed much. You could see that she was ill; yet, even shadowed, her eyes were startling for their size and luster; her mouth still curved in the most perfect bow he had ever seen.

She gave a bitter laugh. "Don't look at me in daylight," she advised. "I'm yellow."

He carried her in, despite her protests that he should give her to the footman. She weighed nothing; it was terrifying. He had to keep looking at her face to reassure himself. Her eyes were flashing with indignation; that was good. Perhaps he simply didn't remember how much she had weighed when they were younger. No, he had to be honest. His body remembered the heft and weight of hers all too well. This new Pauline felt like she was made of wire and paper.

Camillo had prepared an entire set of rooms for Pauline on

the first floor of the palace. In one corner, there was a bedroom for her, and a smaller one for a maid or nurse alongside it. The bedroom opened into a large sitting room; the sitting room, in turn, connected on one side to another bedroom, for Sophie, and on the other to a square room he had fitted up as a dining room, with a table that could seat eight. The bedroom faced inward, toward the courtyard; the sitting room and dining room looked out over the street. He thought Pauline would enjoy looking out on some activity.

He carried her through every room, pointing out the various things he had brought for her comfort: a fire screen, pillows for the sofa, footstools, a painting of Napoleon (donated by a Florentine official who was only too happy to get rid of it), a set of china cosmetic boxes that someone had given them as a wedding present, which had been forgotten in the attic of the palace in Rome. Then he took her into her bedroom and showed her his great triumph: a bath, opening directly off the bedroom, with two tubs. "One is for milk," he said proudly. "The other for water. And there is a tank of water above the milk tub, to rinse you afterward, just as you like."

She didn't say anything, but when he finally set her down carefully on the bed, he saw that her eyes were full of tears. Then Sophie came in, and he thought he must have imagined it, because she clapped her hands, laughing.

"Sophie! Come and look at my bathroom! If you are very nice to me, I may let you use it."

He left her then to rest and refresh herself, and did not see her again until the early evening, when she received him as formally as her condition permitted. She was lying on the chaise in the sitting room, with Sophie seated nearby. The lamps were turned low, and the candelabra stood behind her on the hearth. The myriad shawls had been replaced by a dress and matching coat of deep blue, a color which had always looked well on her. She wore diamond earrings and a diamond band in her hair, and her tiny feet were encased in blue slippers with small diamond buckles. On one hand was a large emerald ring; on the other, two narrow bands studded with sapphires.

He noticed all of these things in great detail, because he was afraid to look at her face.

She patted the chaise. "Come sit here by me."

How many times had she said that to him! Usually she was on the bed, of course. But he remembered distinctly their first meeting, in Paris, in the half-unfurnished room, with the single daybed and two chairs, and all the Bonapartes standing around the walls. Those had been her first words to him: "Come sit here by me." He remembered them so clearly because he had expected her to speak French and instead she spoke in Italian. And also because from the moment he saw her, he was hopelessly infatuated with her.

He perched gingerly at the foot of the chaise and finally looked at her face. It was yellow, there was no gainsaying it. She wore some powder, but the sallow tinge showed through it. Her cheeks were hollow, and there were deep lines beside her eyes. He knew those lines from his two years in the army; they were the mark of someone living with constant pain.

She lay back, watching him read the tale of her disease in her face. "I told you I was yellow."

"Not so very much," he lied.

"It isn't so noticeable when I wear blue," she conceded. "But green is out of the question now."

She sat up a little straighter and held out her hand to him—the pose was familiar. After a moment, he smiled and got up, returning with a pear from a bowl of fruit and nuts on the table. "No apples," he said, putting it in her hand. "But you still win the beauty contest."

"Oh," she said, realizing what he meant. "The statue." She grimaced. "It's locked away, you know. I asked your steward not to let visitors see it any longer. I'm jealous of her. Of the old me. And I don't particularly like her. She was not a nice person."

Camillo had been jealous of the statue, too. The thought of strangers eyeing his naked wife had not been very pleasant. He sighed. "I never managed to have you and the statue in the same place, you know."

She handed him back the pear. "She's prettier."

"I'd rather have the real you." He looked down at the fruit. "Would you like some? I could cut it up for you."

She shook her head. "I don't eat much these days."

"Are you comfortable? Is there anything more you need?" He could see, through the open door of the bedroom, a small table already covered with medicine bottles.

"I am fine; I just need to rest for a bit."

Sophie had tiptoed away and closed the door to the sitting room. They were alone together for the first time since that terrible scene in Turin.

"What now?" he said. "What should we do?"

She kicked off her shoes and wriggled into a slightly less upright position.

"Now we wait for me to die," she said. "I don't think we need to do anything. I think it happens by itself."

* * *

Life in Florence settled into a bizarre rhythm. There were the sleeping times and the awake times. The sleeping times would run for a period of four or five days. Pauline would doze—she never really slept any longer—for twelve or fourteen hours at a stretch. Her face was constantly puffy; her movements languid. She barely ate at all during these episodes. At first, Camillo thought she was taking laudanum, but Sophie told him that it had been like this for months. The fatigue was so overwhelming that it trumped the pain; she needed very little laudanum until she came "awake" again. Then she would revive, sit up, demand to be carried downstairs, to be dressed, to have music or conversation. The daggers at the corners of her eyes would deepen every hour, but she refused the drug as long as she could. "I have slept enough for five people already," she would say. Camillo's chef learned that during the awake times he could tempt her to eat, especially if he made the dishes of her childhood: cod cheeks, or kid stewed in milk, or cheese-and-brandy tarts.

During the awake times, Camillo and Sophie would sit with her far into the night. She liked to talk, and Camillo and Sophie were her audience. Her favorite subject was Elba. She would describe in minute detail the balls she had given for Napoleon, the plays and musicales she had organized, the respectful behavior of all the French and British officers. Sometimes she would tease Sophie about her husband. Camillo thought this was cruel; the man was dead, after all. But Sophie didn't seem to mind.

"Charles was a brute," Pauline said one evening. "Sophie's husband," she said, in an aside, to Camillo.

"Yes, I know." He frowned at her. But it was too late.

Sophie looked up from the letters she was sorting; Pauline was being deluged by sympathetic letters from former connections who had heard of her illness. And, thought Camillo cynically, who realized that she was childless, dying, and wealthy. "You only thought he was a brute because he didn't speak French," she said.

"You didn't speak much English," retorted Pauline.

Sophie grinned at her. "We didn't talk much." Then she sighed. "Really, when we were not in bed, he was a very boring man. Hunting and shooting. And everything had to be *English*. Hunting was only good in whatever silly county it was he came from; shooting was only good with a pistol made in London."

"You should have listened to me," Pauline said, looking smug.

"What did you tell her?" Camillo asked.

"That she should take him as her lover; he wasn't good for anything else."

"Well, I didn't listen, did I?"

"Because you wanted to show me you were independent."

"Yes, and because I thought I wanted children."

Pauline looked down. "Sophie, I'm so sorry," she said in a low voice, her bright mood suddenly gone.

"I know." Sophie went back to her letters. "And really," she added, "Charles's children might have inherited his brains. Or lack thereof. And *that* would have been a challenge."

Camillo knew they should leave this subject, but he was suddenly curious. "What did he look like? Was he handsome?"

"Oh, yes." Sophie smiled. "He looked a bit like you, only very English. Rosy cheeks and lighter hair. But tall, and rode like a god."

His eyes automatically went to Pauline.

"No, I did *not* flirt with him," she said, indignant. "I didn't flirt with anyone on Elba, did I, Sophie? I was Napoleon's hostess; I had responsibilities."

Perhaps that was why she liked to talk about that brief six months in the exiled emperor's miniature kingdom, he thought. It was safe. No lovers to avoid during the reminiscences. Sophie had a different theory; she told Camillo that it was the only time in her life Pauline had ever felt that someone truly needed her. She was the only one of Napoleon's seven brothers and sisters to join him in exile ("ungrateful beasts" was Sophie's judgment of the others), and she had created an entire mock world on Elba for her brother, down to a tiny theater replicating the Comédie-Française.

Other subjects usually led back to Elba, too. One evening Pauline got out all her jewelry and began trying it on.

"I look like a hag," she said cheerfully. "But oh, how pretty they are!"

Necklaces were draped over the backs of chairs; bracelets and tiaras sat on the tables; earrings and rings rolled around in the saucers Sophie had brought in to hold them. Camillo stared around at the largesse; many were pieces he had given her. But there were some notable and very valuable absences.

"What happened to the large diamond necklace?" he asked. "And the collar from Napoleon's wedding? And the emerald parure? You still have the ring; I saw it. What about the necklace and earrings?"

"Oh, I sold all those pieces." Pauline lowered a tiara carefully onto her head and looked in the mirror. "Napoleon had very little money after he abdicated. I sold the emeralds and the collar right away, to help buy some property on Elba, and when he left the island, I gave the diamond necklace to his valet. It was the most valuable piece I had, and I thought he might need it. In case anything should happen." She glanced over to her brother's portrait, which had been hung in the place of honor above the fireplace. "I never saw him again, you know. I tried and tried, but the British wouldn't let me go to St. Helena."

"I know," he said.

"You shouldn't have married me, Camillo." She gave him a wry look. "You should have been my brother. I am a terrible wife but a very good sister."

"I don't think of you as a brother does," he said lightly.

She laughed.

In December, the sleeping days began to outnumber the awake days by larger and larger margins, and Camillo woke every morning with a black abyss gaping in his stomach. And then suddenly, in the middle of January, she was awake. Awake without pain. Sleeping again, instead of dozing. The yellow in her skin receded, as did the lines around her eyes. Everything about her seemed to come back to life—her hair, her posture. Even her fingernails, which had become cracked and discolored, began to heal.

None of them trusted it at first. Two days went by, three. She was eating at every meal. Sophie reported, glowing, that Pauline's stools were normal—they discussed such things openly now, even at the table. On the fifth day, Pauline asked Camillo to take her out in the carriage. She had only been out once or twice, for very short rides, since her arrival. They drove along the river first, and then to the park. Camillo winced inwardly at every bump in the road, but Pauline had tilted her head back, drinking in the sky and the clouds. It was late afternoon, and the sun was sinking behind the trees on the avenue, casting long shadows onto the paths and bare flowerbeds.

"We should come back when the flowers are blooming and the fountains are on," she said.

"That isn't until May," he replied absently, and then could have bitten his tongue out.

Cautiously, they began to entertain. Pauline had been receiving callers on her awake days all along, but only one at a time and only in her own rooms. Now they invited two or three people and greeted them in Camillo's spacious drawing room, with its deep-gold walls and frescoed ceilings. Next, they hosted a dinner. Soon they began to go out, at first to small, brief events. In early February, they tried the opera and did not go home, as planned, after the first intermission. Pauline hung heavily on his arm in their box, but as people pointed her out from the pit or came, bowing, to pay their respects, he stopped asking her whether it was time to leave. She was flushed, laughing, brilliant. She was happy.

"Camillo," she said the following day. "Doesn't Carnival begin soon?"

"Next week." A month ago, he had planned to move her out of Florence into a house in the hills; Carnival in Florence was a nonstop riot of noise and commotion. But he didn't think she would want to leave now, and he was right.

"Let's have a ball."

"What?" he said, taken aback.

"A ball. A masked ball. Please, Camillo."

He didn't have the heart to remind her that at the last Carnival ball they had hosted, she had disappeared with another man.

It sometimes seemed unfair to him that he had a better memory of her many lovers than she did. "Oh, him," she would say. "I had forgotten all about him." Camillo hadn't.

"A masked ball," he repeated.

She gave him a dazzling smile that would have been unthinkable three weeks earlier.

"Why not?" he said, feeling as though he were living in some bizarre dream where life and death were all mixed up together and no one could tell which was which.

Pauline woke every morning and went to bed every night obsessed with the ball. Sophie and Camillo and Camillo's secretary and majordomo tried to persuade her to let them do more of the work, but she fixed on every detail as if she would collapse back into her old lethargy the moment she stopped thinking about it. She designed masks for herself and Camillo, a pair of turtledoves. ("Don't you dare say one word" was Camillo's comment to Sophie when she saw them.) She ordered hangings for the ballroom, interviewed musicians, drilled the footmen on their stations for the evening, and frowned over menus.

"This is what she was like on Elba," Sophie told him one afternoon. Pauline was fretting over the guest list. "But there, we had three and four events every week. She wanted to distract Napoleon."

"No wonder you ran away and got married," he said gloomily.

Pauline lifted her head. "Dearest, can we invite your mistress and her oldest daughter?"

He was shocked. "Of course not. It would be a terrible insult to both of you."

"But we will all be masked." Her voice took on a familiar,

coaxing note. "I want to see her. I want to imagine you with her after I'm gone."

"No."

She pouted. God, he had never thought to see her pout again. But he held firm. The thought of Livia and Pauline in the same room was insupportable.

As the fateful Tuesday drew closer, he and Sophie seemed to be holding their breath. How long would the respite last? What if she fell ill again today, or tomorrow, or the next day?

On the morning of the ball, Pauline did not emerge from her bedroom until two in the afternoon. Camillo and Sophie were both waiting for her, in a state of near panic. She had not slept this late in months. But her maid had assured them she was merely sleeping, not ill.

"What's wrong?" she said, looking at their worried faces.

Sophie pointed to the clock.

She glanced over. "I needed my beauty sleep," she said, very *grande dame*. She began to laugh. "Look at the two of you! Mother hens! Honestly, Sophie, sometimes I feel as though you are older than I am." She made a shooing gesture at Camillo. "Go away. You're not allowed to see me until tonight."

Obediently, he left. He went for a walk, he read, he wrote a few letters, he ate, he took a bath. At some point, he decided, Pauline's obsession must have become contagious. He could think of nothing except the ball. He didn't even like balls.

He took special care with his toilet that evening, letting his valet fuss as much as he liked and adding a few touches he thought Pauline would like: a ribbon awarded him by her brother and a stickpin she had given him right after their wedding. His jacket was blue, which meant, he suspected, that Pauline would also be in blue. His waistcoat was a dull gold, embroidered in blue thread. His smallclothes were white, as were his stockings and shoes. He settled the mask over his eyes and went downstairs to wait for his wife. Sophie was there before him, with her escort for the evening, a distant connection of Camillo's who had hinted lightly, and then not so lightly, and then very plainly, that he was available for the job. He was a widower, a few years older than Sophie, with two small children. Not for the first time, Camillo wondered what would become of Sophie once Pauline died.

"This feels familiar," Sophie said, looking up the staircase. Her mask, a shimmering band of fish scales, was dangling from its straps around her neck. Then she gave him a rueful glance. "No, I forgot. You were at the top of the staircase with her, last time. In Turin."

Turin. The banquet. Their last, most terrible fight. Really, didn't he have *any* happy memories of balls with Pauline?

"She told me that men like to see women descending to them," Sophie informed him.

At the top of the staircase, with her gloved hand just skimming the banister, Pauline appeared. She was in blue, as he had anticipated, and as she floated down, he thought he had been transported back in time. Her dress was cleverly cut to conceal how thin she was, and all one saw as she came forth was a graceful sweep of sky-colored silk below the cameo of her face. She had her mask in her hand, and as she came up to him, she held it out to him. "Would you help me put it on?"

Her maid could have done it. Would have done it, normally. But now he stepped closer and tied the strings in her dark curls. She bent her head, and he smoothed the ends of the ribbon down over the back of her neck. He could feel the bones at the top of her spine. She was wearing perfume. That was his life now. Bones and perfume.

"Well. Shall we go across the courtyard and receive our guests?" she said brightly.

He danced with no one else. When Pauline had another partner, he stood and watched her. It seemed to him that time was spinning away from him so fast that he could no longer even keep track of it. One minute he was dancing, then he was standing, then he was dancing again. Pauline herself never stopped moving. Even when she stood talking with someone, she shifted lightly from one foot to the other, as though she were a bird, about to take off. She ate nothing; she drank a few sips from each glass she took and then set it down and darted away.

He had spent two weeks worrying that she would collapse before the ball; now he began to worry that she would collapse *during* the ball. His eyes stole constantly to the clock. When the orchestra began playing the sequence of dances they had selected for the end of the ball, he breathed a sigh of relief.

"The dummy, the dummy!" everyone shouted as the last dance concluded. There was cheerful confusion as all the guests simultaneously demanded their cloaks and wraps; it was nearly time for the traditional ceremony at the river where drunken Florentines burned the Carnival King made of straw and papier-mâché and tossed fireworks off the bridges.

He practically ran over to Pauline, who was standing, flushed and bright-eyed, bidding farewell to a large group of guests.

"You are *not* going to the river," he said in a fierce undertone, taking her arm and fastening his hand around it like a manacle. "We had fireworks here earlier; that will have to do."

"Yes, Camillo," she said, looking up at him.

"I mean it," he said. "I'm surprised you are still standing."

"I said yes. I meant it, too. We can stay here."

"Good."

Then she smiled.

Pauline had one particular smile that Camillo had never thought to see again. It was her "take me to bed" smile, and when he saw her give it to other men, he wanted to kill everyone in the room, starting with the unlucky man and ending with Pauline.

This time she was smiling at *him*.

No. He shook his head very slightly.

She took off her mask and held it up next to his matching one. Yes, her decisive nod replied.

He carried her up the stairs for the second time in four months. She still weighed nothing, but at least she wasn't tinted yellow and covered in shawls. When he set her down on the bed, he still fully intended to ring for her maid and leave. He was exhausted, and he wasn't even ill. Nor had he danced every dance. Or skipped supper.

She clung to his hand. "Camillo, please don't go." She tugged. "Stay here. Just for a little bit."

"You need to rest."

"I'm going to have a very, very long time to rest." Her expression was wistful. "Right now I have just danced all night at a wonderful ball, and I don't know what will happen when I wake up tomorrow. I know I won't feel this well for very much longer. Sometimes I am afraid to go to sleep; I tell myself that if I stay awake, perhaps it will last."

He sat down beside her and held her hands. "You want me to keep you awake."

She nodded.

"We could just talk."

She gave him a dark look. "Camillo, I have not been a very good wife. But one thing even you cannot accuse me of. I do *not* talk in bed."

He had to laugh.

"You're afraid you will hurt me," she said softly. "You're afraid you'll make me ill again."

His face must have given him away.

"Maybe you will. So what?" She turned his hand over and traced the half-sphere of flesh below his thumb. The Mound of Venus, palmists called it. "I want to remember you as my lover, not my nurse. Is that so wrong?"

"Perhaps not." He was weakening.

"Just think," she said. "For the first time in seventeen years you can make love and not have to go to confession afterward."

They turned down the lamps—her request, not his. She did not want him to see her body naked. "And I will not have sex with my clothes on," she informed him. "I never have, and I am not going to start now."

He knew that she often had pain in her abdomen, so he curled up behind her as she lay on her side and entered her from the back. Every movement was careful and gentle; he was holding her in his arms and with his hands circling her breasts, but he barely touched them, just letting her nipples brush his palms. Every once in a while he would feel the bones of her spine against his chest and remember how ill she was; he would just rock himself slowly back and forth inside her, making a little soothing noise that was more for him than for her, until the grim reminder receded to the back of his mind. It was very slow, very tentative. At one point they both dozed off for a minute; he came awake again rock-hard from some little movement she had made as she shifted.

"Did I fall asleep?" Pauline sounded indignant.

"We both did. Just for a moment."

"How do you know it was just a moment?"

He nudged her inside with the evidence.

"I've never fallen asleep before." She sounded curious, not upset.

"It was nice." He nudged her again. "Now I think I'm going to keep both of us awake."

His hands shifted down to her hips, then folded in and cupped her as he pressed into her more firmly. He could feel her respond, feel her pushing back against his thumbs. His thrusts deepened, and she began to move with him.

"I have nothing to hold on to," she gasped. "I want to grab you somewhere." She groped down and found his hands, notched between her thighs. Her small fingers curled over his thumbs and pressed them deeper and deeper as he rode her from behind. The sensation was exquisite.

"Don't stop," she panted. "Don't be afraid of hurting me, Camillo, don't."

That was all he needed. He lifted her upper leg slightly and pulled back to get a better position. Then he drove into her, hard and fast, feeling her hands tightening on his and clenching with the rhythm of his thrusts. She came just as he did, with a series of shuddering pulses that reverberated through his fingers all the way up to his wrists.

They lay there panting for a few minutes, still entwined.

"Thank you, prince husband," she said at last.

"My beautiful princess." He smiled. "You had your way with me, as usual."

"Oh, this was the easy part." She rolled over so that she was facing him. "You can turn the lamp back up."

"What was the easy part?" he asked, climbing back into bed. He didn't turn it up very much. He didn't want her to be self-conscious.

She didn't answer right away. She studied his face, his chest, his shoulders. "When I found out I was dying, I decided I needed to do three things," she said, looking carefully at his collarbone. "I needed to persuade you to take me back. I needed to make love to you again—if I could."

He thought she would go on, but she didn't.

"And?"

She shook her head. "I've been lucky so far. Luckier than I deserve. I don't want to ruin it."

SIXTEEN

She was never the same after the ball. They had all known it would happen, that she was clinging to her temporary gift of health with both hands and refusing to let go until the ball was over, but it was still hard to see her sink back into the cycle of sleeping days and awake days. By the end of March, she was worse than she had been in December; there were not many awake days, and they were so painful that she sometimes gave up and let laudanum send her back to sleep. By mid-April, she was in nearly constant pain and would fret for hours at the slightest noise outside in the street, or if a maid set a bowl down on the wrong table. Her brother Louis visited and, after one afternoon of watching his sister toss and turn, agreed with Camillo. It was time to leave the city.

Camillo rented a villa on a hill to the south of Florence, a pretty, square stucco house with gardens just starting to come to life and a sweeping view back toward the town. He hired nurses and maids. He moved furniture from the palace to the villa, including the bathtubs. This time he set up Pauline's rooms on the ground floor, so she could be wheeled outside in a bath chair if the weather was fine.

The last item to be moved was Pauline. He had sent Sophie and the servants on ahead; he wanted to be sure that Pauline's bed and medicines were waiting for her. As he got into the carriage with her, she clutched his hand. Her fingers were like sticks.

"Can we go to the park?"

He was puzzled. "The park?"

"The one with the fountain. You said they turned it back on in May."

It was the second of May.

She gave him a bitter, triumphant smile. "I'm still here. And I want to see the fountain and the flower beds."

"It's in the wrong direction." He thought that the ride to the villa would already be longer than she could tolerate without serious discomfort.

"I want to see it."

Nobody was as stubborn as a Bonaparte, he thought. They drove slowly to the Cascine and pulled up in front of the fountain. Thank God, it was on.

She looked out the window. "It doesn't look like much," she said, disappointed. "But the flowers are nice." She lay back, exhausted and gray with pain, and didn't say anything else until they pulled up in the drive of the villa, half an hour later than expected.

"I saw it," she said defiantly. "That's what counts."

* * *

By the second week of May, she was no longer able to go outside, even in the bath chair. Sophie went out every morning and cut fresh flowers for her room. She seemed to be fading right along with Pauline, paler and more strained every day. He saw Pauline watching Sophie sometimes when Sophie wasn't looking and knew Pauline was worried about her. But since Sophie never left Pauline alone for more than five minutes now, he had no chance to ask her about it.

One evening he was sitting with a brandy in the garden, watching the moon rise behind a grove of olive trees.

"Your Excellency?"

It was one of the footmen.

"Yes?"

"The princess sent me to tell you that she is feeling a bit better and hopes you will come sit with her for a few minutes."

"Let's bring her out here," he said suddenly. It was so beautiful. The air smelled like warm dust and flowers, and the olive leaves looked like they were made of silver.

"Shall I get the chair, sir?"

"No, we'll have to carry her. Go get Matteo and bring a bed out here."

It took twenty minutes to set everything up, and he cursed himself for a fool during every one of them. But when they brought her out and laid her on the bed, she looked around her like a child, delighted.

"It's lovely," she said softly.

"You would have been more comfortable in your room," he said gruffly.

"I'm never comfortable." She said it calmly, without any bitterness. "And Sophie thinks you are being romantic, so she won't follow me, for once, and I can finally talk to you about her."

"Ah."

"Yes." She sighed. "Camillo, you've done so much for me already. I hate to ask anything more. But—"

"You want me to take care of her after you are gone."

"She doesn't need money," Pauline said quickly. "Napoleon gave her a generous dowry, and I am leaving her a large sum as well. Plus"—she gave a little cackle—"you won't believe this, but the British army pays her a widow's pension. Like clockwork, every quarter-day."

"She needs a home," he said.

"I did something terrible to her," whispered Pauline. "I've never forgiven myself. I gave her—I gave her some medicine in Turin, and it was too strong for her. I thought she was better, but after she married, she found out—she can't have children, Camillo. She got very sick after Waterloo; she was pregnant and some damage from those doses I gave her made everything go wrong. I don't know if she'll ever marry again. Watching the two of us can't have given her a very good opinion of the institution of marriage. Her husband's family abandoned her after she miscarried; her father died five years ago, and her brothers couldn't even be located for his funeral. I picture her wandering around Europe, like a ghost, always on the edge of things."

"I won't let that happen," he said.

"Do you promise?"

"I promise."

"Promises made to a dying person are sacred," she reminded him. She looked at the moon. "I don't think I'll die tonight. It's too lovely out."

She was quiet for a while, then she asked him, "Is Jerome coming?"

"Yes."

She asked every day now. Her youngest brother was at the moment the only one of her siblings within reach of Florence.

Hurry, Jerome, he said silently.

Sophie paused in the doorway of Pauline's room. One of the roses she was carrying was digging its thorns into her wrist, but she just shifted it slightly and stood as still as she could. Pauline was sitting up in bed, leaning against the pillows, her eyes closed. She wasn't sleeping; Sophie could tell. She was waiting for her next dose of laudanum, willing herself not to take it yet. Camillo was sitting next to her, holding her hand. She was gripping his fingers so hard they were swelling slightly at the tips. The two of them sat like that for half an hour at a stretch sometimes, saying nothing.

Camillo had taken her aside last night, after the doctor had left.

"Pauline is worried about you," he said without any preamble.

"I am fine."

"What are you going to do after—afterward?"

"I don't know." She knew they were going to ask her this question sooner or later; she should have had an answer ready. "Go back to France, perhaps. Stay here." She added stiffly, "I have money of my own, you know."

"She asked me to look out for you," he said. "Tell me, Sophie. What would you like to do? Where would you like to live? You will be very well dowered; I could arrange another marriage for you if that is your preference. My brother Francesco divides his time between France and Italy; he has written me that he would be very eager to have you join his household. And you would be welcome to stay with me, as well."

"What of the duchess?"

"She is very generous and kind-hearted."

Sophie thought that even a saint might have some difficulty welcoming her rival's ward into her own home. "I can't talk about this now," she said. "I won't." The doctor had said Pauline had only a few days to live.

He hesitated. "I should mention one thing. Since you say you have thought of returning to France."

"You wish to remind me that the Bonapartes are not very popular there?"

"Look." He handed her one page of a letter.

It was from his brother Francesco. He warned Camillo that a series of books about the fallen imperial family had been published, most anonymously, but some "authored" by former confidantes of Napoleon and his family. The most popular and successful of these books were all attacks on Pauline. She was the new Messalina, the Whore of Babylon, she had slept with Napoleon, she had taken Negro slaves as lovers, she had walked on the necks of her ladies-in-waiting, she had posed nude for a roomful of men, she had forced Napoleon to divorce Josephine. "I warn you," wrote Francesco, "so that you may do your best to protect her from these books and those who have read and believed them. I am told it is even worse in England."

Sophie handed it back. "She knows all about them."

"She does?"

"Her English friend, Lady Holland, sent her an excellent selection of quotations from both the French and the English versions."

He was horrified. "And you gave her the letter?"

"I don't open letters from friends like Lady Holland," she said. "But I did read it, afterward. She showed it to me. She thought it was very funny."

"You didn't."

Sophie had gone off and cried.

"Don't forget what I said," he had told her, folding up the letter and putting it back in his desk.

"I won't." She had added, after a moment, "Thank you."

She hadn't slept much last night, and when she did fall asleep, she had dreamed that someone was speaking to her in French and she couldn't understand them. Most of her dreams were in Italian now. She even thought in Italian. Was her dream a sign? Pauline would have thought so. She was very superstitious.

Pauline stirred on the bed, and Sophie came in and found a vase for the roses. Camillo was flexing his newly liberated hand.

"Jerome will be here tomorrow," she told Camillo quietly.

"Good," said Pauline, without opening her eyes. "I'll have a Leclerc, and a Borghese, and a Bonaparte. All my families."

Camillo could have told the doctor not to announce her own death date to Pauline. "You should send for a priest, Your Excellency," he had told her last night. "At once."

"It's 'Your Imperial Highness,'" she had corrected him. "And I'm not ready for a priest."

He had strongly advised her to have a priest brought as soon as possible.

At that point Camillo had decided she would somehow make it to the next day out of sheer spite.

"I don't want to die at night," she had whispered, after the doctor had left. "It's dark."

"We'll wait until tomorrow morning, then." He settled into the chair by her bed.

"Are you there, Camillo?" she said a few hours later.

"I'm here. What is it?"

She shifted on her pillow. "I'll wait until daylight."

"For what?"

She didn't answer.

He barely slept now, afraid he would miss something, some word or gesture. Some last bit of Pauline. When he did doze off, he woke listening for her breathing, afraid she might have slipped away in the five minutes he had lost.

The curtains in her room were open all the time now, night and day. "Don't shut the world out," she complained when the maid tried to draw them. "I like to see it." So he saw the sky gradually turn the color of slate, then granite, then pearl.

Pauline's eyes were open. "This is the last one," she said, watching the sky brighten.

"Do you need more medicine?" He started to reach for the bell rope.

She shook her head. "No. It doesn't hurt. Or rather, everything hurts, but in a different way. My body is saying good-bye." Her eyes closed again, but her hand slipped into his. This time she didn't squeeze.

The sun rose, and Pauline stirred again. She turned her head and looked out the window. "All right," she said. "Send for the priest. And my maid. And Sophie. I'm not dying in my nightgown."

He rang the bell but didn't get up.

"Go away," she said gently. "I'm going to have a bath, and then my maid is going to make me pretty one last time. Get some rest, get something to eat. I promise not to die without you."

Sophie got to pick Pauline's final outfit. In theory. First, she picked a blue robe; Pauline told her blue was the color of the Virgin Mary and she couldn't think of anything less appropriate. Then Sophie picked a rose-colored silk; it had been one of Pauline's favorites.

"No," said Pauline after a moment's reflection. "I think I seduced Pacini last year wearing that."

The maid held up four more gowns; Pauline shook her head.

"White?" said Sophie. "You want to wear white?" There was only one gown left in the armoire.

Pauline tilted her head to one side and studied the dress. "Why not?"

Because you are paler than the fabric, thought Sophie. Pauline was still wrapped in towels from the bath, and she was exactly the same off-white as the linen. But Sophie didn't say anything. There was always the rouge pot.

It took both of them to get Pauline into the dress, since she could not really stand up without help, and she was breathing hard when the last button was hooked. But she looked triumphant as they helped her back into bed.

"Now my hair," she said. "And then some paint." Her maid was an old hand at this now; in a few minutes, Pauline looked almost healthy.

"Jewelry," she announced after studying her reflection. "Something gaudy and distracting." She directed the maid carefully in placing earrings, two necklaces, and a diadem, and then held up the glass again. "Very good!" she approved. "What do you think, Sophie? Do I look like a princess?"

Sophie thought the gown and the jewels, perhaps not by accident, bore a remarkable resemblance to the outfit Josephine had worn to be crowned empress.

"Now," said Pauline to the maid, "go fetch something. I don't care what. Just tell all the others that I am not dressed yet and go away for ten minutes."

When the door closed behind the servant, Pauline looked at Sophie. "No one is coming back in here until you tell me what you are doing."

"What do you mean?" said Sophie, suddenly feeling cold and sick.

"What are you doing tomorrow? And the day after that? And the week after that?"

Sophie shook her head, helpless.

"Camillo spoke to you; I know he did."

"He did." Sophie didn't want to remember that conversation. She didn't want to be having this conversation. While they were choosing gowns, it was a game. This wasn't a game.

"Sophie, look at me." Unwillingly, Sophie met Pauline's eyes. They glittered fiercely above her hollow cheeks. "I'm dying. Now. I can't feel my feet. My hands are going numb. Do you understand me?"

"Yes." No.

"I am not letting anyone else in until I am sure that you will have a life after I am gone."

"I don't know!" shouted Sophie. "How can you ask me to answer that question now, of all times? How can I think about anything else? I have only been apart from you for fifteen months in the last twenty-two years! And I was miserable for every single day of those fifteen months!"

Pauline grimaced slightly in pain and shifted her position. "If I die without talking to Camillo and Jerome," she said, "they will be very upset. And I need to dictate my will. Stop being so stubborn and just answer me."

"What do you want me to do?" said Sophie, starting to cry at last.

"I want you to be happy," said Pauline. Her voice was very low. "I want you to belong somewhere. We were always wandering, the two of us. So where do you belong? Do you want to try to be French again? Or do you want to stay here and be a Borghese?"

"Borghese," Sophie choked out.

"Good," said Pauline. "That's what I thought."

Camillo changed his clothes and swallowed some coffee but arrived back at Pauline's room before she was ready and had to wait outside the door. He paced back and forth impatiently until he realized that anyone seeing him would think he was an expectant father outside his wife's confinement. It was a birth of sorts, he thought, then went and sat in a chair, his head in his hands. Jerome came a few minutes later and stood by the wall, his face set. The priest was here now, too.

Pauline admitted them an hour later. She was wearing a magnificent white gown, a full set of rubies, and what he suspected was some very cleverly applied makeup. She was pale but not sallow and was sitting up in bed. She looked almost well enough to go outside. For one minute his heart leaped; she was better again; she would laugh and dismiss the priest, as she had done several times earlier. But she didn't. When he watched her swallow the wafer, he felt himself go numb. Her voice, intertwined with the priest's, seemed to come from very far away.

"Now the notary," Pauline told her maid. In front of the five witnesses, she made a long list of bequests. Camillo recognized some names: her nieces and nephews, Dermide's nursemaid Carlotta. When she came to Sophie, he went over and stood next to her while Pauline dictated the names of four properties that were now hers. Sophie was crying silently, not even bothering to wipe the tears away.

Then he heard his own name. "To my husband, Prince Borghese, the villa known as Villa Paolina, in Bagni di Lucca, in gratitude for his care and devotion during my illness."

He looked up, startled. It hadn't occurred to him that she would leave him anything.

"It's so beautiful there in the summer," she said. "I wanted you to have it."

When the notary had finished, she signed her name. Her hand shook. For the first time, Camillo began to believe that this was real, that Pauline was leaving him. He could see now that under the makeup she was growing paler and paler, that her whole body was trembling slightly with the effort of holding herself up.

"Thank you," she said to the maid and the notary. "You may go."

Now, he thought. *Now she'll lie down.*

No. She beckoned Jerome over and spoke with him for a little while before embracing him. Then she turned to Sophie. Her voice was getting softer and softer; Camillo couldn't hear what she said, and Sophie was unable to reply; she simply sobbed. At the end, Pauline said something to her that produced a nod. Then Sophie kissed Pauline's hand, not once but twice, and fled.

Jerome looked at his sister, then at Camillo, and withdrew.

Pauline was still sitting up. He strode over and dropped to his knees beside the bed. "For God's sake, lie down," he said, his voice rough. "It hurts me just to look at you."

"No," she said. "I have to do this sitting up. If I thought I could stand, I would." For the first time, he saw tears in her eyes. Her voice was weak, but it was steady and clear. "I have no right to ask this of you. You have already been more than generous." She stopped. "I don't know if I can do this."

"What? What is it?"

"Ask you to forgive me. I know God has forgiven me, and that is all I should care about, but I loved you, and I was so horrible to you, I know I don't deserve—"

"Stop." He put his hand over her mouth. "Stop. I won't listen. Of course I forgive you." He blinked away tears. "I forgave you a long time ago. The fault wasn't all yours, you know."

"Am I your wife again?"

"You were always my wife."

"And you don't mind that I asked to be buried in the Borghese chapel?"

"You're a Borghese princess." He kissed her forehead.

She sighed. "Now I can lie down. Will you stay with me for a bit?"

"Yes." He pulled up his usual chair.

He sat and held her hand and listened to her breathe. "I love you," he whispered after a little while.

She smiled.

EPILOGUE

June 9, 1845

The lamps were burning in the Borghese chapel, reflecting off the statues of golden angels cavorting behind the altar. The angels, for their part, were supporting an ancient and revered image of the Virgin, dark with age. In theory, the angels were merely the frame; in practice, their glittering bodies completely eclipsed the painting.

Sophie stood to the side; the others were still kneeling in prayer at the altar. She liked staring at the antique Virgin, who stared right back, frowning. Not for her the typical adoring, submissive gaze down at her divine child; no, she looked right at you, daring you to tell her she was a bad mother. Legend said she had been painted by Saint Luke, from life. Sophie liked that idea.

After a few minutes, Agnese got up, genuflected, and

came back to stand by Sophie. "Aren't you going to pray at all, Cousin Sophie?" she asked hesitantly. "If you don't like priests, he's gone now."

"You asked me that last month, at the mass for your Uncle Camillo."

The girl pursed her lips. "You might have changed your mind since then," she pointed out.

"Aunt Paolina used to say the same thing when she bullied me to come to church," Sophie said absently. "Only it wasn't a month in between—it was more like three days."

Agnese shifted from one foot to the other. She was getting restless; the commemoration service had been a long one. And Bettina, still determined to save Pauline from her just deserts, was not going to leave the altar until she had said one hundred Hail Marys.

"I'm going to go and look at the little house on the other side of the church," Agnese announced finally. She darted off.

The "little house" was, in fact, an elaborate vessel for consecrated wafers in the chapel on the other side of the nave, built for Pope Sixtus V. The vessel was a very detailed two-foot-high model of the chapel that housed it, complete with bas-reliefs on the tiny doors and miniature statues on the domed roof. It was held aloft by yet another team of gilded angels.

Sophie wondered sometimes what it would be like to be a Borghese, to have basilicas like this one as your family church, your playground even, in the case of a child like Agnese. To have your ancestors staring down at you from niches in the walls, wearing the papal miter, surrounded by all the gold and paint and marble that centuries of Catholic wealth and power could command. To have a gold ciborium as a sort of sacred doll's house.

She had hated the place when Pauline was first buried here. She had stood at the side of the chapel then, too, seething with grief and anger at the thought of confining Pauline inside this pious jewel box. She felt as though someone had stolen the body of the real Pauline and replaced it with someone else. Her joyous butterfly of a Pauline, her reckless, irresponsible, impatient Pauline, did not belong here. But it had been Pauline's last wish, and Camillo's, too. Sophie had gradually made her peace with the idea. After all, for twenty years now, Pauline had been a faithful Borghese princess. Camillo had been resting alongside her for thirteen of those years.

Of course, he wasn't the only Borghese who had been buried here recently. Sophie wondered how Pauline was getting along with Agnese's mother, the saintly Lady Gwendolyn.

"Are you watching us, Pauline?" she whispered, leaning against a pillar. "Do you like it here? Does it make you laugh when Bettina says prayers for you?"

The old servant was struggling to her feet, assisted by Matteo. It was time to go. Sophie looked around for Agnese and spotted her a few feet away, right by the silk rope across the entrance to the chapel.

"Cousin Sophie, come look," she said, beckoning. "I just noticed something."

Sophie went and stood beside her.

"See?" Agnese pointed to the sign next to the rope. "Look at the name of the chapel!"

CAPPELLA PAOLINA was the heading, in large block capital letters. Then, in smaller script underneath, *The Cappella Paolina is closed this afternoon for a private family memorial. Visitors to the basilica are asked to remain on this side of the rope.*

Sophie smiled. "It's not named for Pauline," she told Agnese.
"It's the pope who built the chapel, Pope Paul. The one who was
also named Camillo Borghese."

"I *know* that," said Agnese. "But don't you think it's nice? That
a Camillo is a Pauline? Don't you think it's a sign that they are
happy together, now?"

Another Borghese romantic in the making, thought Sophie. *Just
like Camillo.*

She reached instinctively for the folded paper at her chest. It
had been sent to her on the first anniversary of Pauline's death,
and when she had opened it, she had thought there must be some
mistake. Why would Camillo send Sophie a letter addressed to
a ghost? But he had.

Dearest Pauline,

the letter said,

> *You wrote me so many letters that I never answered, and
> now it is my turn. I wish I had answered those letters. I
> wish I could have been more like Sophie. She was honest
> enough to admit that she loved you all along; I was too
> proud, too careful of my dignity, until it was almost too late.
> You never had dignity, Pauline, and I thought it was a ter-
> rible flaw in your character. Now I ask myself why I valued
> it so highly. You had joy, you had passion. Dignity isn't
> worth much in comparison with that.*
>
> *I miss you. I miss your body, and your voice, and the
> way you tilt your head sideways. I miss your eyes. No one
> else has eyes that large and dark. I miss your ridiculous, ex-*

travagant habits. A few months ago I discovered what I had
spent on milk for your baths while you were in Florence.
I could have bought an entire herd of cows! But I laughed
when I saw the accounts.

I went to Lucca in August, to the villa you left me in
your will. It's perfect. I was happy and sad there, both at
once, because the whole place was so much like you. I'm
going back there in a few weeks, to be happy and sad again.

Do you know where I am right now? I'm sitting across
from you, with four dozen candles shining on your naked
body, just the way you liked me to see you. It took me
a while to get up my courage for this. After you died, I
couldn't even think about the statue for a long time. But
today, on the anniversary of your death, I made myself
go and visit you. I arrived in Rome just before sunset,
and when they unlocked the room the light was coming in
sideways and firing your skin with a hint of pink color. You
looked so beautiful. The candlelight is more spectacular, but
not as lifelike.

I'm no longer jealous. I think I'll open the room more
often, let people see you. You always enjoyed having admirers. Perhaps I'll even move you to the villa, where you can
have other lovely statues for company in the quiet hours
when the salons are closed. Sophie can go visit you there; she
always liked the villa better than the palace. I'm sending this
letter to her, in fact.

She is the only one who will understand why I wrote it.
Your husband, Camillo

THE HISTORY

BEHIND

THE STORY

AFTERWORD

It was the summer of 1988, and I was headed to Rome. I was to spend two days there with my family prior to what would be, in my mind, my "real vacation," a trip on my uncle's yacht, *Valentine*, through the Mediterranean.

Although I was born in Italy, I hadn't spent much time there since moving to the United States at the age of seven. This was going to be my first trip back to Rome in a long while. To be honest, I didn't know much about my family history at this point, nor did I really care. I was the type of kid who was excited to go to Rome because there was no drinking age. I was a punk. Really. I remember I had a pierced ear with a big colored parrot hanging from it. My poor parents! The weather was sunny, hot, and humid—a typical July day in Rome. My father and mother were taking me to Villa Borghese, Rome's largest park, which was owned by my family until 1903; in that year, the Villa Borghese (the park itself, the villa, and my family's art collection) was nationalized by the state and then handed over to the municipality of Rome.

I remember when I first saw the entrance to the park. Two massive stone pillars framed the gate, one decorated with an eagle, the other with a dragon. As I walked in between these twin symbols of the Borghese clan, I could see lawns, fountains, and statues spread out in front of me. Bicycles rolled down the concrete pathways; Italians were sprawled on blankets kissing; street vendors were selling gelatos and beverages. From the trees overhead birds chirped, drowning out the city sounds just beyond the stone walls that separated the park from the central districts of Rome.

The park was enormous, the landscaping beautiful. Terrace led to fountain led to grotto led to avenue. After an hour, when I thought we had seen everything, my father took me to the center of a path and pointed up a slight hill. A building gleamed white in the sunshine. It was perfectly proportioned, one of the most elegant mansions I had ever seen.

"The Galleria Borghese," my father said quietly. "Home to your relatives until 1903." (Perhaps, in some sense, it is still my family's home; the history of this magical place is filled with my ancestors' stories, statues, and paintings.)

I followed him along the paved walkway past what seemed like hundreds of trees and flowering shrubs. It took a full five minutes to reach the entrance of the Galleria. Up the marble steps, through the door, across the atrium, down a hall, into an elegant square room—and there she was.

Even to a teenage philistine, that statue was spectacular. The white cold marble, the finely crafted couch, the apple, and

Paulina. How stunning! It really was one of the most beautiful works of art I had ever seen. I stared.

"That is your relative, Paulina Bonaparte Borghese," my father said. "She was Napoleon's sister; she married Camillo Borghese."

That was my first introduction to Paulina.

After our tour of the Galleria Borghese, my parents took me to Santa Maria Maggiore, one of Rome's five basilicas and home to the Borghese chapel. Although the chapel was splendid (my brother would get married here thirteen years later), nothing was more moving to me than the Borghese crypt, which was beneath the chapel. As this is a private area in the church, open only to members of the Borghese family, my father had to ask Monsignor Cocuzza to unlock the massive wooden doors and let us in.

The crypt is at the bottom of a long flight of steps, deep beneath the basilica. There, on the marble floor, spread out across the entire expanse of the crypt, was my family tree, all beautifully carved (the names, the crests, the tree with its leaves . . . everything). Flanking the tree on both sides were tombs, each inscribed with the name of its occupant. When I saw Paulina's name, I was actually quite shocked. Why would a Frenchwoman (especially a Bonaparte) want to be buried in Rome surrounded by all the Borgheses? And that was when my father told me the story of Paulina and Camillo.

Theirs was not a fairy-tale marriage; the story is sad, even tragic. And yet it is also beautiful and romantic, and it contains a very important lesson about love, a lesson I wanted to share with all who cared to read this book: love is about understanding, forgiveness, and communication. Without these elements, love simply cannot work, nor can it grow. This was true with Camillo and Paulina. It was understanding, forgiveness, and communication that reconciled the unhappy couple in the end, but it was the absence of those elements that poisoned their love for so many years. Only when it was too late did they realize what they needed to make their marriage real.

Today, all that is left to remind us of this tragic story is the beautiful statue of Paulina. If you happen to visit Rome, go pay Paulina a visit. Perhaps you will even be lucky enough to do so accompanied by someone you love. You can tell them the story of Paulina and Camillo. Then I encourage you to take a romantic walk through the Borghese gardens. In that lovely setting, you can remind your companion of how much they mean to you, of how much you love them. Paulina and Camillo would approve.

If you enjoyed reading this book,
please visit the book's official website:

www.PrincessOfNowhere.com

Here you can learn more about Pauline's life,
view the list of characters surrounding her,
see pictures of the beautiful palaces she lived in,
have discussions with other readers,
and much more!

Elvin Boer

PRINCE LORENZO BORGHESE is an Italian and American citizen who has resided in Manhattan since 1997. His storied paternal ancestors include Napoleon's sister Paulina Bonaparte Borghese. Lorenzo graduated from Rollins College in Winter Park, Florida, and has an MBA from Fordham University in New York. In 2006 he starred on ABC's reality TV show *The Bachelor—Rome*. An avid animal lover and founder of Royal Treatment, a high-end pet line offering a vast array of pet supplies, Lorenzo is also creator and founder of RoyalPetClub.com, a discount pet luxury website that sells pet supplements and organic grooming products manufactured in Italy.

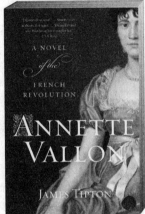

DANCING WITH MR. DARCY:
Stories Inspired by Jane Austen and Chawton House Library
Edited by Sarah Waters
978-0-06-199906-2 (paperback)
An anthology of the winning entries in the
Jane Austen Short Story Award 2009.

DARCY'S STORY
by Janet Aylmer
978-0-06-114870-5 (paperback)
Read Mr. Darcy's side of the story—*Pride
and Prejudice* from a new perspective.

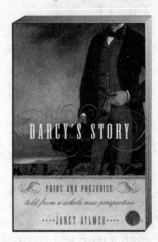

DEAREST COUSIN JANE:
A Jane Austen Novel
by Jill Pitkeathley
978-0-06-187598-4 (paperback)
An inventive reimagining of the intriguing
and scandalous life of Jane Austen's cousin.

THE FALLEN ANGELS: A Novel
by Bernard Cornwell and Susannah Kells
978-0-06-172545-6 (paperback)
In the sequel to *A Crowning Mercy*, Lady Campion Lazender's courage,
faith, and family loyalty are tested when she must complete a perilous
journey between two worlds.

A FATAL WALTZ: A Novel of Suspense
by Tasha Alexander
978-0-06-117423-0 (paperback)
Caught in a murder mystery, Emily must do the unthinkable to save her
fiancé: bargain with her ultimate nemesis, the Countess von Lange.

FIGURES IN SILK: A Novel
by Vanora Bennett
978-0-06-168985-7 (paperback)
The art of silk making, political intrigue, and a sweeping love story all
interwoven in the fate of two sisters.

THE FIREMASTER'S MISTRESS: A Novel
by Christie Dickason
978-0-06-156826-8 (paperback)
Estranged lovers Francis and Kate rekindle their
romance in the midst of Guy Fawkes's plot to blow up
Parliament.

THE GENTLEMAN POET:
A Novel of Love, Danger, and Shakespeare's The Temptest
by Kathryn Johnson
978-0-06-196531-9 (paperback)
A wonderful story that tells the tale of how William Shakespeare may have come to his inspiration for *The Tempest*.

JULIA AND THE MASTER OF MORANCOURT: A Novel
by Janet Aylmer
978-0-06-167295-8 (paperback)
Amidst family tragedy, Julia travels all over England, desperate to marry the man she loves instead of the arranged suitor preferred by her mother.

KEPT: A Novel
by D. J. Taylor
978-0-06-114609-1 (paperback)
A gorgeously intricate, dazzling reinvention of Victorian life and passions that is also a riveting investigation into some of the darkest, most secret chambers of the human heart.

THE KING'S DAUGHTER: A Novel
by Christie Dickason
978-0-06-197627-8 (paperback)
A superb historical novel of the Jacobean court, in which Princess Elizabeth, daughter of James I, strives to avoid becoming her father's pawn in the royal marriage market.

THE MIRACLES OF PRATO: A Novel
by Laurie Albanese and Laura Morowitz
978-0-06-155835-1 (paperback)
The unforgettable story of a nearly impossible romance between a painter-monk (the renowned artist Fra Filippo Lippi) and the young nun who becomes his muse, his lover, and the mother of his children.

PILATE'S WIFE:
A Novel of the Roman Empire
by Antoinette May
978-0-06-112866-0 (paperback)
Claudia foresaw the Romans' persecution of Christians, but even she could not stop the crucifixion.

PORTRAIT OF AN UNKNOWN WOMAN: A Novel
by Vanora Bennett
978-0-06-125256-3 (paperback)
Meg, adopted daughter of Sir Thomas More, narrates the tale of a famous Holbein painting and the secrets it holds.

THE PRINCESS OF NOWHERE: A Novel
by Prince Lorenzo Borghese
978-0-06-172161-8 (paperback)
From a descendant of Napoleon Bonaparte's brother-in-law comes a historical novel about his famous ancestor, Princess Pauline Bonaparte Borghese.

THE QUEEN'S SORROW: A Novel of Mary Tudor
by Suzannah Dunn
978-0-06-170427-7 (paperback)
Queen of England Mary Tudor's reign is brought low by abused power and a forbidden love.

REBECCA:
The Classic Tale of Romantic Suspense
by Daphne du Maurier
978-0-380-73040-7 (paperback)
Follow the second Mrs. Maxim de Winter down the lonely drive to Manderley, where Rebecca once ruled.

REBECCA'S TALE: A Novel
by Sally Beauman
978-0-06-117467-4 (paperback)
Unlock the dark secrets and old worlds of Rebecca de Winter's life with investigator Colonel Julyan.

THE SIXTH WIFE: A Novel of Katherine Parr
by Suzannah Dunn
978-0-06-143156-2 (paperback)
Kate Parr survived four years of marriage to King Henry VIII, but a new love may undo a lifetime of caution.

WATERMARK: A Novel of the Middle Ages
by Vanitha Sankaran
978-0-06-184927-5 (paperback)
A compelling debut about the search for identiy, the power of self-expression, and value of the written word.